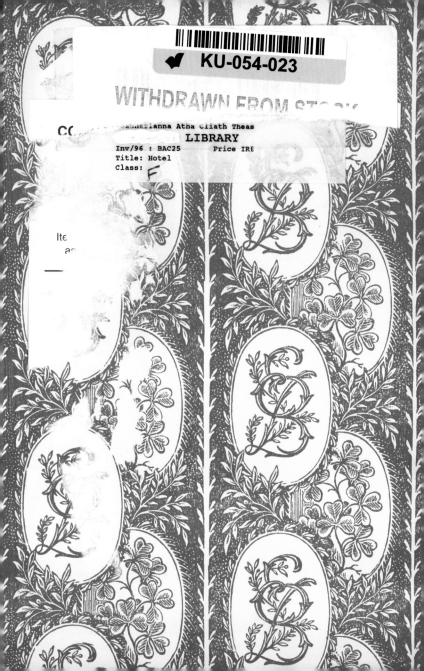

THE HOTEL

Sydney put down her plate

CONTENTS

CHAPTER I

QUARREL

MISS FITZGERALD hurried out of the Hotel into the road. Here she stood still, looking purposelessly up and down in the blinding sunshine and picking at the fingers of her gloves. She was frightened by an interior quietness and by the thought that she had for once in her life stopped thinking and might never begin again. Ladies under discs of coloured shade from their parasols came walking down the middle of the road; they deflected their course to pass her. Their faces conveyed nothing, but now and then they would smile, and Miss Fitzgerald felt her throat and chin contract as custom wrenched from her a small, stiff bow. She stood there helplessly, as though she were waiting for a friend.

That Miss Fitzgerald should, after so violent an exit, simply continue to stand there had been beyond the calculations of Miss Pym. *She*, after a short blank pause of astonishment up in her room, had begun to creep down the stairs warily. She listened; she clung to the banisters — tense for retreat at every turn of the staircase. The lift-shaft rose direct from the lounge and the stairs bent round and round it: she stared down for a long time through the wire-netting case of the shaft to assure herself that the lounge was empty. It was. There was not a soul down there; not a movement among the shadows, it was eleven o'clock and everybody would have gone out to the shops or the library, up to the hills or down to the tennis-courts. Not a shadow crossed the veiled glass doors of the drawing-room to interrupt the glitter from the sea. Not a sound came up from the smoking-room. Miss Fitzgerald was not there.

Miss Pym had been quite sure she would not be there, but all the same she let out a sigh of relief. Miss Fitzgerald had gone out: having discharged with such bitterness of finality that last shot in her locker she would have fled. At this crisis of ungovernable agitation Emily (how well they knew each other!) would have taken to the hills. Miss Pym could see plainly her figure stumbling up in the glare towards the shade of the olive trees, breast to breast with the increasing slope. She must be given a little longer to get away.

Miss Pym, waiting about in the lounge, glanced back diffidently at the last few minutes, then turned round square and faced them. She was surprised to find herself cool, explanatory and reasonable. Her wait prolonged itself, the minutes seemed interminable; now and then she glanced at the lounge clock. She read the announcements pinned to the notice-board, looked along the letter-rack and read the names on the envelopes stuck prominently on the concierge's desk to await new arrivals. These long-forecast shadows for ever darkening the threshold of the Hotel excited Miss Pym; for some new arrival that never arrived she was storing up tenderness. She found that they were to expect (quite soon, perhaps) a clergyman, a Rev. J. D. L. Milton – *John?* Three letters for him and something that looked like a bill (or perhaps a receipt) had been forwarded from an address she knew quite well, a country house in Derbyshire. Gratifying how one's intimate world contracted itself, how one's friends wove themselves in! Society was fascinating, so like a jigsaw puzzle!

Miss Pym heard somebody beginning to come downstairs and moved quickly away from the notice-board. Those firm steps coming down unhurriedly in a light, continuous, increasing ripple sounded like Mrs. Kerr's; it was Mrs. Kerr herself who appeared at the turn of the stairs, drawing her loose white gauntlets over her wrists. Without troubling to look down into the lounge she called 'Sydney . . . Sydney,' as though she did not care to question or need to command but expected Sydney to take form somehow out of a limbo to which forgetfulness had consigned her, and be drawn up the stairs to where her friend stood beautifully, balanced either for advance or immobility.

'Miss Warren isn't here,' said Miss Pym. 'She'll have gone on down to the courts, I dare say: she went past me in the corridor with her racquet quite a little time ago.'

Mrs. Kerr said 'Thank you,' smiled and accepted this; she did not seem really to care whether Miss Warren were there or not, her 'Sydney . . . Sydney,' must have been quite perfunctory. 'Well, *I* shall go down to the courts,' she said, and came on down to take her parasol out of the rack. She was accustomed to leave her nice parasol leaning up in the rack there quite casually, for anybody to borrow, instead of taking it up to her room with her. Miss Pym watched eagerly, and Mrs. Kerr must have felt a conjunction to be inevitable, for having made a show of hesitation between three parasols not at all like each other, and feeling Miss Pym still behind her, she asked charmingly, hopefully: 'And are *you* going down?'

Miss Pym never went near the tennis-courts, but a prospect of walking down there and appearing publicly with Mrs. Kerr was delightful (poor Emily, scrambling alone in the hills!). She abandoned a plan she had, still embryonic, of going down to the shops, and wondered whether their two names -- her own and Mrs. Kerr's -- might not, henceforward, begin to be coupled. She had a queer little thrill and held open the swing-door with

13

gratitude, almost with reverence. Mrs. Kerr with a vague inclination of the head passed out before her. They crossed the gravel together under the hundred windows of the Hotel.

When they turned out of the gates, however, Miss Pym flinched and felt giddy. For there stood Miss Fitzgerald, twisting her fingers together and staring straight at them. Had she been awaiting them there, malign and patient? Had they walked into an ambush? Then she saw how drained-out, how void of intention, Emily was. She seemed hardly to see them. She might have crept out here to bleed – but her wounded presence still was an outrage. Miss Pym looked away.

'There's Miss Fitzgerald!' said Mrs. Kerr pleasantly.

'Oh? – Yes.'

'Mustn't she be waiting for you?'

'I – '

'You mustn't let me be selfish,' said Mrs. Kerr.

Miss Fitzgerald, who must gradually have brought them into focus, wheeled round nervously and hurried away. Everything that, abroad, an English lady takes out with her swung from her arm and bumped as she fled: the coloured straw satchel, the native umbrella, the golf-jersey, the net bag supplementing the satchel. There streamed from them, to Miss Pym's perception, a pitiful wraith. With all these, in shining readiness for the day's excursion, Emily had presented herself at her friend's door – less than an hour ago.

'Going all by herself?' observed Mrs. Kerr.

'Yes,' agreed Miss Pym, and after a moment cautiously licked her lips.

Mrs. Kerr, balancing her parasol on her shoulder, walked on, looking ahead serenely. She did not seem to be wondering what on earth one of them was to say next; she did not look as though it even remotely con-

cerned her. There were so many things that she might
have said just now that Miss Pym could have taken up
easily, but she did not say one of them, only exposed with
indifference her profile to the sidelong, zealous research
of Miss Pym. Her profile did not commit her: it expressed
an ironic indulgence to fashion in the line of a hat-brim,
the soft undulation of hair, an ear-ring's pendulous
twinkle, the melting suave lines of a scarf round the
throat. Mrs. Kerr took fashion in and subdued it and
remained herself.

Miss Pym, with a welling up in the depths of her, was
moved to tell Mrs. Kerr everything and did not know
where to begin. She was a timid woman, but had for
a moment the sufferer's arrogance. She hesitated, pondered, debated with herself, and again with reluctance
looked back.

It had been what she would have to describe as a
quarrel. It had been a Moment, not a succession of
moments, not a gradual divergence of herself and Emily
from the path of loving forbearance. It had been a
flare – or a blotting out, how could she better describe
it? – like the horrible blackness of spilt ink, suddenly
everywhere, that makes one crinkle one's face up. They
had seen each other crudely illuminated, and they had
seen each other as *vulgar*. She could not remember how
it began; she could not remember anything leading up
to it; just that there had been something intolerable
about Emily from the moment she came to the door . . .
That is the worst of anger, that terrible clarity. They
had had, at that moment when everything tottered,
worse than a sense of destruction: they had felt the whole
force of a doubt in that moment: had there ever been
anything there? Isolating doubt which coming upon
them suddenly had sent Miss Fitzgerald blindly downstairs and left Miss Pym, trembling, to put away the

sketching-blocks and newly sharpened pencils and empty the steaming coffee from the thermos flask into the slop-pail . . . If Miss Pym were to tell Mrs. Kerr all this, she couldn't imagine what Mrs. Kerr would be likely to say.

She realized that she had not made any remark for a long time, and wondered in agony what Mrs. Kerr must be thinking of her. A slight turn of Mrs. Kerr's head, the ghost of a smile, the quickened twinkle of an earring made her feel all at once she could not tell Mrs. Kerr: she was afraid.

'I think many people might maintain,' began Miss Pym laboriously, 'that this was an ideal place to pass the winter.'

'I'm sure it is,' said Mrs. Kerr.

'Except, of course, those *Spartans* who enjoy the sleet and fogs, or say they do, because they maintain that endurance, that is, endurance practised as an act in itself, *constitutes* enjoyment.'

She had pulled out a fine, full stop of sarcasm, but Mrs. Kerr seemed to ignore it and said quite seriously: 'Oh, but does anybody think that?'

'I – I suppose they must,' said Miss Pym, flustered. 'But I do think that to the Straightforward Persons who can be frank with themselves and admit that they do like to escape the difficulties of Life and the unpleasantness – if they can do so without depriving themselves of experience or evading Responsibilities, or hurting Other People – *then* . . .'

Where was she? What had she been going to say? This was the way that she and Emily talked all day long, climbing the hills or sitting among those warm rocks that fringe the Mediterranean. They drew in each other's ideas and gave out their own by a gentle process, like breathing. They had pinned down the most slippery,

ethical subtleties for absorbing, tireless analysis. Everything they said to each other was so *true*. Now this was
all becoming nonsense, futile in the ears of Miss Pym.
Her waves came back bewildered, broken against something. She could not endure the ordeal of this gracious
listening. Was Mrs. Kerr like this when Sydney Warren
talked?

She drew a desperate breath and continued: 'As I
say, to the Straightforward Person – and I think, you
know, that the more one is that the more one is bound
to admit to oneself that one is a Hedonist, and that it is
better not to fight or to drive oneself, but to lead and
develop——'

'Ah yes,' said Mrs. Kerr, 'I think you are so right.
One's first duty is, I'm sure, to be warm. Other people
may pose about their reasons for not coming abroad,
but you and I are much wiser.'

The road ran straight ahead of them, parallel with the
coast and planted with two regular lines of chestnut trees.
To the right the hills rose up with their climbing villas;
to the left the town with its gardens crowded down to
the sea. As Miss Pym walked on, distressed but concentrated, confessing herself a Hedonist, Mrs. Kerr touched
her lightly on the arm and said, 'No, look; this way.
We're missing the turn to the tennis-club!' She kept a
hand on Miss Pym's sleeve for a moment longer and
guided her gently. Their path struck off at a right-angle
between high garden walls, a funnel of sunshine so
narrow that two could not walk abreast. Miss Pym,
elated, deprecating, plunged down it ahead of her companion, who had to pause for a moment to disentangle
her parasol from a long spray of creeper that swung down
over a wall. Miss Pym felt the heat on her thin back as
she hurried crabwise, incoherently talking, but she did
not dare to put up her parasol, because parasols are so

awkward when one is nervous, and how should she feel if she poked Mrs. Kerr in the eye?

She approached the tennis-courts and heard the cries, the ping of the balls, and saw the shining, darting figures and the shaded balconies of the pavilion. Miss Pym felt behind her a drawing away of Mrs. Kerr and knew that she was now to be abandoned. Mrs. Kerr was looking through the wire-netting; her eyes went from court to court, then turned dissatisfied to question the pavilion, then the benches underneath the wall where players sat in groups or couples, waiting for their courts. She watched these benches for some time, and Miss Pym watched her.

'Well, it's been so nice . . .' said Mrs. Kerr. Her voice trailed off into a valedictory murmur. It had been so nice. . . . Miss Pym could never have brought herself near the tennis-courts: she was shy of all the people; she would never have come along. They wore blazing, immaculate white, and bright woolly wraps huddled round them professionally. The quality of their hard, cool stare of indifference yet so penetrating was enhanced for Miss Pym by the glare of the courts, the air charged with sunshine, the treelessness, a kind of positiveness everywhere. She had a sense, so acute from her own ill-health as to become intolerable, of the stored-up, schooled, directed energy in all these fine bodies. She turned in a panic, abruptly, upon Mrs. Kerr. 'I'll be going back,' she said. 'I——'

The other stood still by the turnstile. Her eyes now rested in passivity, as after a home-coming, on a face they had discovered.

'I'll be going back . . .' Yes, it was Miss Warren who, over there with a scarlet handkerchief bound round her head, had been galvanized by awareness, half risen, and remained staring towards them across the courts. Miss

Pym spoke again, louder, but Mrs. Kerr, who was passing through the turnstile, gave no sign of attention. Only when Miss Pym was half-way up the path in retreat did Mrs. Kerr recollect her companion and, turning, make some vague gesture, some unheard sound, of farewell.

CHAPTER II

SYDNEY

'BUT they told me you had come on down!' cried Sydney Warren. Slipping along the wall, at the edge of the courts, she gained the pavilion and the back upper bench where Mrs. Kerr had seated herself. Mrs. Kerr smiled and looked leisurely round her. From these high seats one had an excellent view of the courts and could hardly be seen from them, sitting far back in the shadow. At one's feet a packed row of spectators leant forward into the sun.

'I waited for nearly an hour,' said Sydney. 'And Colonel Duperrier swore he had seen you go down. I couldn't make it out, but I came. If I'd ever imagined——'

'It never occurred to me you would wait. It would have been dreadfully silly. And, anyhow, it was nice to walk down with Colonel Duperrier.' (Sydney repudiated Colonel Duperrier with a grimace.) 'I walked down with Miss Pym,' Mrs. Kerr said contentedly.

'I know – I was horrified. One of the pussies!'

'Oh, is she? She seemed intelligent. She was telling me she is a Hedonist.'

'A *how*-much?'

'A Hedonist.'

'How Victorian!' Sydney said crossly, and hacked at the toe of her shoe with her racquet.

'Do you think so?' said Mrs. Kerr. 'I suppose,' she confessed, 'one forgets: we *are* rather old pussies.'

'*Don't* be so——'

'My dear child, I'm her age. We do date when we

talk. She had quarrelled, I think, with her friend, the
other artistic one. I came on her down in the lounge,
nearly crying, and the other, still nearer it, was out in
the road. You know, women's lives *are* sensational.
Aren't you inclined to be intolerant with us all?'

Sydney seemed surprised at this quick little gush of
humanity. She stared at her friend, who was brilliantly
earnest, then turned away gloomily. 'Oh, women's
lives . . .'

'Well, I suppose it's inconsistent of me,' said Mrs.
Kerr. 'I'm not a Feminist, but I do like being a woman.'

Any approach to the personal seemed to be difficult.
Sydney said airily: 'Oh, of course if one's one kind of
woman——'

'Well, so are you,' said Mrs. Kerr, looking abstractedly
at her young friend. Sydney, at a probable twenty-two,
had a clear pallor and regular features of which the
lines were now, as too often, strained and broken up by
an expression of over-eagerness. An exaggerated attention to what was being said or suggested would arch up
the eyebrows tragically, harden the eyes and draw in the
mouth to a line that prefigured maturity's. The forehead was broad and lovely and could have been bland.
The scarlet handkerchief bound round the head accen-
tuated her darkness and pallor; it had in common with
other details of her dress and appearance a faint kind of
nervous swagger.

'You could be charming,' said Mrs. Kerr. 'But I dare-
say an indifference to one's company which doesn't
comprehend the desire to please is really the safest —
won't you go and play tennis?'

'I'm waiting for the people on E Court to finish,' said
Sydney, and got up slowly, not quite knowing whether
to resent this as a dismissal. Mrs. Kerr, with the air of
a return to solitude, a cheerfulness rather suggestive of

release, leant forward and signalled to someone below who had been looking up for a long time trying in vain to catch her eye. 'Oh yes,' she replied, 'do go and play tennis. Surely it wasn't wise to come away from your partner when you were expecting a court?'

'But what are you going to do?' asked Sydney. Mrs. Kerr did not answer. 'I mean, do you want me to go?' she began again. She did not want to leave the pavilion, this 'girl of your age' tone which was being used to her really did give her something to resent. She did not want to go down to the courts again; she knew that if Mrs. Kerr sat on here, watching her meditatively, her play would all go to pieces.

'I have heard so much of your service. Today I am really going to watch it.'

'This is one of my off days.'

'Dear Sydney, whenever I come you tell me it's one of your off days.' Mrs. Kerr laughed. 'I'm unlucky.'

'Oh, do you notice that? From the moment you come here I never hit anything.'

'What on earth do you mean, my dear Sydney! How terribly sinister! It had never occurred to me that my eye might be evil. I meant something much more prosaic – that I happen to miss things.'

Sydney felt foolish. How like her (Mrs. Kerr would agree) to have drawn so far-fetched, so morbid an inference. How unlike herself to have been betrayed into so bald an assertion.

'Luck's funny,' she said. 'I don't think it's constantly good or bad, but it's sun-y or moon-y, if you know what I mean, and one's born with one kind or the other. Mine's moon-y – I'd better go down.'

'Yes, I shouldn't have kept you.'

Sydney played so badly that Colonel Duperrier was astonished. Now and then he permitted himself a 'tut-

tut' – by implication a tribute – an 'Et tu, Brute!' at which she ironically chuckled. They crossed and re-crossed one another grimly. Along the margin of her vision, distended by nervousness, shoulders were shrugged, and disappointed onlookers strolled away. At a net that grew ever higher Colonel Duperrier's opponent, Chinesely grimacing, crouched and sprang incredibly. His partner, a long way behind him, nonchalantly flipped at her balls. Away at the back of the pavilion Mrs. Kerr remained sitting; the edge of her skirt, the tip of her parasol, came out into sunlight. From out of the black shadow that hid the rest of her, her scrutiny like a live-wire was incessantly tugging at Sydney's consciousness.

The set was over, quickly over. Colonel Duperrier's play had been affected by the collapse of his partner; now, as their opponents strolled off, he laughed deprecatingly, stooping to let the balls run up on to his racquet. He had several pleasant remarks in reserve to brush away Sydney's discomfiture, but some kind of an explanation from her was needed to unlock them; he did not know how to begin. She did not apologize, and his embarrassment grew. No one could have been sorrier than he for the poor girl – a fine player subject to this deplorable kind of paralysis. He thanked God that he had not yet asked her to play with him in the tournament, and resolved never to do so, yet was filled with a special, protective benignancy for her.

'Terrible glare,' said he.

'There generally is.'

'I thought particularly bad today. . . .'

'I didn't notice,' she said indifferently, wondering where to go now. Anywhere, she thought, but back to the pavilion after all this.

'We ought to move off,' he said, rousing her; 'they

want the court. Well, I vote we take those two on again and get some of our own back. Don't we?'

Though he continued to admire Miss Warren, he could be no longer surprised that she was not popular in the Hotel. There was a certain dark stare of aloofness . . . He told himself that she was curiously dammed up: there was certainly something *in* the girl. Generally speaking, he preferred people who came out easily: she was not his type. He came up abreast with her dutifully as they walked from the court; then his face brightened: he knew he would soon be relieved of her as Mrs. Kerr smiled and nodded down at them from the shade of the pavilion. 'Come on up!' he said eagerly, and Sydney was forced to precede him.

'We-ell?' said Mrs. Kerr, as though they had been a pair of victors.

'The glare is awful,' said Colonel Duperrier.

'I expect it is,' she agreed, and made room for them both. Colonel Duperrier cheered up; soon, in a quiet way that diffused itself across his features and attitude and the expression with which he watched the players below, he was very cheerful indeed. When he had left them, Mrs. Kerr asked Sydney to walk with her to the library. 'Unless,' she said, 'you are going to play again.'

To go to the library one turned to the left instead of the right at the top of the footpath; the same procession of chestnut trees arched one over with their boughs. At this hour the road was more frequented; lunch-time had made perceptible its earliest magnetism. Visitors strolled gravely hotel-wards; villa residents were proudly distinguished by the possession of dogs. There was no traffic, and a long-legged English child in the middle of the road was able to read as she walked without menace.

'What a nice man, that Colonel Duperrier!' said Mrs. Kerr.

'Yes. Very patient.'

'*That* seems a curious quality to attract you.'

'Anyone else would have killed me this morning. I suppose he has learnt to be patient: that wife——'

'Poor woman!'

'It would be kinder if neurotics were to be chloroformed – did you admire my service?'

'My dear child, don't be heroic! I don't remember it as anything terrible. I don't know, of course, how well you can play.'

Sydney was silent, stung by a sudden suspicion that Mrs. Kerr did not really believe in her tennis at all. If she did not exist for Mrs. Kerr as a tennis player, in this most ordinary, popular of her aspects, had she reason to feel she existed at all? It became no longer a question of – What did Mrs. Kerr think of her? – but rather – Did Mrs. Kerr ever think of her? The possibility of not being kept in mind seemed to Sydney that moment a kind of extinction. Mrs. Kerr had many friends; all these demigods would leap up at a reference to one of the least of them, shadowy and menacing. Men and women of supreme distinction and beauty, they never appeared in person, were never described and so were never allowed to diminish. The very fact that Mrs. Kerr never praised them – seemed, in fact, rather flatly to take them for granted – was fresh reason for self-laceration. 'A delightful woman . . . rather a charming person . . . I thought, an amusing man . . . ' These haunted Sydney, aloofly inimical, these friends of her friend. People one did not know remained on a different plane, inaccessible to one's criticism. Sydney professed herself (to friends of her own age) a Realist, and it was perhaps because of this that her imagination, which she dealt with austerely, was able to revenge itself obliquely upon her.

After a pause she said, 'Well, you know one thing now

about my play – if it interests you. You do know how bad it can be. I think that was the depths.'

'Oh dear, oh dear,' her friend said benevolently. 'Will you kindly choose me another book?'

'Did you finish that last?'

Mrs. Kerr shook her head and looked sideways at Sydney in a way of her own. She sighed, her eyelids delicately and sadly fluttered – she was a lovely thing.

'Oh,' said Sydney, in a secret ecstasy, 'you are incorrigible. Then why do you go on asking me to choose you books?'

'I know there must be *something* in them.' The way this was said might have stamped out of being, for Sydney, for ever the friends of her friend. 'I know, you see, there *has* to be something. I want so much to be able to read them – I hope so much that I may.'

'I shall give up choosing you books.'

'Oh no, don't do that . . . Sydney darling. I suppose I *may* be incorrigible. I still seem to read for amusement.'

'But that was just it – I was so certain that man would amuse you. He's got a brilliant mind like – like what would appeal to you.'

'I'm sure he has. But you see, he was much too clever for me that he only seemed to me dull. And I do still like books to be – what shall I say? – decent. Though I know it isn't the thing to admit: you all have such pure minds . . . I'm sorry.'

'You don't look a bit penitent. Tell me – has Ronald got a very "pure mind"?'

'Alarmingly,' said Ronald's mother. 'But he's learnt to respect my limitations.'

Sydney, who was herself at times conscious of these limitations – remotely, as in a dream – smiled at the thought of Ronald, a long-limbed, intense-looking adolescent she was unlikely to meet. Ronald was a long way away, in Germany. (She had put together her Ronald from two photographs his mother possessed: a blurred snapshot and a shadowy portrait-study.) One could smile over Ronald; to imagine him was not distressing; he was not among the demi-gods. It was amusing to see one's own qualities in him pilloried in smiling maternal allusions. Ronald was 'young'. Yet all this might not have counted so much in his favour if it had not seemed certain that Ronald was to remain in Germany.

'I should like to meet Ronald,' Sydney said benevolently. 'And, by the way,' she added, 'I must bring back Tessa another book. Anything that's bright and very loving, with a certain amount of illness in it, will do her beautifully, provided she doesn't remember having read it before ... Now you're not to say I'm horrid about Tessa: she's as much amused at her own taste in books as I am. She hasn't got much time for novels now – she's reading Baudouin.'

'It would never do,' said Mrs. Kerr, 'to bring back Mrs. Bellamy one of your depressing books.' She slipped an arm through Sydney's for a moment as they turned together up a flight of cold steps to the library.

CHAPTER III

LATE FOR LUNCH

TESSA BELLAMY did not feel so well again
today, and lay wishing more than ever that she
knew what were the matter with her. Several
complaints had, it is true, been suggested to her by her
doctors before leaving England, and she had come abroad
with a perfectly open mind as to the possibility of most of
them. Not one of them had proved itself entirely satisfactory. She wanted something that would settle down
with her, simple and unexigent like an old family
servant, so that they might get to know each other and
understand each other's ways. She was distressed by any
suggestion of impermanence; she was a lonely woman.
One had to have Something in one's life. She lay on a
velvet sofa in her bedroom with the head pulled round
away from the window and wished that she were a
religious woman and that it were time for lunch and that
Sydney would soon come in.

Tessa had made a special arrangement with the
Management about dieting, if that should be necessary.
She paid an extra five per cent to have the menu for each
meal brought up in advance, but so far she had liked the
sound of everything so much and hated so much to give
trouble that she had not asked for anything to be changed.
She was not sure now whether she should continue the
arrangement; by which, of course, one did deprive oneself of the pleasures of curiosity and suspense. On the
other hand, the arrival of the menu gave one something
to think about during the morning. She wished so
much that she could make up her mind about this,

turned her head among the cushions and with a sigh refolded her hands on her bosom. In Life one seemed always to be making decisions.

When Sydney came in she thought that Tessa, lying with closed eyes in the thick green dusk of the closed jalousies, must be asleep. She stood looking down for a moment and pretended to herself (to heighten a sense of her real security) that Tessa was dead. She was fond of Tessa, but imagination often divorces itself from feeling; all that occurred to her now was that in such a contingency she would have to leave Mrs. Kerr and the sunshine and go back to London because Tessa, whose guest she was here, would no longer be able to pay the bills. Later, however, she produced a real pang of distress – how her own irritability and coldness would glare back at her when Tessa was gone!

Tessa put a hand up and patted her front hair, then opening her eyes looked up at Sydney thoughtfully, not as one who has just been awakened.

'I've been thinking things over——' she said.

'Good!' exclaimed Sydney with the geniality that endeared her to Tessa. 'If it's the menu, you know I should keep that up. It's an excellent principle and I'm sure the manager respects you for it.'

'Oh, do you think so?' said Tessa, and looking up with round eyes thought how untrue it was that intellectual people did not make pleasant companions. 'But you know I do hate——'

'Giving trouble? But that's what they're paid for . . . How are you feeling?' Sydney looked down with solicitude. To think one felt ill, to think only of that, to be so netted down must be terrible.

Tessa, drawing in her chin upon its many duplications, lay still and considered a moment, then began to tell Sydney exactly how she did feel. While she was still

talking the gong sounded; she got up and patted her hair
again, this time in front of the looking-glass. Breaking
off with a sigh she began to powder her nose. Sydney
meanwhile pushed open the jalousies; if she did not do
this, Tessa would quite contentedly make up her face in
the half-light and go downstairs like a nice little clown.

Sydney's relations had been delighted that she should
go abroad with her cousin Tessa. It had appeared an
inspired solution of the Sydney problem. The girl passed
too many of these examinations, was on the verge of a
breakdown and railed so bitterly at the prospect of a
year's enforced idleness that the breakdown seemed
nearer than ever. Now an ideal winter had offered itself:
sunshine, a pleasant social round. Sydney could be out
of doors all day long; she might distinguish herself in
tennis tournaments; she might get engaged. And
Tessa was so kind; she was forty, married, motherly; she
had no nerves, she had no children. Her inside kept her
happy and interested, she would be the ideal companion
for anybody inclined to be neurotic. She admired Sydney
whom she maintained to be cheerful and amusing; it
would be good for Sydney to be with somebody who
refused to consider her as anything but cheerful and
amusing. Sydney seemed as a rule to be so unfortunate
in her choice of friends.

Sydney untied the red handkerchief and combed back
the hair from her forehead. She frowned at her own
reflection: Was this what all these people really saw when
they looked at her? She was accustomed to stare at
people as from a point of vantage, forgetting she too had
a face. They had thoughts, too (with these she often
forgot to credit them); did *they* also think as they looked
at oneself? The strangeness is that a cat can look at a
king and *see* him; we kings forget so often that cats are
more than objective.

'– a lucky girl you are,' Tessa was remarking, 'to be able to walk about like that in the sun without burning your face . . . We're to have an asparagus omelette, Sydney: you know, "á l'asperge". We might come on down, if you're ready: they bring in the omelettes at once, you know, and it really isn't fair to the waiters. . . .'

Very few people cared as much as this about being fair to the waiters; the rest came trickling into the dining-room gradually, by twos and threes. The table Tessa had secured for herself was in a good position, near the door but not too far away from a window. By turning her head a little Sydney could feel the cool air on her face, and see, under the awning, palm-fronds rising up from the garden below, an orange tree in fruit and the roofs of the town behind it, vivid against the sea. Mrs. Kerr's table was off to the right at such an angle that, from where they sat, without being too much observed, Sydney was able to watch it. It was generally empty the longest of all. Behind Tessa the double doors were spread wide in an hospitable gesture, like the hands of a *maître d'hôtel*. Beyond, down the long perspective to the foot of the stairs, one could see visitors take form with blank faces, then compose and poise themselves for an entrance. Some who thought punctuality rather suburban would gaze into the unfilled immensity of the room for a moment, then vanish repelled. Others would advance swimmingly and talk from table to table across the emptiness, familiarly, like a party of pioneers. Men came in without their wives and did not always look up when these entered. Women appearing before their husbands remained alert, gazed into an opposite space resentfully, and ate with an air of temporizing off the tips of their forks. When the husbands did come in it seemed a long time before there was something to say. It seemed odder than ever to Sydney, eyeing these couples, that men and women should be expected to pair off for life.

During intervals between the courses women reft from intimate conversation looked across at each other's tables yearningly. Mrs. Hillier held out by the fringe for a friend's admiration a beautiful crêpe-de-chine scarf she had bought from the shops. She had chosen it for a wedding present, but it was such a lovely green that she could not resist wearing it, just till this evening, to take out the creases. The three pretty daughters of a London doctor at a table in one of the windows maintained their high level of uproariousness. They were the first to be interrupted by Mr. Lee-Mittison, who was going a round of the tables with an open botany-case. He showed them the roots of a very uncommon anemone, found in the hills. The three Lawrences turned their shining heads to wrinkle up their noses at the botany-case, but Mr. Lee-Mittison was not to be discouraged. He dangled one of the roots at them; his teeth and his glasses glittered benevolently.

'My wife and I,' he said, 'hope to make another expedition to the hills tomorrow, taking with us provisions for a picnic. We shall be delighted for you three young ladies to accompany us.' He rested a hand on Veronica Lawrence's chair and beamed down on the top of her head. The Lawrences made round eyes at each other and tittered unabashedly. Their father, to show that he was in no way responsible for them, leaned back and looked out of the window. 'There is a special invitation,' continued their friend, 'for Miss Veronica, whom I know to be an excellent walker.' He clicked the lid of the botany-case, winked respectfully at Veronica and passed on to another table.

The Lawrences had appropriated for general use the

principal young man of the Hotel, young Mr. Ammering, who, having been unable to find a job since the War, was said to be suffering from nervous depression in consequence and had come out here for a rest with his father and mother. He seemed to be one of those young men of thirty (Public School and University education, active, keen sportsman, good general capacities) who advertise their willingness to try anything in the Personal column of *The Times*. Enforced inactivity must come very hard on poor Mr. Ammering, who played tennis all day long with a set face and went out at nights with the Lawrences to dances at other hotels, where he talked to his partners most beautifully about the War.

Mr. Lee-Mittison after a moment's pause – not diffident, only embarrassed by the richness of his acquaintanceship – veered left towards the Ammerings' table. But Victor as he approached took up the local paper and began to read the visitors' list aloud to his parents, who listened attentively. The nearer Mr. Lee-Mittison came the louder Victor read and the more eagerly his parents listened. Something about the group of them rather too exclusively domestic offended Mr. Lee-Mittison's social sense vaguely: he turned away. The Ammerings should not see his anemones. He paused for a word with Mrs. Hillier, who shook out the fringe of her scarf at him, seeming delighted to talk; and decided to cut out the visit to the Mellarshes who, quite newly married, were, though not talkative, still solicitously watching each other eat.

The Honourable Mrs. Pinkerton and her sister-in-law the Honourable Miss Pinkerton had professed to be interested in anemones; they had an extremely fine garden at home which Mr. and Mrs. Lee-Mittison hoped to visit. But though the two families were on excellent terms, in fact becoming quite intimate, Mr. Lee-Mittison still did not like to approach the good ladies at meal-times. They seemed somehow enclosed as they sat there, moated about by their patent honourableness. Distinction drew a bright line round their woolly white heads, detaching them from the panorama of faces; distinction flowed down with their sleek satin draperies into dark folds. Bowing towards their placid obliviousness, Mr. Lee-Mittison passed on.

Sydney's eyes went over Tessa's shoulder, fixing the doorway; Tessa's little smiles at her withered unnoticed.

'Hasn't Mrs. Kerr come in yet?' said Tessa at last, her penetration innocently revenging the death of the smiles. 'How vague she is! I'm afraid she will miss the omelette.

'She doesn't like omelettes,' said Sydney, looking solemnly at Tessa with her strained dark eyes. She could have screamed when Mr. Lee-Mittison, coming up unheard behind her, laid a hand on the back of her chair. Putting down the case on the table he showed them his roots. He liked Tessa, to whom he had talked a great deal, but it was to Sydney that his invitation was to be addressed. 'My wife and I——' he began, and glanced again at Tessa regretfully. She was not young enough . . . '– provisions for a picnic,' he concluded.

'When?' said Sydney abruptly.

He flipped the air with his hand to enjoin patience. 'I was about to say; we shall be glad if you will join us tomorrow——'

'Oh, thank you, I can't. I am sorry, I have an engagement.'

'O-oh!' said Tessa, who thought this would have been nice for Sydney. Mr. Lee-Mittison stared incredulously.

'Tut-*tut*,' he said. 'Well, think it over . . .' Sydney's strangeness bothered him; the Lawrences had seemed so *glad*. From behind a screen that hid the service-lift the

waiters with their steaming dishes debouched suddenly
and sped like bees to distribute themselves among the
tables. Excusing himself quickly, Mr. Lee-Mittison
hurried back to his own table, where his wife, who
rejoiced in Herbert's popularity, had sat all this time
knitting. Now she leant sideways and pulled his chair
farther out for him, tucked her knitting away in a bag
and gave him all her attention. The return was in the
nature of a home-coming; she was the kind of wife who
can always create this atmosphere.

'Well?' said she.

Behind Tessa the doorway still framed emptiness.
The meal clattered on. Nearly everybody here was
English: the air was allowed to come in pleasantly
through the open windows under green-striped awnings
and feel its way, cool-fingered, from flushing face to
face. Nobody was hurried or constrained; time put out no
compulsion and the afternoon might have stretched
ahead, as it seemed to stretch, brightly blank. Over it,
however, habit had spun her web of obligations; a web
infinitely fine and fragile from which it was yet impossible to break without outrage. Beyond the dining-
room, along the expanses of the lounge, people risen early
from their tables were awaiting one another, meek under
the rule of precedent, to fulfil a hundred small engage-
ments. Leisure, so linked up with ennui, had been
sedulously barred away. Each armchair, each palm and
bureau had become a trysting-place where couples met
to hurry off or groups were reunited.

Meeting, with an air of effort that made her seem to be
breasting a current, the desultory trickle of the exodus,
Miss Pym came in, very late. She was scarlet-eyed, the
last tear must have been recently wiped away. Something
wobbled in her throat, round which she twisted and
untwisted an anaemic string of turquoise beads. She

seemed constrained to look at everybody, then to look quickly away again. Sydney, leaning her cheek on her hand, turned from the door for a minute or two to study Miss Pym. She had never seen what she still called to herself a 'grown-up person' so visibly ravaged by emotion. The emotional range of her elders seemed to Sydney narrow and stereotyped; they reacted without variation to stimuli from without. But Miss Pym gave an impression, somehow, of having been attacked from *within*.

Miss Pym looked diffidently at the waiter. She had cut herself off from the omelette, so he shrugged his shoulders and brought her up a plate of macaroni from the servants' lunch. This the bruised creature pitifully but with evidence of hunger began to eat; the traditional British struggle with macaroni brought her down sharply from tragedy to farce. Sydney sighed impatiently and turned away.

Mrs. Kerr, half-way across the dining-room, looked about her in surprise. Discounting her own lateness, she seemed to wonder if the other visitors had been dispersed miraculously. Her eyebrows said 'How odd!' but did not seem to ponder over this. She sat down and looked out at the orange tree; then took up her Tauchnitz and without another glance at the room began to read.

Tessa and Sydney had been sitting on interminably; they had watched from rise to fall of the curtain the whole drama of lunch. The fact was, Tessa did not think it wise to hurry. She turned round and round pensively their basket of fruit, took each orange up, pinched it, and put it back again. The nicest-looking were never the softest: another of life's perplexities.

'I think,' she said at last, 'that I *will* take another orange, but I won't eat it here. I shall take it up to my room with me and eat it there. I'm quite sure, you know, that oranges are *good* . . . But don't let me keep you, Sydney, if you want to go and talk to Mrs. Kerr.'

'Why should I want to go and talk to Mrs. Kerr?' asked Sydney in an unconcerned voice that echoed round the big, deserted, crumby, orange-scented dining-room.

CHAPTER IV

BATHROOM

T H E Honourable Mrs. and Miss Pinkerton occupied
two wide-balconied rooms at the end of the first-
floor corridor. Five times across the Hotel, each
on a floor, these corridors ran – dark, thickly carpeted,
panelled with bedroom doors. The front rooms looked
over the town into dazzling spaciousness, sky and sea;
the back rooms were smaller, never so bright, and looked
over the road with its chestnut trees on to the side of the
hill. Into these the north light came slanting; no sky was
visible until one leant far out, only the scrambling olives
and scared little faces of the villas. Eyes from the villas
could have peered down into the vacant eyes of newly
awakened sleepers. At this side of the Hotel, screened by
opaque glass from the possibility of observation, were the
bathrooms.

Mrs. and Miss Pinkerton were of course on the sunny
side, with their balconies from which the view could be
patronized. The view was their own; they were to enjoy
the spiritual, crude and half-repellent beauty of that
changing curtain, so featureless but for the occasional
passing of a ship. They barricaded themselves in from
the assault of noonday behind impassable jalousies. No
private suite with a bathroom was available; it was
possible, they brought themselves to comprehend dimly,
that in hotels of this type none existed. They therefore
had had reserved, at some expense, the bathroom
opposite to their doors for their exclusive occupation.
One says 'occupation' advisedly: here in white-tiled
sanctuary their bowls of soap, their loofahs, their scented

bath salts could remain secure from outrage; here, too, their maid could do their smaller washing and hang the garments up to dry before the radiator. There generally were garments drying there; the two distrusted foreign laundresses, perhaps with reason.

Other visitors on the first floor respected this arrangement which had a certain beauty for them, the accretion of prestige. They bathed at the other end of the corridor; if that bathroom was full they went up to the second floor where people could not afford to have baths so often. James Milton, a clergyman, was, however, unaware of this, and going upstairs directly after his arrival locked himself into Mrs. Pinkerton's bathroom. Here he hoped to remove by steaming and by prolonged immersion the grime, ingrained in one till one is almost polished, of a transcontinental journey. This was the bath that he had been promising himself for the last thirty-six hours: it had come to shine before his numbing intelligence as in itself the journey's bourne. He did not notice the bath salts, but, unthinkingly, made full use of the loofah, which he was surprised and pleased to find there.

He had arrived late, having dined on the train, and few people were at hand to witness the arrival: a big man talking Italian above the folds of a muffler and making abundant, baulked gestures at the boots and concierge. He seemed unwilling to admit how well they could speak English. The few onlookers, by hanging poised in their talk for an infinitesimal second's observation, bore in a sense of his squalor upon him sharply. He was aware of the glow of clean faces, the glaze of immaculate shirt-fronts. He felt them averting their eyes considerately. Relegated, alien, blinking like an owl after his dark drive in the light's untempered scrutiny, he stood for a moment, then fled upstairs on the way to Mrs. Pinkerton's bathroom.

He took in enough of his No. 19, when the chambermaid switched the lights up, to know that it faced out the wrong side, offered no space for his baggage, and was so furnished as to confuse thought, distract contemplation and impede the movements of the body. The lace-veiled window was pallid against the dark; pushing it open a little he let in some cold air and heard the rustle of a palm tree. Unwinding his muffler and throwing off his great-coat, he waited only to take out his sponge bag and dressing-gown and sweep his towels along with him; then made off down the corridor, calling back to the chambermaid in three languages that he was going to have a bath. He was an independent man with a bump of locality on which he had grown with years increasingly reliant, and he brought himself without difficulty to the door of a hospitable-looking bathroom.

Mrs. Pinkerton and her sister-in-law never sat for more than a minute or two in the drawing-room where other ladies forgathered. They withdrew early to their own rooms where they would embroider, eat little pastries and drink coffee. No one else had ever been invited to join them there; such an invitation was hardly to be expected, though the Pinkertons had consented to be present once or twice at Mrs. Lee-Mittison's coffee-parties. They felt, perhaps, a little lonely these evenings; the comfortable feeling of enclosedness would fall away when there was nobody to be enclosed against. In the high room among marble-topped furniture they sat listening with well-bred attentiveness to one another's breathing. Through the thin walls every footstep, every shutting of a door should have been audible in the velvety silence of the corridor. Yet the ladies had this evening no inkling of what was to occur; no premonition seems to have troubled them.

The Honourable Edward Pinkerton had died before

his father, Lord Parke. Though he had not been young when he died, such a frustration of life's high purpose for him – he was an only son – had lent him the pathos of youth. Had his widow been less substantial and less palpably recent he might have passed, by the references made to him, as having died before his majority. He remained 'Poor Edward', embalmed like a dead child in the pity and patronage of the living. He was making a third with them, this evening as ever, his mild be-whiskered face, with that expression of awe on it with which fancy is wont to invest the pictured faces of the dead, looked out from a vast scrolled frame that over-shadowed the silver-stoppered bottles on the dressing-table. A similar photograph commanded the bedroom of Rosina, his sister, to the exclusion of other relationships. Rosina sat in an armchair pulled out under the light with her work held up to her eyes, embroidering diligently. She and her sister-in-law had grown very like one another, coiffured and dressed by the same hands, worked upon from within by similar preoccupations. They were more closely allied to one another in the memory of Edward than they had either of them been to Edward himself. Somehow, up to the moment of death, Edward had eluded both of them; it was after death they had closed in relentlessly. Cherished little animosities reinforced their ties to one another; Rosina maintained to herself implacably that if *she* had been Edward's wife she would have borne him children; Louisa was enough aware of this to be a little markedly generous to Rosina, who was not in a position to refuse anything that might be offered.

Mrs. Pinkerton sat turning over the pages of *The Tatler* and talking to Rosina while she embroidered.

'I see,' she said, 'the Wyntons' girl is to be married.'

'Ah?' remarked Rosina, snipping with her gilt scissors. 'Who is he?'

'A *Barre*, apparently.'

'Are there Barres? I never heard of any. Where does it say he comes from?'

'It says here,' replied her sister-in-law, looking at the paper closely, 'Hampshire.'

'There are no Barres in Hampshire,' said Rosina definitely.

'Then it is another of these marriages.' They both sighed.

'Elissa Howard,' Mrs. Pinkerton went on more cheerfully, 'writes a very pleasant, cheerful letter. She is so considerate when one is abroad or ill. She is a woman that I always like to hear from. She is coming out next month, to Nice, you know.'

'It will be pleasant to have Elissa within reach: one feels very isolated.'

'Oh, I'm sorry, Rosina, that you don't *like* the Hotel . . . I cannot understand how anyone can go to Nice: they say it is a kind of French Brighton.'

'They say the Carnival is very pretty . . . But I dare say,' Rosina unguardedly added, 'that it's more expensive than we——'

'It's not a question——' Mrs. Pinkerton was beginning. '*Come* in!' she cried in an exasperated voice.

Lurgan the maid put her long wedge of a face round the door. 'I beg your pardon, Madame, I'm sure,' she said, 'but I put the Shetlands to air an hour ago and now I cannot get into the bathroom. . . .'

Three or four minutes after this announcement Tessa, thoughtfully taking her hair down with Baudouin propped up before her, was surprised by the entrance of Sydney, unusually animated.

'Mrs. Pinkerton and Rosina,' said Sydney, 'cannot get into their bathroom. They simply can't. I've been watching. Both their doors are open and they take it in turns to come and rattle incredulously at the bathroom door. It is really funny; I wish you would peep out and look. That determined little rat of a maid of theirs is being the man of the party; she heaved her shoulder against the door just now as though she were going to force it, and Rosina cried, "No, don't, I forbid you — there may be somebody there!" '

'Oh, poor things,' said Tessa, 'how awkward for them! Do you think they will send for the manager?'

Tessa, with her fluffy hair falling down round the innocent, interrogatory O of her face looked younger, looked really rather — there was no other word for it — sweet. She wrapped her kimono closer round her and followed Sydney into the dusk of their end of the corridor, from whence they expected to watch unobserved. But a moment later Miss Pinkerton, down at the other end, turned in their direction a wild face of appeal. She hesitated, then something in the essential Tessa brought her towards them. She ignored Tessa's deshabille. 'Oh, Mrs. Bellamy,' she began, 'I wonder if you . . . It is rather embarrassing. . . .'

'I *know*. I am so sorry. Have you any idea?'

'We cannot understand,' said Miss Pinkerton. 'We *cannot* believe——'

'It can't be deliberate,' said Tessa consolingly.

'Why don't you ring for the manager?' asked Sydney, anxious to precipitate a crisis.

'I think it would be better for us, under the circumstances, to send for Madame.'

'But it may be a man.'

'It cannot be a *gentleman* . . .'

Mrs. Pinkerton appeared at the door of her bedroom.

She looked expressionlessly out from under an Olympic cloud of hair and seemed immense. She said: 'My sister may have told you of our own difficulty?'

'You've *no* idea?' Tessa said again hopefully.

Mrs. Pinkerton shook her head. 'One doesn't like to be seen standing here,' she said, and, an invitation seeming to be explicit, they followed her back into her room. They must have been the first in the Hotel to cross that threshold; it was a tribute to the humanity of Tessa. Keeping the door a little open, they listened and heard the uninterrupted crash of water from two taps turned full on. Sydney covertly pulled *The Tatler* towards her and glanced at its pages, but the stricken air of the two ladies pervaded the room and began to oppress her. She realized that this must be something worse for them than not, simply, getting what they paid for. It went deeper than that. They were stupid but not, she felt, vulgar; all this lace and leather, monograms everywhere and massive encrustations of silver meant less to them, probably, than to herself, to whom wealth and position would have been conveniences to be made use of. They were part of the immense assumption on which the Pinkertons based their lives. The Pinkertons imposed themselves on the world by conviction. The damage at which they now stood aghast was not a personal affront, and they were ennobled by the absence of personal resentment. The poor old things had, after all, ventured out into the world along a kind of promontory.

Lurgan came in and stood by the door. 'You would 'ave thought,' said she, 'that 'e would at least 'ave noticed Madame's Shetlands, 'anging by the radiator.'

'I don't see why you should assume that it's——'

''Ark!' said Lurgan, putting up a hand peremptorily. The taps had been turned off and a fine baritone voice

44

rose clear at the cessation of the water. 'Hail, gladdening Light . . .' he sang: it was an evening hymn.

'Singing!' said Lurgan. It was inexpressible.

'It's a lovely hymn,' Tessa said, propitiatory. Her face lighted up; she looked round at them. 'I expect,' she said, 'it's the clergyman. There was that Mr. Milton.'

'One would have expected greater delicacy,' said Mrs. Pinkerton, and indeed on that score Tessa did feel Milton to be indefensible. The testimony of the radiator . . . She looked helplessly at Sydney who, overcome at the moment by a simultaneous desire to yawn and to laugh, suggested that they should go back to their rooms – since there seemed nothing at all to be done – and leave the Pinkertons and Lurgan to their vigil.

'One could take steps . . .' Mrs. Pinkerton was saying, frozen into an attitude of reflection.

'Or would you wait till tomorrow to do so, and just let him finish his hymn now and come out?'

'There are situations in life,' said Mrs. Pinkerton, 'face to face with which one is powerless.' Though she only meant that in the struggle for life one is sorely handicapped by the obligations of nobility, Tessa and Sydney gathered that Mrs. Pinkerton was prostrated. After a blank little silence intended to express the inexpressible they murmured a solicitous 'Good night' and slipped through the door.

James Milton met them coming out. The asceticism of a lifetime in such matters had drawn him after ten minutes from his bath. He had stood and steamed in the warm air, then scrubbed himself dry and got into his dressing-gown sooner than he had expected. The water now receding from a rich black rim along the sides of the bath had done its work; he felt his own man again, clear-brained and vigorous. He looked forward to stretching out his limbs – cramped by last night in the train – in a

bed again, when once he had unpacked and come to terms
with his ridiculous room. He hoped to sleep till the
palm trees outside were posed in blue air and white sunshine; when, on opening his eyes, a first picture should
spring to them brilliantly, vivid, as he leant from his
window, with all the vividness of ideality. He still had
a childish pleasure in arriving at places at night, as
though he had been brought there blindfold. Humming
a Gregorian chant he clicked back the bolt sharply and
came face to face with two ladies, one in a dressing-gown,
emerging simultaneously from an opposite room.

Tessa, horrified, fled down the corridor; they heard
her door slam. Sydney stared. She did not see why she
should retreat, as she momentarily expected Milton to do
so, and she could not help being amused at his discomfiture. Milton looked boiled, his face, neck and ears were
bright scarlet; his fine thin hair stood erect and his damp
moustache drooped at the ends like a sea-lion's. He
clasped his clothes and towels against him in an ungainly
bundle.

Milton also stared; it did not occur to him to retreat
and there seemed nowhere to go to. He felt quite sure
he had met Sydney before. Her dark eyebrows, square
forehead and arrogant chin seemed already familiar. On
this evening of strangeness and new impressions she was
out of place, stepping out as she did from among his
own recollections. Unaware of himself he bowed gravely,
while in the doorway behind her horrified faces appeared
for the moment, then vanished again.

CHAPTER V

PICNIC

THE party for Mr. Lee-Mittison's expedition was assembling as directed in the lounge, at the foot of the stairs. They stood in a group, eyeing one another a little blankly. Veronica Lawrence came downstairs, twisting her scarf round her throat nonchalantly and pulling down her felt hat over her eyes. Mr. Lee-Mittison clicked the lid of his watch at her playfully.

'Oh, sorry!' cried Veronica. 'Am I keeping you all?'

Victor Ammering heaved himself out of an armchair and came sauntering up, hunched and indecisive-looking, ruffled about the head like a young thrush. He stood tugging at the flaps of his pockets, and Mrs. Lee-Mittison, hurrying to and fro in a last ecstasy of preparation, stumbled over his feet.

Mr. Lee-Mittison, his panama hat in his hand, was counting heads, making quick calculations, and checking over the parcels of lunch in the concierge's desk. He called to his wife, who was advising everybody to take some kind of an alpenstock in case of difficult walking. 'Now, are we all complete? Is there anyone else? I believe they've put out one too many packets of lunch.'

'Better than one too few,' observed one of the girls, and the rest laughed politely.

'Three – five – six – eight—— No, there is no one to come, they have made a mistake. Now, Herbert, the girls are all ready, I think.'

'Then forward – march!' cried Mr. Lee-Mittison and the five girls, followed by Mr. and Mrs. Lee-Mittison, filed through the swing-door held back by James Milton,

who brought up the rear. Glancing back through the
glass he saw Victor, whose rather marked exclusion from
the picnic-party he was at a loss to understand, pocket
the remaining parcel of sandwiches. This was done
calmly and not with the air of sudden resolve. Mr.
Milton, puzzled, alert for experience, hurried after the
others.

They went forward at a swinging pace, well spread
out across the middle of the road. Carriages jingled past
them, and a motor rushed by containing Colonel and
Mrs. Duperrier and Mrs. Kerr, who were driving over
the frontier to visit some friends. They all waved and
smiled at Mr. Lee-Mittison's party. This was a moment
of keen pleasure for Mrs. Lee-Mittison. She carried a
mackintosh over her arm in contempt of the sky, a bag
of knitting in case they should sit down for long, and a
basket of delicacies, dates and chocolates, with which
Herbert liked her to supplement the lunch. Under her
hard hat she shone with happiness; she refused to allow
Mr. Milton to carry the basket.

'Oh no, please,' she implored, 'it's *our* picnic,' and he
saw that her day would be spoilt if she were not able to
be the Martha.

Mr. Lee-Mittison was pleased with his wife, as with
everybody, and now and then patted affectionately the
folds of her mackintosh. The departure, always a fidgety
piece of organization, had gone off magnificently with never
a hitch, and he looked with satisfaction at the five girls
with their short skirts and neat ankles walking in front
of him. No one could have been less of a horrid old
satyr than Mr. Lee-Mittison, but he loved to surround
himself with bright faces, and the faces of young women
are admittedly the brightest.

He knew himself to be a success with young people:
he could spin yarns and imitate animals by the hour,

and tell graphically of life in the East, bearing his descriptions out with photograph albums. He found that he need never want for young society; girls seemed to take to him naturally. He did not care for young married women, while widows depressed him – poor little souls. On this occasion, the capitulation of Sydney Warren had been a particular triumph. She walked before him with her characteristic quick step, a little out of time with the others – her hands pushed deep down into the pockets of her jersey. It was true that in the glimpse he had had of her face she had not looked merry and that her back now did little to correct that impression. But if so, Mr. Lee-Mittison thought, a jolly day in the hills would be all the better for her.

The five girls had been all rather silent, but suddenly Eileen Lawrence burst into song; a chant in tune with their marching:

> I had a good home that I lèft – lèft – lèft.
> Now don't you think I was right – right – right?
> Me father was drunk, so I packed up me trunk,
> And I left – left – left——

'Oh, get into step, Sydney!'

'Really, Eileen!' said Mrs. Lee-Mittison, smiling with gratification at this burst of high spirits but glancing up at the villa windows under which they were passing. The Lawrences were such dear girls, Herbert loved them so, but she did hope they were not going to be too rowdy.

'This feels like school again,' said Eileen. 'Left –left – left.'

'I can't think what one would do,' observed Veronica, 'if one's father really were drunk.'

'Doctors daren't——'

Two other girls, a pair of pale Miss Bransomes, giggled ecstatically.

'Specially Dad,' continued Eileen. 'But as far as I know Dad's never killed anybody.'

'Oh, *Eileen*!' said Mrs. Lee-Mittison.

'I dare say,' said Veronica, 'that if we pretended to everybody here that Dad did drink everybody here would believe us. They're a cheery crowd.'

'Not a very *kind* joke, I'm afraid,' said Mrs. Lee-Mittison, pink with diffidence.

James Milton, in whose late parish most of the people had been elderly, looked with interest at these modern girls. Sydney, turning round suddenly, caught him watching them all with pleased curiosity, and felt as his eye lingered hopefully on her that he was expecting a further contribution, still more picturesque, from herself. She was silent sardonically, partly to disappoint him, partly because she never felt in line with the Lawrences, and partly because she was self-conscious and felt stiff and clumsy at this sort of ragging.

Mr. Milton had been introduced to them all in the lounge by Mr. Lee-Mittison, who commended him to their good graces with a general wave of the hand. The Lee-Mittisons always went out of their way to be pleasant to strangers, making efforts to draw them as soon as possible into the social life of the Hotel centring round Mr. Lee-Mittison. They had been predisposed in Milton's favour by the fact that he had come downstairs to break-fast and ordered an egg: this seemed to them virile. Very few people came down to breakfast, a discouraging meal to which the Lee-Mittisons by a punctual appear-ance and bright nods round tried in vain to impart an atmosphere. Accordingly they had buttonholed Milton and told him that he positively must join their expedition this morning; they would take no denial. Milton looked flattered and bothered. 'As jolly a set of girls as you'll meet anywhere,' said Mr. Lee-Mittison, winking chastely.

Milton was a big man of about forty-three with the clear, ruddy-and-white complexion of a wax model from which the moustache and expressive mouse-coloured eyebrows unconvincingly sprouted, looking darker than they were. He was long-limbed and strongly built but evidently out of training, for he began to pant and be silent sooner than any of them when they took the steep path up the side of the hill. He had intelligent, bright eyes, creased at the corners with humour, and the assured, affable, occasionally rather inane manner of the innately shy and diffident man who has never had to venture outside a society where he is secure and appreciated, and who has brought himself to believe, in spite of a deep-down protest, that such a society is the world. One felt that it should be easy to impress, affect, or discompose Mr. Milton, and yet that he had seldom been impressed, affected or discomposed.

The path was cobbled; it went up glaring white beyond the edge of one's vision, relieved only here and there by the shadow of an olive tree. After some time it intersected a road that ran high up along the side of the hill, and the party staggered a short way along the road and sat breathlessly down on the parapet. James Milton and the Lawrences took out their cigarette-cases and Milton offered his round.

'Oh, you girls, you girls!' cried Mr. Lee-Mittison, 'you do it charmingly, but how I wish that you wouldn't!'

Sydney merely bent forward to the flame of a match that Milton was sheltering for her, but the Bransomes, a pair of pale cousins, turned paler still with dismay. They had recently arrived and had been much gratified by an invitation to the picnic; they did not care if they smoked or not, having only wished to resemble as closely as possible the Lawrences and the alarming Miss Warren. They waved the cigarettes away and shook their heads mulishly.

Mr. Lee-Mittison ignored their sacrifice. He was sitting astride on the parapet facing his protégées; now he leant forward, extending and thumping his chest. 'Look at me!' he shouted. 'Sixty-four and never smoked, never touched a drop in my life. Sixty-four, I tell you!' He stuck out his chest still farther and invited one of the Bransomes to thump it also, but she declined. 'Regular habits, the fear of God, and water from the spring!'

'– Perrier when we are abroad,' said Mrs. Lee-Mittison, knitting.

The olives below the parapet sighed and twinkled; between the branches the party looked down at the miniature roofs of the town and realized how far they had come. Little distinct shadows from branches above their heads shivered over their figures and faces. Veronica moved closer up to Sydney confidentially. She thought Sydney queer, rather interesting, and wondered what she could possibly be thinking so hard about all the time. Sydney's remoteness intrigued the fêted Veronica. She supposed with sincere generosity that the sort of men who did not admire herself might find Sydney very attractive. The absence of such a man here seemed bad luck on Sydney. But then, on the other hand, Sydney had curious ties.

'I never thought he'd get *you*,' said Veronica. 'You always seem to be doing something else.' She placed a foot of her own beside a foot of Sydney's and noted that while Sydney's was the better-shaped her own must be by half a size the smaller. 'You seem to be wonderfully busy,' she said with a sigh.

Sydney glanced into the irreverent, sentimental boy's eyes of Veronica. There *was* something pleasantly hard about her; at every contact one was conscious of the blade in her deep down with a fine edge on it.

'Constant dripping,' she said. 'For twenty-four hours I seemed to meet no one but Mr. Lee-Mittison and every time we met he was so *sure*——I wonder if she, or the first wife, ever wanted to marry him, or whether they *had* to.'

'How *do* you mean?' said Veronica with a spurt of laughter. She never waited to grope for one's meaning, which instinct generally prompted one to offer her on the flat of the palm, like a lump of sugar to a pony. 'I can't think,' she continued, 'why he's so determined to have you. You don't effervesce. You're not breathlessly modern (on his level!) every minute like we are. You can't think how tired we get. That's why Joan struck at coming this morning. She said she felt *old*. . . .'

Sydney looked along at Mr. Lee-Mittison. '*Ape!*' said she. Mr. Lee-Mittison was trumpeting like an elephant and waving an imaginary trunk at the delighted Bransomes.

'Oh, I don't know; the old blighter rather amuses me,' said Veronica tolerantly, and squinted down at the tip of her cigarette. 'Joan's off colour; as a matter of fact,' she suddenly confided, 'I believe she is keen on Victor Ammering.'

'But isn't he——'

'Yes, he's keen on me,' said Veronica indifferently. 'But you get used to that if you're three sisters more or less the same age. Between us, we generally manage to keep people in the family.'

Sydney pondered; she had no sisters, and the ethics of the situation were beyond her. 'You mean,' she said, 'it would be more trying for Joan if *I* wanted Victor Ammering?'

'Oh, *I* don't want him, if that's what you mean,' said

Veronica, with the crudeness of sincerity. 'Anyone can have him, as far as I am concerned.' She dangled an imaginary Victor airily, as though he were a marionette. 'But I can't imagine what you and poor old Victor would find to say to each other,' she added.

'He did once try and kiss me, ages ago, at a dance,' Sydney said, reminiscently smiling.

'I know, he told me: he said you were rather annoyed.'

'I know I was – I hate being messed about.'

'I said to him at the time: "Victor, you are the limit: you've no instinct."'

'I should have thought he had heaps.'

Veronica looked at her sideways. 'By the way,' she said, 'why didn't you go for that drive with Mrs. Kerr? They must have had heaps of room in the car, and I should have thought——'

'Oh, I'm sick of motoring,' Sydney said, and threw her cigarette away into the olive trees. 'Besides,' she added sombrely, 'I don't know their friends over there.'

'Didn't she ask you?'

'Not exactly – no. Why should she?'

'Oh, my dear girl, *I* don't know why she should!' Veronica shrugged her shoulders. A queer girl this, Veronica thought, well turned-out, clever, presumably, with a complexion she might have done more with, and awfully jolly feet, to sit brooding cheerlessly on a parapet because a middle-aged woman hadn't asked her to go for a drive.

'Well, come on,' she said, 'Moses is getting the tribes together.'

Sydney thought this surprisingly witty: she chuckled. 'What do you think of our Aaron?' she asked, but Veronica did not hear. Mr. Lee-Mittison had swung his leg back over the parapet; his wife was putting her knitting away. They all got up rather unwillingly and began to climb the next path, which left the road only too soon and was steeper than ever.

They came up at last on to the brow of the hill and found themselves at the extremity of a long ridge that stretched ahead of them, going down sheer at each side into a valley. From where they stood the ground dipped away again slightly, then rose in a series of undulations to a point of rock whereon a pale-coloured village balanced itself improbably. A mule-track, which must have made a more gradual ascent up the side of the hill, looped itself over the ridge a little ahead of them and vanished again. Beyond the village more hills, a disheartening infinity, rose blade-like, without shadow, against the vapourless and metallic brilliance of the sky. From the grass, among the twisted shadows of olives, flame-bright anemones spurted; Mr. Lee-Mittison precipitated himself upon them with a cry of pleasure and triumph. A scent of thyme stung the nostrils, reinforcing the glare with its pungency till two of the senses reeled.

The picnic-party had not halted, doggedness had forbidden them even to pause, since they had left the parapet now immeasurably far below. Veronica Lawrence, wildly exclaiming 'The Promised Land!' stumbled forward into the thyme and lay crucified. Eileen, incapable of more than a gesture, knelt down and stared in dismay at the hills which now promised no bounds to the activities of Mr. Lee-Mittison. The Bransomes, half-obliterated by the strain of the ascent, flopped sideways and in self-conscious abandon stood hugging an olive tree.

Sydney found Mr. Milton beside her; his face was glazed and dark, and in spite of his ceaseless mopping the sweat streamed down so that he could hardly open his eyes.

'*You* don't look hot at all,' he said reproachfully; and Sydney, who was enduring the burning discomfort of those who cannot perspire, said snappily:

'Well, we can't all express ourselves.'

'I wish,' he said ruefully, pushing a handkerchief round the inside of his collar, 'that my self-expression were not quite so fluent.'

She pushed back her hat and put up her hand to her forehead; it felt hot as a pebble on an August beach. They had straggled a little nearer the village, so that the brow of the hill rose behind them, cutting away the horizon, and the sea, when they turned to look for it, was only visible in a triangle at the mouth of the valley below. She felt him waiting for her to speak and reluctantly asked, 'Do you like the village?' nodding ahead.

'Yes,' he said, after a pause which gave the unhappy impression that he had sealed the village with his approval. 'It's jolly. It's out of some background – looked at, you know, through an arch or the slit of a window. Look at the track leading up to it – there's even a donkey.'

'Yes, some Flight into Egypt!' said Sydney. She gathered from the lightness of his manner in making the allusion that he was anxious not to appear unduly familiar with the National Gallery or the Uffizzi, and wanted to ask him, 'Haven't you lectured on the Renaissance?' But she knew how inexorably the Hotel would refuse to let him escape from all that he was, and had pity on his innocent holiday taste for incognito, foredoomed from its birth on the threshold of the Hotel. Everybody could see at once that he had lectured on and perhaps even taken people round the National Gallery. She looked disparagingly at the village with its toppling campanili.

'I think,' she said, 'that it's rather too like a cruet.'

'It may have inspired the cruet,' he gravely amended.
'Can you tell me why it is walled?'

She glanced suspiciously at him, but his limpid gaze
held a real curiosity.

'Against the Saracens. They used to land along this
coast and ravage the valleys, so they built the villages
as high as possible and fortified them. I pity any Saracen
that ever got into them, for they're perfect honeycombs,
and the people I think are cruel – in a leisurely sort of
way.'

'Ah!' said he with an air of pleased receptivity. 'It
would be interesting to get in touch with local records.'

'I don't know whether there are any. Do you remember the Decameron lady who fished in the sea near
here and was carried off by a pirate whom she liked from
the first moment better than her husband?'

'Husbands' shares were not good in those days,' he said
tolerantly. 'I ought by the way, to re-read my
Decameron.'

She wanted to ask him whether the *Decameron* had
really been dedicated to him by a friend. 'Wouldn't it
be nice,' she said, suddenly smiling, 'if the Saracens were
to appear on the skyline, land and ravage the Hotel?
They all take for granted – down there – that there
aren't any more Saracens, but for all we know they may
only be in abeyance. The whole Past, for a matter of fact,
may be one enormous abeyance. But I wonder,' she
added while a cloud of depression crept over her, 'how
many of us they would really care to take away?'

He did not know how she wished him to answer and
risked: 'It would be an embarrassing choice.'

She sighed flatly. The dust, panic and ecstasy with
which she had filled for a moment the corridors of the
Hotel subsided. Once more she saw her fellow-visitors
as they were to remain – undesired, secure and null.

'Not many,' she said, and turning away from him seemed to be gazing down some distant, barred-away perspective of feminine loveliness. 'Women must have deteriorated.'

She half expected from Milton a flutter of protest, then noticed that she must have lost his attention, he was thinking about something else. He flushed and looked hard at her suddenly.

'Excuse me,' he said. 'Haven't I met you before?'

'Only last night,' said she, and grinned at the recollection more or less overtly. Then she wondered whether he knew that by just such a question do young men – at dances and elsewhere – strike for the first time the personal note. It is asked leaning forward intensely with the implication 'Your ever-remembered face!' He could not have said this to many young women; he said it this time too awkwardly.

'Ah yes, last night,' said he. 'But surely before? . . . It occurred to me then.'

'I don't think so. Unless you are the sort of person who remembers faces he has sat opposite to in a bus.'

'Ah well,' said James Milton. 'It may have been that!'

CHAPTER VI

THE KISS

MRS. LEE-MITTISON sat with the packets of lunch piled up around her like some homely goddess. She had spread out the mackintosh, on which she hoped she might later persuade Herbert to arrange himself – unobtrusively, for she did not wish to humiliate him before these dear girls who, unlike the girls of her own generation, seemed to be able to sit on questionably dry grass without after-effects. She sat with her hat tilted forward to protect her eyes from the glare, looking down at her work but not knitting, her whole being in a state of happy suspension, a pause as distant from life as a trance. The sun wooed her persistently and at last, with a gesture from her almost dionysiac, she undid and flung open the woolly jacket buttoned across her chest.

Herbert had taken the girls ahead with him farther along the way to the village; she could hear his voice upraised in a sustained and happy monologue and now and then a thin exclamation from one of the Bransomes. They must be picking anemones. Surprised at herself, she sat with bliss in her little oasis of solitude. She looked down the slope beside her into the valley below and saw a little house, with a blue door whose colour delighted her, beside the bed of a river. Two lemon trees were beside it, and this little house which she seemed at once to inhabit gave her the most strange sensation of dignity and of peace. She saw herself go climbing up the garden from terrace to terrace, calling the goat, and the goat, beautiful in its possessedness, come loping down to meet her, asking to be milked. At this she paused in perplexity, for she had never milked anything and turned cold at the thought of touching the udders of an animal. But in a moment this was over and she carried the milk frothing warm in the pottery jug inside, into the dark interior of the house which would not be dark from within. Here something turned her back and she could not follow herself; she saddened, feeling excluded from some very intimate experience. The house was lonely and in autumn, when the river was brimming, the rushing past of the water must be terrifying; its echo would line with sound the upright walls of the valley. On still spring nights the thud of a falling lemon would be enough to awake one in terror.

The villino suddenly dropped away from her eye as though she had put down a telescope, and as her life sprang back into focus she must have been dizzy, for she felt sick at the thought of their hotel bedrooms that stretched, only interspersed with the spare-rooms of friends, in unbroken succession before and behind her. She felt sick at the thought of for how many mornings more she would have to turn the washstand into an occasional table by putting away the basin and jug in the cupboard and drape with Indian embroideries the trunk in which they concealed their boots.

Mrs. Lee-Mittison saw that Sydney Warren and Mr. Milton had wandered away by themselves, and that Veronica Lawrence, apparently unattached, was strolling among the olive trees a little way down the slope This did not seem like Veronica, and it was not like Veronica, either, to remain so persistently unaware of the ascending Englishman in the grey flannel coat coming so rapidly up towards her. Mrs. Lee-Mittison, with faint misgivings thought she recognized the set of those shoulders and, leaning forward a little, saw from the shape of the head that this was indeed Victor Ammering. She quivered; the hill was too small, there were too many other hills for her to believe that this could be anything but a deliberate intrusion. Herbert particularly had not wanted Mr. Ammering. He did not care at all for the young man, who was unintelligent, too talkative and did not bring at all a nice atmosphere into a party. Herbert was quite sure the girls didn't like Mr. Ammering either and would not wish him to be invited; that was the most delightful aspect of modern girls, they all liked just being jolly together.

'Veronica,' she called sharply, 'here, just a minute, my dear!' She might have been calling back a paddling child from under the menacing curve of a breaker.

'What for?' Veronica looked up at her astonished.

'Mr. Ammering seems to be coming up the hill. I think he must be making some mistake.'

'Well, it isn't a private hill,' said Veronica. 'I suppose he's simply going for a walk.'

'Don't you think we had better tell him,' said Mrs. Lee-Mittison, 'that his friends are not up here? It would save him the climb.' She fidgeted and swayed slightly; she was gathering Herbert's happiness, all his little plans for the day, for protection under her feathers, and she gave such an impression of being ruffled-out, apprehensive and angry that she did actually make Veronica think of a hen, with head a little on one side and blinking bright eyes.

'How odd,' said Veronica, sitting down on the grass still a little below her, 'that Victor should have hit on this hill. I thought he was playing tennis. However, it's his walk, and I suppose it's his hill as much as ours. I can't see that we can do anything about it, Mrs. Lee-Mittison, except be rude.' She took off her hat and shook back her fluffy cropped hair.

'I hope I shall not be *rude*,' said Mrs. Lee-Mittison with a quiver in her voice.

'Hullo, Victor, I thought you were playing tennis!'

'Do I look as if I was playing tennis?'

'Fool! You can't come here, it's somebody else's picnic.'

'Well, I suppose I can walk about on the hill!'

'Fool – you do look hot! Go and walk about on one of the other hills.'

'It does not matter to *us*, Veronica,' called down Mrs. Lee-Mittison. 'Mr. Ammering's plans for the day are his own, of course. I think you had better come up here, if you don't mind, and help me put out the lunch. Then we will call back the others.'

Veronica pulled three pieces of bark from an olive tree and threw them in Victor's face, then she turned her back on him and came scrambling up the hill. Mrs. Lee-Mittison produced from her bag and spread out a printed paper tablecloth; her smile of competency usual to these occasions was a little dimmed by a still apprehensive consciousness of Victor's presence below. With Veronica's help she arranged the eatables. Veronica piled up the oranges in the middle of the cloth and ringed them round with Mrs. Lee-Mittison's little biscuits and the chocolates wrapped in scarlet and gold. 'There: "The young housewife"!' she cried, sitting back on her heels complacently. Mrs. Lee-Mittison thought of the cottage below and had once more the queer little pang.

Sydney and James Milton returned by the loop of the road, which they had followed, they said, for a short distance in order to look into the farther valley. She conveyed by the manner of her walk and by an air of serene inattentiveness that it was nothing to her that he should choose to accompany her; it must be his mistake; she had nothing to offer. Looking and feeling like her friend Mrs. Kerr, she sat down and turned her face to the view. Mr. Milton was not so hot now, but he had been bouncing half a dozen conversational balls assiduously, and it was in evident relaxation that he lay down on his back on the grass like a dog and smiled up at the sky.

'Here, we can't all lie down, you know; it's dinner!' screamed Veronica. 'Who do you think's going to drop the hard-boiled eggs into your mouth? *Gerrup!*' At the indescribable sound she made he sat up astonished. He had never been spoken to like this before and it deeply gratified him. By the time the others had assembled he was smiling and passing the food about and chaffing Veronica, perhaps a shade laboriously.

'I say, I'd no idea you were a parson.'

'Don't I look like a parson?'

'Oh no. I'm perfectly staggered. You may be a bishop or anything. Was I terribly disrespectful? Well, it's not fair, anyway; you ought to wear *that* kind of collar.'

'The dog-collar? Dear me, you think I ought to advertise?' He was elated to find himself so much at ease, so disarmingly secular. 'You spotted me, didn't you?' He turned to Mr. Lee-Mittison, hoping to be contradicted.

'My dear fellow, that is neither here nor there. I have always said that there is no reason why a parson shouldn't be a sportsman.'

'That's what my father says,' contributed one of the Bransomes. 'I mean that there is no reason why a clergyman shouldn't be a *man*. A Man of the World, you know.'

'What on earth do you mean by "a man of the world"?' asked Eileen Lawrence scornfully. She had no patience with other people's vocabularies. The Bransome coloured and seceded from the conversation. She resolved that when she returned to England she would cultivate a manner like the Lawrences'.

'Speaking as a churchwoman——' tendered Mrs. Lee-Mittison, busy with the sandwiches.

'Anything at all, in fact,' said Sydney, 'so long as he is nothing of the priest.'

'God forbid!' said Mr. Lee-Mittison seriously. He was a Protestant.

'Well, it's God's affair——'

'Oh, there's Victor!' shrieked Eileen. 'I say do look, Veronica, there's Victor down there in the trees . . . Look, he's eating an orange. Hi, *coo-ee*, Victor; come up!'

'Oh, we don't want Victor up here,' Veronica said, 'he's a bore. Oh, shut up, Eileen; leave him alone with his beastly orange. Messing it about all over his face, too, like a kid in a train.'

'I think, as Mr. Ammering is evidently on his own, Eileen, we ought not to interrupt his walk.' Mrs. Lee-Mittison had spoken with authority, but Eileen took no notice and already the foundations of the picnic shook. Everybody stopped eating, rolled over sideways on their elbows and looked down. The Bransomes were intensely interested – how pathetic! 'Why not ask him up?' said Sydney. James Milton suggested, 'Would you like me to go down?'

'I think we had better not interrupt Mr. Ammering's walk,' repeated Mrs. Lee-Mittison despairingly. They all pointed out to her that he was already sitting down. She looked across at Herbert, the roof of her mouth turned cold; Herbert seemed so very much put out. She knew so much better than he did how often Herbert was hurt. Now all that lovely circle in which he most completely came alive had wavered, bulged and broken. She began a little wildly to recruit for attention. She tugged at

Violet Bransome's sleeve, she leaned sideways and tugged at the cousin's; she signalled lavishly to Veronica and to Sydney. 'I think Mr. Lee-Mittison has a story to tell you. I think he is going to tell you all a story now . . . Mr. Milton,' she whispered across, 'do ask Eileen Lawrence to stay quiet. And ask Herbert (he's so far away from me) ask him to begin. . . .'

Mr. Lee-Mittison began the story, which was about Malay. He raised his voice, drew out his words and was emphatic. One by one the girls returned their eyes to his face reluctantly. The more suggestible among them took their cues from Mrs. Lee-Mittison and echoed her small exclamations. Herbert's wife, with tightly folded hands, was leaning forward eagerly. It could not have been thought possible that she had heard this story before were it not for the glance around with which at the approach of any salient point she would gather up the attention of the circle, and the dissyllabic titter with which she anticipated the humorous passages. Once she gripped a Bransome's hand convulsively – 'Isn't it exciting?' After about ten minutes of this recital, Victor Ammering appeared on the outskirts of the circle, stepped across the botany-case and sat down. 'I say,' he said – '(excuse me, sir!) – have any of you got a match?'

'Then we saw the native crawling out from the darkness of the bushes, most impenetrable darkness, into a patch of moonlight. He had a knife between his teeth. It was a ticklish moment. My friend Murphy whispered, "Don't fire!" We prepared——' Hanging breathlessly on his own words, Mr. Lee-Mittison looked immensely round at them. Their attention had again been distracted. Only Violet Bransome, now uniquely faithful echoed:

'You prepared—— And then——?'

'I will wait,' said Mr. Lee-Mittison, staring straight

before him, 'until the young ladies over there have finished talking.'

'Oh, thanks most awfully,' Victor was saying, his voice heard bleakly in the silence. Sydney, saying 'Bounder!' in a soft aside beneath her breath, had handed him across her matches. 'And, oh, look here,' Victor added, 'do go on and all that. It sounds thrilling. I didn't mean to interrupt.'

'A story interrupted half-way through can hardly be of interest. Pray don't let us keep you from your walk.' Mr. Lee-Mittison glared; none of the party felt comfortable.

Victor, who was not really such a bad young man, and who had been simply dominated by the most developed of his instincts, heaved himself off the ground and declared himself ready to depart again. 'As a matter of fact,' he said, 'I simply came to say that if any of you wanted to wash your hands and faces after eating oranges, I've found a tank down there among those gardens, quite clean, not a bit slimy and with no frogs.'

'We have handkerchiefs, Mr. Ammering,' said Mrs. Lee-Mittison.

'Have I got orange on my face or anything?' asked Veronica, and she turned her face up to Victor suddenly, away from the others, so that they could only guess by his expression what he saw there.

'You have,' said he. 'You've got orange right up round your ears. And you've got little bits of egg and stuff along your mouth.'

'We have handkerchiefs,' repeated Mrs. Lee-Mittison.

'I'll wash,' declared Veronica, and suddenly, incredibly, outrageously she had gripped Victor's hand, hoisted herself up by it and walked away with Victor down the hill. She left a gap across which the others looked at one another, and which they felt unable to draw up and fill. Mrs. Lee-Mittison wished that they would all go away now, for moment; she wanted to move up closer and sit next to Herbert. There was an uncertain silence. Then James Milton, who had been subject all his life to a kind of idiocy of nervousness, burst out laughing. The horrid sound which he could not contain appalled him, till at last to cover it he said to Mrs. Lee-Mittison, 'Youth calls to youth, doesn't it?' She replied, 'I'm afraid I do not understand you.' They all stared, Sydney with such contempt that her face remained imprinted burningly upon his memory. Presently, intending no offence but entirely forgetting that the story was to be continued, she also got up and strolled round the hill. She wanted to enjoy her own thoughts, which seemed all day to have been ceaselessly interrupted.

Veronica and Victor scrambled very companionably down towards the tank. The descent was in places almost precipitous; they had to lower themselves from tuft to tuft of grass. Once, coming to an empty slope, they lay and rolled down it; at another point they sat and slid. When trees interposed, they swung themselves joyously, like young apes, from trunk to trunk. Every now and then they reappeared into sight of those above, who, never ceasing to be aware of them, watched with covert but passionate interest. Their indifference, their recklessness, stirred something in the beholders, either envy or anger. At last, almost simultaneously, they leapt, with a dual cry just audible to their friends, into the soft tilled earth of a peasant's garden. The little terrace projected like a shelf, like an apron-stage, over the depths of the valley. Here was Victor's tank, round which, forgetting to wash, they soon began a most delectable water-battle.

'Look,' cried one of the Bransomes irrepressibly, 'they're splashing each other with water.' The rest remained perfectly blank; Mrs. Lee-Mittison knitted.

Veronica paused, and did her reputation the credit of a long, inquiring, guarded upward glance, which the steepness of the ground, the long grass, and the closeness of the trees at a point combined to baffle. One's own visibility is impossible to calculate. Then she scooped something out of the tank and put it down Victor's neck. He seized her wrist and doubled it backwards. She writhed, and with a voluminous and graceful movement kicked him. As in a dance he whirled her round him suddenly and kissed her ear and her cheek. She hesitated, balanced against him, then appearing reconciled to his change of tactics, flung her head back and allowed him to continue. He must have kissed her lips then for the first time; their stillness for some moments was profound.

Sydney's imagination had failed her, she found herself disappointed in her own society and was coming back slowly to rejoin the others. To her, looking down unawares, the couple gesticulating soundlessly below her in the sunshine appeared as in some perfect piece of cinema-acting, emotion represented without emotion. Then she wondered by what roads now unknown to her she might arrive at this: to be seen swinging back against a man's shoulder in that abandon of Veronica's. She wondered whether at such a moment she would be cut off from herself, as by her other emotions. She watched the miniature unreal Veronica toss back her hair and walk away. At Victor she forgot to look again; she had not thought of him.

She descended upon the others, who seemed to be stupefied by something and to be at the same time scrutinizing one another and avoiding each other's scrutiny. Then with a burst of talking they all came alive again and began clearing up the lunch, collecting pieces of paper which had strayed away and sweeping up orange-peel and egg-shells from among the grass.

Eileen Lawrence whistled, Mr. Lee-Mittison sang. He
was singing angrily a song that nobody knew. His wife
was everywhere; she thanked the girls profusely as they
heaped the debris into her basket. James Milton offered
cigarettes about spasmodically. His cheeks burned. He
kept striking matches, burning his fingers with them
and throwing the matches away again with exclamations of unnecessary violence. He had never seen a man
and woman kiss before and was battering in a kind of
despair against the glass wall that divided him from experience. He was thankful, with a tinge of regret, that
Sydney had not been among them; then he turned and
saw her behind him, talking to Eileen Lawrence. He
could not tell how long she had been there. Sydney
was saying, 'Do you mean to *tell* Veronica?' Eileen surprised him by saying, 'Not unless she asks me – what's
the good?'

To the Lee-Mittisons, married, of an older generation,
it was only possible for their guests to attribute one
opinion. 'Shocked!' they all assured themselves and
instinctively moved away. James Milton found himself
between two of the girls and walked with them along the
side of the hill, the others distributed themselves ahead
of him. He realized that the party had been divided
against itself transversely into generations rather than
vertically into sexes, and he was flattered to find himself
accepted in this camp. They all moved off together, talking vaguely about anemones, the village and the view.

Mr. and Mrs. Lee-Mittison remained alone. She did
not look at her husband, as she was afraid she might look
at him stupidly, sympathetically, and knew that this
would annoy him. After a pause, through which her
needles clicked, she said: 'Well, I think it's going off well,
don't you? They all seem to be happy.'

He was walking restlessly round a small circle in which

he seemed to be enclosed. His thumbs were tucked beneath the lapels of his coat and he stared round him critically at the expanse of day to be seen from the top of the hill. To left and right the sky sagged down to lower horizons.

'Happy? I dare say. I guaranteed to keep you thoroughly happy.'

'They're dear girls. They'll be coming back soon, won't they?'

'Of course,' said Mr. Lee-Mittison, still unable to catch sight of any of his party, whom the hills seemed to have devoured. 'I had suggested their going off on their own for a bit.'

'Oh, I expected you must have. The lunch was nice, wasn't it – the little biscuits?'

'Excellent.'

'It is nice to be alone a little. Oh, Herbert, sit down on the mackintosh – wait, I'll bring it over to you.'

'The hills are a bit lonely – I don't quite like them going away so far.'

'Oh, they'll be quite all right together – English girls. What a long bright day! We are always lucky in our weather.'

They were sitting side by side on the grass like a young couple, and for a moment she thought he might be going to pat her hand. She stopped knitting and waited, then, after a glance at his profile, quietly continued. She was saying to herself, 'Oh, my dear Herbert, my poor Herbert!' and her mind grew dark with resentment against the others. If one might only, in intimation of what one felt, have pressed up ever so gently against his arm. But he had always to be considered successful; his head, though frequently bloody, might never be admittedly bowed. '*Very* lucky,' she repeated, 'in our weather.'

'*Halloo!*' he shouted all at once, his hands, like a Triton's, making a cave round his mouth. 'Halloo-alloo-alloo-alloo!' They listened and heard only an echo at the end of the valley: He shouted again; still nobody answered.

'I'm a bit disappointed in Milton,' said Mr. Lee-Mittison. 'I didn't take him for that sort of fellow. I don't think I'll ask him to come with us again.'

'Perhaps better not,' said Mrs. Lee-Mittison.

CHAPTER VII

OUT OF ORDER

THE lift was out of order. Mrs. Hillier, who was in a hurry, had for some time been pushing the third-floor button unavailingly: the lift did not even tremble. She then pushed the second- and fourth-floor buttons as an experiment, but to this also there was no response. She slid back the iron gates again and stepped out into the lounge so suddenly and so angrily that Miss Fitzgerald, who had been watching sympathetically, was quite frightened.

'The lift is out of order,' she said tersely. 'Where can the concierge be?'

'He is always out at this hour. They say he has a wife in the town.'

'I do not see why we should be prevented from going to our rooms because the concierge happens to be married.'

'Anyhow, he is no good with the lift. They ought to keep a boy who thoroughly understands it.'

'He would have an attachment, too,' said Mrs. Hillier, who was really a cheerful and humorous person. With renewed determination she got back into the lift, and Miss Fitzgerald, getting in also for company, sat down beside her on the narrow seat. This was the most comfortable, intimate and exclusive corner of the Hotel and Miss Fitzgerald dreamily desired it. It was the kind of place in which one could have talked. They pushed each button successively, and even struck chords of two or three at a time. A wire twanged somewhere above and a chain rattled, but one did not move an inch.

'At any rate,' said Miss Fitzgerald, 'it is better than to

be taken half-way up and then stuck between two of the floors. My friend told me she once saw that happen to some ladies in a hotel at Switzerland. They were there for more than half an hour with their feet just visible below the ceiling of the lounge. The hotel was full of foreigners and it was most unpleasant.'

'Dreadful,' said the Anglo-Indian lady. She at all events could congratulate herself on her feet. 'Oh!' she cried, peering bird-like through the bars of the gate, 'can't some of you help us?'

Colonel Duperrier and a Mr. Miller had risen and were approaching politely from different corners of the lounge. The ladies got out of the lift and the gentlemen, getting in. assured themselves that there was really something very wrong indeed.

'I *cannot* see,' said Mrs. Hillier mutinously, 'why I should have to do without my scissors.'

Colonel Duperrier felt very sorry for her, she seemed to be beating her wings. 'Couldn't I——?' he began.

'Oh no, thank you.' The scissors were in her bedroom, as they both knew. One was drawn up from here out of ken, feet last, into the region of intimacies. 'And I cannot see why they should expect one to walk up. *I* shan't,' said Mrs. Hillier, flinging her gauntlet, to applause, in the face of the Management.

'I can't see why they should,' agreed Miss Fitzgerald, while Mr. Miller, sighing over this insoluble enigma, returned slowly to his patience-board. Colonel Duperrier rang twice for the Management, then looked into the dining-room to see whether the head waiter were there and could be asked to do anything. At three o'clock in the afternoon the Management and the personnel seemed to be equally inaccessible. They were perhaps asleep, like many of the visitors.

Sleep, the thin uneasy sleep of daylight, had today been

the refuge of many, for cold rain fell ceaselessly past the
windows. It was a transparent rain without mist, like
summer rain in England, through which trees and
buildings for a great distance could be seen distinctly in a
Japanese conventionality and flatness. Leaves and long
palm-fronds shone and trickled. Curtained in this pale
gloom, the Hotel seemed permeated by a sense of the
rain's despairing persistency, against which the reasonable conviction of visitors that the sun, bound by contract
with the locality, must soon appear again put up cold
walls around an inward emptiness. In many rooms the
tick of travelling-clocks, the stutter of rain along the
balconies, were being listened to attentively.

Mrs. Hillier snuggled up her woolly wrap round her
ears, nodded to Colonel Duperrier and went back into the
drawing-room. She seemed, from the desolation, dusk
and excludedness of the lounge, to return at least into
something. As she opened and shut the glass doors he
heard a kind of gasp of feminine conversation, and saw
his wife and many other ladies sitting round in a semicircle with a firelight on their knees. There was one
open fireplace in the Hotel and it was in the drawing-
room. She must have told them at once that the lift was
out of order, for there arose staccato indignation which
the door shut off from him. The lounge with its grouped
furniture was of an isolating vastness. A man, from here
unrecognizable, sat leaning his back against one radiator;
Mr. Miller with his patience-board had drawn up as
close as possible to another. One longed for the disorder
of firelight among the orderly shadows. One missed
one's dog. One missed the tug of association and habit
towards one chair: there were too many, groves of chairs
through which Colonel Duperrier wandered sadly. He
could not even remember where he had been sitting
before.

Miss Fitzgerald, standing on tiptoe, peeped over the lace blind through the glass of the drawing-room doors, sighed and shook her head. The room presented a too unbroken front of matronhood. She was expressing her feelings in dumb show for the benefit of nobody in particular, as is the habit of lonely, self-conscious women. She observed, still to nobody in particular, 'Well, I suppose if piggy *won't* get over the stile, I'll have to walk.'

'I beg your pardon?' asked Colonel Duperrier.

'Oh, nothing,' said Miss Fitzgerald, startled, and began her painful ascent. Her room was on the highest floor. She disappeared.

A girl with fair hair proved on closer inspection to be one of the Lawrences. She was hunched over a writing-table, trying to write a letter with a Hotel pen that screeched and staggered. She leant on her elbows, tilting her chair up. At an impatient movement from her two or three sheets of letter-paper, thinly covered, fluttered to the ground. 'Oh, *Lord*!' she exclaimed, and dived after them.

'Let me!' said Colonel Duperrier, hurrying across the lounge.

'Got it, thanks,' replied Joan Lawrence, once more arranging the sheets round her elbow so that the slightest movement must again disturb them. Her writing was enormous, and watching her absently he could not help seeing 'the very limit', 'macaroni' and 'torn it'. He looked quickly away.

She twirled her pen and stared at the nib resignedly. 'Pen's the limit.'

'It looks it. You might find a better one in the drawing-room.'

'I dare say. Thanks very much, but I'm not going into the drawing-room.' She was being friendly and pleasant with him; they both laughed. When she laughed, the

sunburnt copper-pink of her cheeks deepened. She was
not so difficult, after all, to distinguish from her sisters.

'Oh, come,' said he, 'you've never turned your back on
don or devil! Go in and look for a pen. They won't eat
you.'

'If you were a kind man, *you* would.'

'Look here, take my Onoto.'

'Oh no, thanks. Nothing but grief and bitterness
comes of borrowing other people's Onotos. *Do* go and
get me that pen. I dare you . . .!' She drew down her
upper lip and stared at him with solemnity. Both liking
each other better than ever, they laughed again. He
was a tall brown man with long legs, a little younger
than the Lawrences' father. His hair was going white
round the temples; strictly speaking, it was pepper and
salt. He was one of their finest tennis-players, and
waltzed beautifully in the old-fashioned manner,
holding one gingerly. His wife was the limit; she was
one of the drawing-room set.

'Go on, I dare you to!' repeated Joan.

He stood a moment longer, tugging his short moustache, then braced himself, magnificently squaring his
shoulders. 'Oh, very well,' said he. He hesitated in front
of the lace-hung doors, whose appearance seemed to
appal him.

'Funk!' called Joan excitedly, and he pushed the doors
open and went in. She heard wave after wave of exclamations arising. The door, which had swung to after
him, did not open again; she could no longer see his
shadow on the glass. She began to wish she had not
thrown her glove into the lion's den. Joan had a healthy
contempt for women like Miss Fitzgerald, but she was a
little daunted by the habituées of the drawing-room,
who played bridge crushingly well, were impeccably
manicured and had a hardish eye that negatived one's

importance. She sat watching the door anxiously. After all, he belonged to those people; it was possible he might not reappear.

But Colonel Duperrier respected these ladies too deeply to wish to remain among them. He came out again modestly, but with an air of achievement.

'Here you are! But I don't know that it's really much better.'

'I'll pretend it is, anyway. Did they mind your taking it?'

'No,' said he, uncommunicative. He drew up a chair and sat not far away from her while she scribbled experimentally with the new pen. It gave him a restful, anchored feeling to sit beside somebody who was doing something. He looked at the back of Joan's neck, from which the cropped hair fell away, with uncovetous appreciation. What he believed himself to be feeling was that it would have been jolly to have had a daughter. If Colonel Duperrier's wife were to die, he would marry some girl of twenty-three who would be very much in love with him and with whom he would be very happy. Colonel Duperrier had never thought of this, but it was evident to any woman. As she continued to draw profiles on an envelope and showed no signs of going on with her letter, he inquired, 'Have you any idea how long that lift's been out of order? I rather wish they'd let me overhaul the thing. Of course, I don't profess to know anything about mechanics, but I've always had a bent that way. I can't help feeling I——'

'It's been getting sicker and sicker since this morning. I think the people going upstairs after lunch must have finished it. You see, Veronica and Victor were playing hide-and-seek with the Barry children, and some of them got into the lift and sent it up and down full speed about four times without stopping.'

77

'Very high-spirited of them,' said Colonel Duperrier. '*Can't* young Ammering get a job?'

'No, he can't,' Joan said defensively. 'It worries him awfully. The War's come very hard indeed on our generation. I don't think people understand a bit.'

'Perhaps they don't,' said Colonel Duperrier, who had also fought.

'We have to make allowances for ourselves,' continued Joan. 'You see, nobody makes them for us. I know young people are always supposed to be fearfully idealistic and that sort of thing, but I suppose *we* can't help feeling that, considering how hard things are on us, we aren't really so bad.'

'But do people criticize you all?' marvelled Colonel Duperrier, who was slightly out of the movement. 'I personally can understand very well how hard this is on Ammering – having nothing to do but rot about here for a winter. At his age it would have driven me clean off my head.'

'We think he takes it awfully well,' said Joan, a little flushed. 'Of course, we all like him very much.'

'Lucky fellow!'

'Oh, well . . . Of course, for anyone like you to be out here must be awfully jolly. Everyone approves, and your work's over and nobody wants you to do anything more.'

'No, I shan't be wanted again,' agreed Colonel Duperrier thoughtfully. 'It's a good thing I'm fond of tennis. I suppose that's why one feels strongly about young fellows like Ammering; I mean, seeing them done out of what really is their due.'

'I don't suppose Victor would mind being you. I shouldn't wonder if he sometimes suffered from the same awful feeling as I do, like being sleepy in the morning and wishing it were bed-time. About lunch-time one begins to buck up.' Joan rubbed her chin thoughtfully with the end of her pen. She was more imaginative than either of her sisters. '*You're* just about at tea-time, aren't you?'

'I suppose I am,' agreed Colonel Duperrier. 'Five o'clock tea.' He thought to himself that it was the kind of tea women sat over till it was time for dinner. At this he began to yawn cavernously, shivered and apologized.

'One does miss one's tea out here,' said Joan. 'The tea-gardens are so breaking; we can't afford to go there, and the *pâtisserie* place is stuffy and full of Italians and one does get sick of pigging it up in one's room with a spirit-lamp.'

'I'm too shy to go to the tea-gardens,' said Colonel Duperrier, 'but I should like to. I hear the tea there is quite decent. Will you, some time, come and have tea with me there?'

'Thanks very much, I should like to,' said Joan, in the business-like tone in which she accepted invitations from the opposite sex. She wanted to go on talking about Victor to somebody who did not at once suspect and smile. So she said, 'It must be very nice for you, having no future to think of.' A moment ago she had seemed to understand so well that he almost believed she had said this to hurt him.

'No *future*?' he repeated, and looked at her blankly.

'Well,' said Joan, 'you haven't got to do anything that matters. I mean, there's nobody but yourself to please and, of course, your wife. While a young man, like – well, oh, anyone – say Victor Ammering, has got the whole beastly thing ahead of him. I suppose it won't all be beastly; I mean, he'll fall in love and, I suppose, marry, and sooner or later his father'll die and then he'll have some money of his own; but in the long run it's all rather an effort.'

'He's not ambitious?'

'Oh no,' said Joan placidly, 'he isn't a bit that kind of man. Besides, what's the good of being ambitious? there may be another war. And even if there isn't, disappointed people are dreadful to live with.'

'Why are you so cynical?' asked Colonel Duperrier.

'But I'm not,' said Joan, and smiled at him with troubled but naive blue eyes.

As she spoke, three people in mackintoshes, two women and a man, came in rustling and dripping from the porch. Their collars were turned up and over these they looked repudiatingly at one another. They had not been for their walks together, and they did not wish anybody to suppose that they had. They had followed one another for some kilometres along a streaming road, to close up unavoidably on the Hotel doorstep. Among them was James Milton, wondering why he had ever come abroad, cold, weary, amazed by the weather. Dripping audibly, they all got into the lift and slammed the gates upon their undesired contiguity. Here they remained for some moments shut up in silence.

'I'm afraid it's out of order,' shouted Colonel Duperrier at the risk of appearing officious. Joan had looked on with detachment.

James Milton, only too glad to escape, let himself out at once and walked upstairs, after a wistful, inquiring glance in Joan's direction. Numbed beyond the point of geniality, not one of his fellow-visitors had spoken to him during the day; he realized that this was the third Lawrence whom he did not know and that she was not going to speak to him either. Joan watched him critically till he had disappeared round the turn of the stairs.

'That's the parson,' said she. 'He went with them yesterday, with the Lee-Mittisons' picnic.'

'Oh yes, the Lee-Mittisons' picnic. We saw them start off. Wasn't it rather a fiasco?'

'Yes, it was. After lunch they were bored, so they all went off on their own, and Veronica met Victor and they went off too. When they came back, quite a short time afterwards, the Lee-Mittisons had flitted – there wasn't so much as an egg-shell. So they all hallooed for a bit, and some of them lay down and went to sleep. Veronica and Victor came home on their own, and the others got tired of calling the Lee-Mittisons and came home too, thinking nothing more of it. Eileen likes the parson, so does Sydney; they say he is rather an ass but wonderfully sporting. They expected to find the L.-M.s at home, but the L.-M.s didn't turn up till half-way through dinner, looking fearfully sick. Old L.-M. came over to father between the soup and the fish, simply snorting. He said to father, "I suppose you realize what your daughter has been exposed to?" We think old L.-M. is quite mad. I was awfully glad I hadn't gone.'

'I should think you were,' said Colonel Duperrier absently. He wanted to ask her: 'Couldn't we go off some day for a walk in the hills?' He tried this over and over in his head, but it didn't sound right somehow. He supposed that the suggestion must be unsuitable, and that at all events she would be bored with him.

As if to settle the matter once and for all, Joan said, with an unhappy note in her voice as she thought of the meeting of Veronica and Victor, 'And anyway, I'm not much of a walker. I don't care for walking at all.'

CHAPTER VIII

IN THE DRAWING-ROOM

AFTER Colonel Duperrier had left the drawing-room the ladies round the fire folded back their skirts over their knees again to keep the stuff from scorching, drew their chairs in closer and resumed their discussion of Mrs. Kerr. Their backs were turned in a kind of contempt on three tall windows through which cold light from the sky and the sea poured in on them gravely.

'I cannot think,' said one, 'what a woman of that sort finds to do with herself.' She spoke with emphasis, this remark had been throughout a recurring-point in the conversation. 'She has no interests. She hasn't a large correspondence, she does nothing at all for herself. I personally find the day so very full here, it seems only too short.'

'I wouldn't say *too* short. But as days abroad go, one seems to get through them quickly enough.' To this there was a hum of agreement.

'She sits on her balcony in the sun,' said Mrs. Hillier, 'a thing which I for one should never have time to do. I suppose one has too much conscience. If I ever do go out on my balcony for a minute and look along, there she always is; and if I call out in a friendly way, "Whatever are you doing?" she says, "Nothing", and looks amused and rather superior.'

'She doesn't sketch, or one would understand her staring like that at the view. Of course, it is very beautiful.'

'She may think,' said another of the ladies, looking up

from some *broderie anglaise* over which she had been straining her eyes. She was of some prestige, her speech was slow and weighted down with implications. 'She must think a good deal,' she decided; 'nobody who was not thinking could do absolutely nothing all day and look so very superior about it, like a cat.'

'You mean that she has something on her mind?'

The lady of the embroidery rubbed her sore eyes with two fingers, revolving this slowly. She opened her eyes again tentatively, blinked once or twice and shut them again. 'The light is very poor,' she said aggrievedly.

'Very. Won't you take my place, Mrs. Hepworth? it is nearer the window – you mean to say that she has something on her mind?'

'No, thank you very much, I do not care to move from this side of the fire – I should rather say that she had something *in* her mind all the time, at the back of it. One is never comfortable in talking to her, though she is, I am sure, brilliant. I have said to myself over and over again, when I've been with her: "That woman has something at the back of her mind." '

'I wonder *what?*' asked someone rashly.

'That,' said Mrs. Hepworth coldly, 'would be quite impossible to say.'

There were about seven ladies present, all embroidering something unpractical and therefore permissible, except Mrs. Duperrier, who, poor soul, was too restless, and another lady who with the aid of much gamboge and vermilion was touching up a water-colour, a sunset. At four o'clock they would all retire for tea; after that they would go downstairs to the basement into what was called the smoking-room and play bridge, with the intermission only of dinner, till it was time for bed. Though keen players, the seven were not to be numbered among the enthusiasts. Those, after a perfunctory glance at the weather, had sat down to their tables soon after eleven o'clock. Nobody who smoked but did not play bridge dared enter the smoking-room.

Out of deference to Mrs. Bellamy, who was among them, nobody had so far touched on the aspect of Mrs. Kerr which most profoundly intrigued them – her friendship with Sydney. Tessa, however, now showed herself lacking in that appreciation of their delicacy with which it had pleased them to credit her. Stretching out a plump, pretty foot to the fire and looking down at it thoughtfully, she remarked, 'She seems a very kind woman. She's been so kind to my cousin.'

'Ah, really, yes?' said someone innocently. 'Your cousin's often with her, I believe.'

'Yes, they are a lot together. Sydney is a very clever girl,' said Tessa simply; 'she is too clever for girls of her own age, I sometimes think, though she is so high-spirited and cheerful and amusing that she is always popular. I often forget, when I am with her, how clever she is. Do you know, she studied for years . . . she has passed . . .' Here she enumerated, not accurately, Sydney's academic distinctions, which while not conveying much to her audience vaguely depressed them.

'Ah, yes, it is nice for a girl to have a career. But I shouldn't,' said a lady with some restraint, tempering her suggestion with a smile, 'say that Miss Warren was high-spirited exactly.' The others disagreed too forcibly with Tessa's opinion of her cousin and respected Tessa too much to say anything at all.

Tessa continued: 'Sydney is very affectionate.'

'She is very much . . . absorbed, isn't she, by Mrs. Kerr?'

'I have known *other* cases,' said somebody else, looking about vaguely for her scissors, 'of these very violent friendships. One didn't feel *those others* were quite healthy.'

'I should discourage any daughter of mine from a friendship with an older woman. It is never the best women who have these strong influences. I would far rather she lost her head about a man.'

'Sydney hasn't lost her head,' said little Tessa with dignity.

'Oh but, Mrs. Bellamy – I was talking about *other* cases.'

'And how few men there are out here – can one wonder the girls are eccentric? They say it's the same at all these places – not a man to be had. I can't think why people go on bringing their daughters out.'

'One wonders, indeed, why some types of women ever come out here.'

'Mrs. Kerr? Oh, do you think——?'

'Mmm-mmm.'

'But she may believe in the sun,' said Tessa; 'many people believe in the sun. Of course it's always been known of, but quite recently a doctor at Baden——'

'She is not a sick woman,' pronounced the lady of the *broderie anglaise*.

'N-no?' said Tessa, petering out. 'But I'm sure,' she resumed, after a pause for consideration, 'that she has interests. I would say she was quite independent. Sydney tells me she likes to be a great deal alone.'

'Well, there now,' exclaimed a lady indignantly, dropping her needlework into her lap in holding both hands out. 'Then why should she want to come out to a hotel? She certainly is striking-looking, but I would have every sympathy with her and make every effort to be pleasant to her if she were lonely. One knows oneself that is insupportable. As winter comes on with those long evenings one begins to feel hardly human, sitting evening after evening in an empty room. One can't always be going out or visiting people or inviting people to come to one. If I shut my drawing-room door, I begin to feel restless at once; it feels so unnatural shutting oneself in with nobody. If I open it, one hears the servants laughing, or something to worry one. I am fond of reading, but I always begin to feel that books are so bad; then of course I realize, well, it's not fair, is it, to expect a book to take the place of human society? If the telephone bell rings, to hear a voice and then be cut off simply unsettles one; and if it doesn't ring the whole evening, one begins to worry and imagine things about one's friends. Once I sat with the door open and, believe me, I could hear four different clocks ticking – I counted them – in different parts of the flat. It's not, of course, that I'm nervous, but I really begin to feel – if you'll understand my saying anything so extraordinary – as if I didn't exist. If somebody does come to the door or the telephone does ring, I'm almost surprised to find I'm still there. One would go mad if one were not able to get abroad.'

She looked round with a shiver of retrospection at the semicircle which was her pleasant asylum. The others expressed their entire agreement. What they had all escaped was terrible.

'But Mrs. Kerr,' said one, 'seems to enjoy that – she's a divorcée.'

'No, he died.'

'Fancy! She doesn't give one a bit that impression . . .'

'Isn't there a son?'

'Yes, she has a nearly grown-up son. I can't think why she doesn't make a home for him.'

'But if one does make a home for anybody one is still very much alone. The best type of man is no companion.'

'Still, he is someone *there*.'

'Besides, my dear, make a home . . .! Of course, it's what one would love to do, but it nearly kills one and it's so expensive; and when all's said and done it's still so uncomfortable these days with all these difficulties, one can't expect a man to stay in it. Of course, *we* don't mind in the same way about comfort, but really it is scarcely fit for oneself. So I said to my husband . . . he agreed . . . It is so broadening to the mind, isn't it? to travel and meet people; we have been so fortunate in the hotels that were recommended to us, and we have been passed on from introduction to introduction so that we have always got to know people at once.'

'And as for the son,' put in another lady who had been waiting with parted lips, 'he really may not want her. And I rather wonder about him, too. One of my boys was at school with him and said he was not at all popular. He won't say why, of course, the Kerr boy wasn't popular; you know what boys are, they are so reserved. But one felt, of course, that there was something. Boys, you know, are rather wonderful; they have a judgment that – well, a kind of instinct.'

'Like dogs.'

'Oh, my dear Mrs. Hepworth . . .'

'I must say, if the girl were in *my* charge, were a cousin of *mine* . . .'

'Even then, though I wonder if one would be justified in interfering.'

'It would be difficult. But I do feel strongly . . .'

'Yes . . . *yes*?'

'Well, I know of a case——'

They all broke off as the door opened and Sydney looked in nonchalantly, as though she hardly expected to find whoever she was looking for.

'Oh, Tessa, there you are! I couldn't think why you weren't on your bed. We have no stamps; I have been looking for you in despair. Nobody I've met has a stamp and the concierge must be asleep somewhere.'

She was standing on the threshold, holding the door
open so that the colder air from the lounge rushed in
from behind her. She did not look as though she had
been out all day; her heavy eyes and the way her hair
had been pushed back from her forehead suggested that
she had a headache. She was asked to come right in, if
she did not mind, and shut the door after her, and she
complied absently. She came and stood behind Tessa's
chair while Tessa fumbled with her note-case; they all
remarked her air of not unhappy abstraction and how,
like a shy, self-centred child who has been sent down into
company on a message and wishes at once to escape, she
remained indifferent to their presence and made no
effort to speak to them. Once she put her hand out and
patted Tessa's hair idly. 'Do hurry, darling,' said she.

'So you've been writing letters all day; dear me!'
said the lady of the *broderie anglaise*, looking over her
glasses.

'Nothing would persuade me to,' said Sydney.

'It's dull for you young people on a day like this. No
wonder the Misses Lawrence were romping.'

'Were they? I didn't notice.'

'Oh, as you said, "we" I thought you had been with
Veronica.'

'I haven't seen Veronica all day,' said Sydney, and
while everybody listened intently she turned away from
Tessa's chair and wandered over to the window. 'Doesn't
it rain? I like it!' she was moved to exclaim. 'If I were
Monet and alive now, I would paint this and present the
picture to the P.L.M. as a poster for the Côte d'Azur.'
She smiled out at the rain with an air of complicity.

'Well, what on earth *have* you been doing with yourself all day?' asked Mrs. Hepworth, who was so motherly-
looking that she could ask anybody anything point-blank.

Sydney frowned for a moment as though she were

trying to remember. 'Thinking,' she said at last, 'with great pleasure of the thousands of villas round the hundreds of bays along these hundreds of miles of coast where the couples are living – as one is told they are living – for one another. Think what living for one another at close quarters would be like today. Think specially of what, before they became so rare, it would have been like to be living with a Russian. "It has been raining for weeks, the hay is rotting and we are living on illusions——" But perhaps you don't read Russian plays? Even in fine weather, I must say I think the importance of personal relations is very much over-estimated. Oh, thank you, Tessa; then I'll owe you three lire for the stamps.'

'Yes, we're very shockable in here,' said Mrs. Hillier briskly, 'as I expect you thought. Personally, I think the interest of these improper couples is, in all weathers, very much over-estimated, but for girls of your age they have always a great fascination. I know they had for me until I went to India. You and your young friend must have been enjoying yourselves, chatting away.'

'I haven't got a young friend,' said Sydney, and now, quite unable to refrain from laughing at herself, she guffawed at Mrs. Hillier with a keen appreciation of her own ridiculousness but with unabated gloom.

'Then won't you stay down here and make up the second four for bridge? You see there are only seven of us; we'll be going down directly.'

'Oh, thank you, no; I must be going up.'

'You know the lift is out of order?'

'Is it? I never use it. I put the kettle on for tea just now and I must go and keep an eye on it.'

'Can't Mrs. *Kerr* keep an eye on the kettle for you?' Mrs. Hepworth called after her.

'She forgets about it,' said Sydney as she left the drawing-room.

CHAPTER IX

MY LITTLE BOY

THREE days afterwards the weather along that coast was once more fulfilling the expectation of visitors. Only a little wind remained to disturb the sea, to rustle dryly through the palm trees out on the promontory where the coast road disappeared towards Genoa and to rush to meet one round street corners with a disconcertingly ice-cold whistle. Against an opaque, bright blue sky the expressionless faces of the buildings had again their advertised and almost aching whiteness. The sounds, like the shadows, were exact and clear-cut, no longer blunted by the rain.

From end to end of the town the principal long street ran like a funnel; as Sydney came out of the flower-shop, her side of the street was slate-grey in the shadow of early afternoon. It was characteristic of her as an intelligent young English lady that she should have come to buy carnations during the hour of the siesta, cutting for her a caprice of her own direct across the custom of the land. The carnations, among which, walking slowly, she now was burying her face, were scentless, but gave one an acute pleasure by the chilly contact of their petals. She had an armful of two colours — sulphur with a ragged edge of pink and ashy mauve with crimson at the centre, crimson-veined. Carnations are not costly before they reach the flower-market, grown on terraces that stagger up the hills and picked in the grey quiet of the morning to the accompaniment of singing and of never-answered calls that come dropping down forlornly from terrace to terrace to the coast. On account of their low cost, their strangeness to the Northern eye and the vehemence of their colouring, they have become the vehicle of much emotion. One cannot, however casually, present these native carnations to a friend and remain quite unaffected, while the pleasure with which carnations are received is intensified by some vague agitation.

Sydney's day had been so far as perfect as a bubble; she felt careless of it, as though the bubble could not burst. Happiness, she said to herself, is not to be solicited, but coming, for however short a time, comes with an appearance of finality, to be juggled with offhand. It seems to be some kind of balance, as in riding a bicycle, attempted painfully a thousand times and achieved at last without effort. Her senses were absorbed by the carnations, she barely looked ahead, and she could be conscious of the street only as a sharp distinction between sun and shadow. Crossing over, she walked in the sun, where dogs stretched their lengths in abandon on the hot pavement. She must have been made conspicuous by her abstraction or by her yellow dress; people turned to stare at her and a tram announced by a hum of over-head wires rushed past with a long smudge of faces turned her way. She left the street but delayed her return to the Hotel by following a series of by-paths, pausing now and then to stare idly through some barred gate into a garden. She was mapping out for herself a deep-down life in which emotions ceased their clashing together and friends appeared only as painted along the edge of one's quietness.

At a turn of the footpath she met the Barry children going down to the shore with their nurse. There were several of them, very much alike; their number appalled Sydney, who stood back against the wall. Cordelia Barry, the eldest, walked by herself a little ahead of the others, ostentatiously carrying a book.

'The *whole* family of us all again, you see!' she exclaimed affectedly. 'Oh, dear Miss Warren, what lovely carnations! Oh, I do love them!'

She was a child of about eleven, with long thin legs and an eager tremolo. Sydney, who considered that she had been demoralized by overmuch grown-up attention, said, 'Do you?' unresponsively. She did not intend to give any carnations to Cordelia.

'You *aren't* going for a walk, I suppose?' said Cordelia wistfully. 'Mother said I might go with anybody who would have me, but that I would have to go with Nanny if everybody else fell through.'

'Well, I'm afraid I can't help you. But I expect it will be nice on the shore.'

'Hoo!' said Cordelia, pouncing on this note of falsity. She tilted her head back to stare up at Sydney from under the brim of her hat. 'How stupid you'd be if you really believed that! Nice on the shore!'

'Come along, Cordelia!' called back Nanny in the flat voice of one who is employing the imperative continually and without effect.

Cordelia clutched at Sydney's dress. 'Lovely yellow thing,' she said feverishly. '*Beautiful* Miss Warren, won't you take me for a walk?'

Sydney, who was still near enough to her own childhood to mistrust children profoundly, wondered what Cordelia could be getting at. 'Not today,' she temporized; 'some day, perhaps.'

'Come *on*, Cordelia!'

'Go on, Cordelia; Nanny's calling.'

'She's no Nanny to me,' said Cordelia in bitter repudiation. 'Veronica Lawrence is very fond of children,' she added rapidly. 'She said she'd take me for a walk any day. But I'm not so much interested in Veronica Lawrence.'

'Then you're an ungrateful little wretch,' said Sydney. 'Run along!'

'Do you promise, *some day*?' said the child despairingly.

'Very well, I promise.'

After another long stare that was at once ardent and sardonic, Cordelia, with reluctant steps and backward glances, went after her family. Sydney heard her calling Nanny a devil. But so long as Cordelia came on, Nanny, who was a broken woman, cared for none of these things.

Sydney, who knew that Mrs. Kerr was all this time sitting on her balcony, never more accessible than today, in a mood which the carnations were soon to reflect, still delayed luxuriously. She heightened the sweetness of exile by telling herself how soon the freshness of her carnations would be over, and how at any moment Mrs. Kerr might fall asleep for the afternoon, or get up and go out with somebody else. She even played with a regret at having packed off Cordelia, with whom she might have walked back still more slowly through the town.

When she did at last return to the Hotel the afternoon post had just come in and was spread out on the concierge's table. There was nothing for herself, but a letter for Mrs. Kerr in Ronald's large untidy writing caught her eye. She hesitated for a moment over this, for she had not yet directly tried conclusions with Ronald; then, very confident of her balance, took the letter up with her and tapped lightly with the corner of the envelope on Mrs. Kerr's door.

Sydney knew at once from her friend's conscious air and rather marked immobility that she had been expected. The carnations, into which virtue seemed to have gone out of herself, were at this anticipated moment difficult to relinquish. She laid them down with a degree of awkwardness across the end of the sofa. Mrs. Kerr, who sat with her feet up, looking out at the sea, ex-

claimed: 'Carnations!' incredulously, as though this were
what she had been longing for, and with an unprecedented movement held up her face to be kissed.

'Will you put them in water?' she said, having looked
at the flowers with wistful delight for a moment or two,
and Sydney, with a feeling of surprise that she could
not explain to herself, glanced round her, then began to
arrange the carnations. She chose for the purpose a
rather self-conscious-looking pottery mug that had been
a present from Miss Pym. She arranged the flowers
deliberately, and Mrs. Kerr looked on in expressive
silence.

'Pleased?' said Sydney.

'Very, very much. I had been feeling like that: it
was uncanny of you. Now they are perfect, Sydney;
leave them alone and don't keep fussing round them.'

'That was because I want them to look nice all round.
I'm not restless.'

'No?' said Mrs. Kerr, revolving critically a possible new
version of friend which she seemed slowly to accept.

'No, I am not. I have a capacity for being still that,
left to myself, I would never have doubted, but that no
one else, you specially, will ever let me believe in.
Look——' She knelt down where she stood, then sat
back and arranged herself, leaning her side and elbow
against the side of the sofa. 'I could stay like this for
the rest of the afternoon,' said Sydney.

'Well, then stay still. Why should I disturb you?'

'You will, you are bound to – just now. Where did
you think I had gone?'

'I was not allowed to think. I went out there and
looked over the balcony, and that clergyman, that Mr.
Milton, was walking about in the garden. He took off
his hat and waved it to attract my attention. Then he
began to talk for some time in the friendliest way.'

'Really? That was excessive of him. What did he say?'

'I don't know,' said Mrs. Kerr. 'I couldn't hear. I just smiled and nodded. He is a cheerful, un-self-conscious person. I like him.'

'Un-self-conscious? He feels spikes everywhere and rushes to impale himself. But I feel an interest in him; he told Veronica Lawrence he admired me.'

'Very appealing of him. And so wise.'

'Wise – to tell?'

'No – to admire. Have many people, Sydney?'

Sydney flung round at her, startled into a brilliant flush. 'I don't know: I've never been sure of it.'

'Never mind,' said Mrs. Kerr, staring out at her friend from some profound reverie; 'when you look like that, the question answers itself.'

'I suppose,' said Sydney after an instant's reflection, 'that extraordinary people do. Cordelia Barry – or did you only mean men?'

'No, I didn't only mean men. Don't be so fearfully on the defensive – or do you think I am likely to match-make?'

'I am sorry, that was horribly vulgar of me. It is so much easier to be vulgar and so much less noticed. I mean, you and I are supposed to assume, or to seem everywhere to assume, that that man down in the garden could be more to either of us than the other. Also, one has had it so ground into one that admiration, any exercise of the spirit, is only valuable to its *object*, to drive her, his, somebody's mill.'

' "Exercise of the spirit" . . .' said Mrs. Kerr, while Sydney listened like a stranger to this repetition of her own words. 'If you call admiration *that*, you must agree that it would be allowed another value, even popularly: the value of a gymnastic.'

'Oh. Shaw's Englishman and his moral gymnasium; yes, I know,' said Sydney scornfully.

'Now, there you are, Sydney; you've moved and you'll say I disturbed you. Don't be so out to suffer. Mr. Milton's not the only person who runs on to spikes.'

' "Out to suffer," ' said Sydney, looking down at herself, as it were, from the height of her exaltation. '*Am* I out to suffer?'

'I feel that you are,' said Mrs. Kerr, and pressing her head farther back into the cushions she looked at Sydney again in thoughtful silence. They could hear footsteps, perhaps James Milton's, crunching the gravel below.

'Well, yes,' Mrs. Kerr said, 'put it that way ... Sydney, isn't that a letter for me, over there by the carnations? Isn't it from Ronald?'

'Yes, it is from Ronald. I brought it up with me, but I forgot to give it to you. Do you want it now?' Mrs. Kerr was holding out her hand for the letter, but Sydney did not seem to notice. 'It's a very fat letter; I expect it is his views on Germany. *Do* you want to read it while I'm here?'

'Yes,' said Mrs. Kerr. 'I think I ought to read it. Mothers do.'

'That you know best, of course.' Sydney, rising to her knees, reached across the table for the letter, which she handed to Ronald's mother. Mrs. Kerr put on what Sydney called 'the Ronald expression' and began to read, while Sydney watched her.

'My little boy,' she said at last, 'is coming here.'

'Coming here?'

'Yes, here. Coming to the Hotel.'

Sydney, sitting quite still, remained blank for a moment and did not say anything. Then she got up and walked about the room, which, crowded up with the glare of the afternoon, now appeared to be much constricted. She did not even wonder as usual whether Mrs. Kerr were waiting for her to speak or if she had forgotten her. She looked for some time at the ornaments on Mrs. Kerr's dressing-table, which had at one time, by their profusion, meaninglessness and evident air of being appreciated, 'dated' her friend for her inevitably. She glanced for a moment, but only as if to assure herself of its still being there, at the portrait of Ronald.

Ronald, for the delectation of some circle of friends as to whose extent and nature she had never speculated, had sat to one of those expensive photographers who specialize in portraits of men. A disposition of the prevalent shadows with one fierce escape of light on to the jaw and temple combined, with the Promethean glitter of an eyeball, to bring about an effect of fine ruggedness, of an elemental something curbed. Each copy of this photograph, a sepia matt, must have cost Ronald about a guinea. Sydney turned away from it impatiently. 'Why on earth,' she asked, 'isn't Ronald up at Oxford now?'

She had to wait for an answer until Mrs. Kerr, having glanced back to an earlier page of the letter and smiled to herself over something, perhaps an inconsistency she had detected, folded up the thin sheets casually and let them slide from the sofa to the floor.

'What did you say, Sydney? Ah yes, Oxford. He thought it would be better to travel for a time, you see, after leaving school. He wanted to expand again, he said, and he wished particularly, though I cannot think why, to spend a year in Germany. He would have preferred to go to Heidelberg, but his guardian wouldn't hear of it, unfortunately. So he is going up to Oxford in the autumn, I believe.'

'I suppose he won't mind being older than the people in his year?'

'I suppose not,' said Mrs. Kerr. 'I should have thought it was a pity. However, I know very little about boys of that age. He will be twenty soon.'

'An impossible age,' said Sydney.

'I suppose it really is,' agreed Mrs. Kerr.

Sydney had by this time made up her mind that their future must not be devastated by the descent upon them of Ronald. She looked about her undecidedly, not certain whether to say, 'This is very generous of him,' with irony, or, without irony but with a display of emotion sure to be distasteful, 'Oh, this is lovely for you; I am ever so glad,' or 'It will be interesting to see you together,' with an implication of detachment and of relegating her friend to maternity. She could not guess to which of these observations Mrs. Kerr would be likely to react most desirably, and she felt herself embarrassed by a lack of insight into her friend's personality of which she had always been conscious, but which had till now added charm to their intercourse. Now that she might have to come to grips with the hypothetical mother in Mrs. Kerr, she realized that she was powerless to estimate the force and scope of that relationship of being to being, from consideration of which, as something out of proportion with life as she saw it, she had always withheld herself.

Mrs. Kerr, her hands behind her head, gazed delightedly at the future. 'How very nice,' she laughed, 'how very nice and amusing ... Oh, no, don't laugh like that, Sydney; why should it seem funny to you? It's very natural, only it's so funny that we – he and I – never seem to have happened to be together in a place where there was nothing to look at and no one to visit and nowhere to go. So that I suppose one might almost say we had never been together ... It is absurd for me to laugh,' she went on, in a glow of speculation, 'but I'm so touched; it is so ridiculously touching of him. Fancy him writing like that and wanting to come from *Dresden* . . . I wonder where he will sleep: we must find him somewhere to sleep . . . I think that will be all right, don't you, Sydney?'

'Have I been very dense?' asked Sydney in a tone strange to herself. 'I do not even seem to have realized you missed him, or thought of him much, or would be glad if he came.'

'But I suppose,' said Mrs. Kerr, looking back at the past in surprise, 'that I didn't realize it either.'

'*Has* it been lonely and dull? They all said it must be lonely and dull for you, but I never———'

'Oh no, Sydney dear. You've made such a difference.'

'Have I?' Sydney said hungrily. Mrs. Kerr nodded; she was enclosed in her thoughts, but this gleam of affection emboldened Sydney to ask, with a desperate directness, 'And you *do* want him now – you are fearfully glad?'

'Sydney, you really are too clever sometimes to understand me. Can't I be glad?'

Sydney felt herself beaten back by something that in spite of nature's whole precedent she knew for a falsity; an imposture her immaturity sensed but could not challenge. She knelt down again in bewildered, still angry, submission by the side of her friend. 'Of course I don't mean that you shouldn't be glad. On the other hand, you know that to me the conventions don't seem to fit you, and bar the conventions, why should I *assume* that you are? You see, I'm not a mother and I don't know any mothers well.'

She allowed herself to be reconquered as Mrs. Kerr, putting a hand out and vaguely touching her hair, said thoughtfully, 'No, you aren't, and you don't; that's quite true. Well, won't you be generous enough to take me for granted?'

CHAPTER X

MR. MILTON

FOR James Milton, after his first few days in the Hotel, everybody with whom he had exchanged a word or a glance or been brought even indirectly into contact had already divided themselves into his friends or enemies. Those who had not yet detached themselves hung about the outskirts of his consciousness as a kind of mist behind which possibilities were for ever stirring, to be glimpsed for an instant, then subsiding again. He suffered, as he did at last confess to himself, and began to wonder why he had ever left his parish, where the crippling sensitiveness of his childhood had at least been deadened by the activity of every day, and where in the assured retreat of office he had had no need to ask what he was. But the place was beautiful and completely satisfied him once he had been able to reconcile what he saw with what he had imagined, and to recognize that while an ultimate Riviera could only have existence in the mind of God, this was as fair an imitation as it was reasonable to expect. He walked for the allied pleasures of coloured experience and of hardening his muscles; he tried to talk Italian to the natives, to be answered incomprehensibly in patois or the local French; he played tennis not so badly, and was to be surprised, in consequence, by the friendliness of the Lawrences, and he admitted to some vague attractions which it entertained him to discuss with himself.

He became friendly, comfortably and without attraction, with Miss Fitzgerald and Miss Pym. These two in spite of their experience of clergymen could not 'place' him. From his moustache, one would have been inclined

to take him for an Evangelical; on the other hand, it is
Anglicans who step with fewest scruples into secular
clothes. He had attended the conferences of neither
party and remained irresponsive to the shibboleths of
both. Miss Pym wrote, on an inspiration, to ask par-
ticulars of him from the friend in Derbyshire that he
and she had early discovered to be mutual. But the
friend in Derbyshire was an Anglo-Catholic and did not
acknowledge the finer shades; she simply wrote back that
he was a delightful man, adding a string of messages
for him that gave no key. Colonel Duperrier also liked
Milton; they exchanged stories about fishing in Donegal,
discussed Europe and respected one another's reserves.
The Lawrences made him an apple-pie bed and used to
send him suggestive Italian picture post cards anony-
mously to see how much he would stand.

But he was still avid for· popularity. Though devoid
of the more odious kind of vanity, he had been given to
understand that as an unattached, personable man he
must be *persona grata* anywhere: and he was troubled
to find that this was not the case. He had avoided Sydney
since that day of the Lee-Mittisons' picnic: for some
reason that he could not explain it was impossible to
think of her without embarrassment, though at times
she was nothing more to him than some curious picture
whose worth he could apprehend but felt unable to
analyse. It was with some unavowed idea of a circuitous
approach to her that he sought out her friend Mrs. Kerr;
preparing to find himself to a degree, but not beyond
that degree, disturbed by her.

He was oppressed by some patent hostilities.

'I am afraid,' he said to Miss Fitzgerald, as during the
half-hour before lunch they sat together in the Hotel
garden in iron chairs under an orange tree, 'that I have
done something to offend Mrs. Pinkerton.'

'Oh, I don't see how you could have. Anyhow she's a fearful old snob,' said Miss Fitzgerald, who knew all about the bathroom but had neither the face nor the heart to tell him.

'Oh, do you think so? She is the sort of old lady I have so often been asked to lunch with that I cannot help wondering why we do not get on.'

'She is the patroness of a living——'

'Well, I don't want the woman's living,' said Milton indignantly. 'Does she think I'm going to pick her pocket for it?'

'How ridiculous you are!' laughed Miss Fitzgerald, who was exhilarated by violence. 'You know she would make a splendid Lady Catherine de Bourgh.'

'Ye-es,' said Milton thoughtfully, wondering who should be his Charlotte. He resumed: 'Another person I should like an explanation with is Mr. Lee-Mittison. He took me up a mountain my first day here, lost me and has been looking daggers at me ever since. He seems to have forgiven the Lawrences and Miss Warren who were equally his victims, and I cannot see why I am singled out. After all, I was stranger to the hills than any of them.'

'I am very sorry for his wife,' said Miss Fitzgerald, sighing pleasurably.

'I don't know. I think he's her fault. She mayn't seem a very buoyant woman, but I don't suppose she'd like to be.'

'It's very curious,' said Miss Fitzgerald, turning to look at him, 'most men, I have noticed, are hardest on men, but with you it seems just the opposite. I don't know whether it's personal prejudice' – she sweetened the impertinence with a smile – 'or the curious sombre rigidity of some old school of thought; perhaps Pauline?'

'I can't think,' Milton said vaguely. At this particular

hour of the morning he did not want to talk about himself and was still less interested in St. Paul.

'Perhaps,' she suggested, 'you are brought too much into contact with women, the tiresome type. A clergyman's life——'

'It never really strikes me that there's very much difference. I mean, there are a certain rather limited number of ways in which people can be idiotic – or, if you like, wicked – and men and women seem to fall into them indiscriminately. It always irritates me to see anybody being bolstered up in their own particular kind of insufferableness by the friend who ought to be helping them, and I do think women (for their own ends, which makes it unpardonable) are worse about doing this than men. If that's what you mean by my being severer on women? Otherwise I can't see that, in my department, at any rate, men and women are noticeably different.'

'Or in any department,' said Miss Fitzgerald, earnestly rallying to her standard. 'And it interested me to hear you use the word "friend" in that context. Meaning that friend and husband – or wife, as the case may be – should be synonymous.'

'Practically,' said Milton, looking round and wondering whether it would be possible to order an apéritif, and wishing, since he feared this was not possible, that he had gone down to the town. 'I suppose,' he continued conscientiously though with a slight effort, 'that you think I am intolerant?'

'Oh no, not that: too, too acute . . . One feels at a disadvantage. I suppose one is oneself too much in the habit of *generalizing*.' She broke off and reached up suddenly in apparent confusion to pluck a small, still rather sickly orange from a branch above her. This, without looking at him again, she bit, right into the peel.

'Surely that is rather bitter?' asked James Milton, looking on solicitously.

'Yes,' said she with a wry face, wiping her mouth, 'it was very bitter!' She turned crimson and began to laugh awkwardly. 'Such an extraordinary thing to do: I *do* do extraordinary things sometimes ... without thinking ... when I'm thinking hard.'

James Milton, who did think this was an extraordinary thing to have done, was silent. She glanced shamefacedly at her tooth-marks in the orange, then guiltily up at the windows of the Hotel, then she wiped the orange and tucked it quietly away behind her.

'Look!' cried out James Milton considerately. 'There's Mrs. Kerr again, out on her balcony.'

'So she is – how nice she looks up there! You know, my friend Miss Pym is so fond of her, she says she is marvellously sympathetic. She is certainly an unusual woman, but so very charming. She is very much criticized here by a certain set, but then I am afraid some women have very small minds. Did you hear, her son is coming out next week? We are so glad, it will be delightful for her.'

'I say, is he really? I'm glad.'

'We are wondering,' continued Miss Fitzgerald, 'what he and Sydney Warren will say to each other.'

'Really?' said James Milton, whose mind had leapt at once to this.

'Not of course that I mean anything ... well, you know, sentimentally. The boy is hardly grown up. No, I mean she has been so much in possession, really rather monopolizing Mrs. Kerr, who of course is incapable of not being nice to anybody and is so patient and sympathetic and good.' Miss Fitzgerald sighed. 'She's been victimized. . . .'

Later on, when Milton had followed Miss Fitzgerald

into the dining-room, he stared with renewed curiosity at the back of Miss Warren's head across the dining-room, as though he expected its shape and colour to be somehow different, or expected her to disclose her whole self to him in some gesture or attitude. He sat at his lonely table crumbling his bread exaltedly and wondering how soon Ronald could possibly arrive. He promised himself that, if Ronald were not delayed, it should be possible for him in a fortnight or even ten days to know Sydney absolutely. Then he had to recollect how unfriendly to him she had shown herself, and wonder whether being thrown back on his society would tend to make her like him better. Tessa's bright, vague eyes surprised him in their wandering; he smiled and nodded.

'Mr. Milton keeps on looking at us,' whispered Tessa to Sydney. 'I do wonder what he wants.'

Many people who admired Mrs. Kerr had already congratulated her; others who had still to do so sought her out as they streamed from the dining-room. A small crowd gathered about her as she stood in the doorway, like a tall bride, confused and elated. Many who did not like her at all had also congratulated, as they were anxious to see how she was taking it. 'Splendid!' shouted and smiled Mr. Milton over the intervening heads; his long, rather pink face also towering.

'Yes, it's splendid, isn't it?' agreed Sydney from behind him. She was jostled against him all at once by more people pushing out from the dining-room and he said, putting out a hand to steady her: 'I'm sure *you* must be glad?'

At the end of that afternoon's tennis he waited for Sydney and walked up with her from the club. 'This young man, this Ronald,' he asked, 'do you know him?'

'I feel I do,' said Sydney. 'Mrs. Kerr has shown me his letters, and she laughs at me occasionally and says

I am like him. And there is a photograph, anyway, that one couldn't help noticing. Altogether I feel he is to be a kind of comic character.'

'Oh! Does his mother think he is funny?' said James Milton, slightly jarred.

'But young people are always funny: as we get more sophisticated we can't help realizing that ourselves – I don't know whether that makes us less funny or more so.'

The sun had dipped to the line of the hills, so that the sky had a kind of gold sparkle which reflected itself on figures and faces. Even before the moment of sunset the air was already tingling with cold; the dark, keen, up-standing trees about them seemed slightly to shiver. Sydney flung the folds of her white fleecy cloak across her breast, and holding them gathered against her paused a moment, looking back towards the tennis-courts with a wild, Beatrice Cenci expression which did not correspond with her thoughts, and of which she was wholly unconscious. Milton's heart leapt to his mouth for that moment; then he felt the chill of dusk lay an ice-cold hand on him, and he shuddered. He asked her impatiently if she were waiting for anyone else.

She said 'No' in surprise, and walked beside him up the path to the Hotel, treading noiselessly in her rope-soled shoes. 'It is an alarming idea,' said he, unable to maintain a silence of whose peculiar quality he became intolerably conscious, 'that the young should be getting progressively more and more sophisticated. It is as bad as it is to be told, if one is a reader of adventure stories, that no part of dark Africa remains undiscovered, and that one-inch maps of all parts of the world will be available shortly.'

'I suppose it would be if one ever seriously considered youth were romantic.'

'But I never said *I* did. Romantic – I'm not that kind

of middle-aged man. When I compared it to Africa, I didn't mean I liked Africa; I dislike the thoughts of the wilds intensely, but they make me so appreciative of the state of civilization in which I am living that I should be sorry if they disappeared.'

'So you feel civilized?' said Sydney, beginning to like him. Till now she had been discouraged by his facile (what she called 'professional') manner, and by a middle-aged whimsicality that reeked of the Barrie play.

'Much more so,' said James Milton, cursing himself for going on like this, and for that very manner and habit of mind of his, of which no one could have been more contemptuously aware.

'More than whom?' said Sydney idly; but he refused to continue and she allowed him with unusual complaisance to swing her with him into a new mood. He stood looking up. The rocky crest of a hill to the east, at a great height, had been suddenly ribbed with scarlet. This vivid colour against the profound and quickly darkening sky was to Northern eyes a challenge to credulity: and Sydney looking up after him with admiration and hostility said, 'I should never have believed it.'

'I have always believed it,' said James Milton, 'but it is surprising to see.'

'You'll see a hundred others,' she told him; and they hurried on, discussing in relation to this line of coast the phenomena of sunset. When they had come out into the road they walked more slowly between the lines of chestnut trees, watching the light fade from the enormous faces of the hotels, then from the villas above, which though suffused in dusk still glimmered. Night had come as always, with the catastrophic suddenness which does not for a long time cease to be alarming. They could hear forgotten windows being slammed indignantly, while lights springing up behind the

curtains brought them out in hundreds in their uni-
formity; with here and there some figure passing
regularly as a pendulum to and fro across the screen
of lace. The hill smoked over with olives loomed, by
some *trompe-l'œil* of twilight seemed to topple, above the
larger hotels; but their own, in silhouette against the
sea, stood out as they approached with a greater significance.

She said, 'I have often thought it would be interesting
if the front of any house, but of an hotel especially, could
be swung open on a hinge like the front of a doll's house.
Imagine the hundreds of rooms with their walls lit up
and the real-looking staircase and all the people surprised
doing appropriate things in appropriate attitudes as
though they had been put there to represent something
and had never moved in their lives. Like the cook-
doll that I always had propped up against the kitchen
stove and the father-doll propped against the library
book-shelves and the sitting-up doll in the bath that was
really a china ornament and had no other attitude, and
the limp dolls that wouldn't do anything so had to be
kept in the spare-room beds, which I always think was an
unconscious reflection on the ideal habits for visitors.'

'Yes,' said James Milton, for whom the Hotel was at
once in miniature. 'If one could see people all at once
like that they wouldn't matter so much.' Quite apart
from and yet somehow parallel with the intellectual
conception he had another idea of God of which he permitted himself to be conscious, as of an enormous and
perpetually descending Finger and Thumb. What
Sydney had just said fitted in with this alarmingly.

'If one could see them like that,' she continued, 'one
could see them so clearly as living under the compulsion
of their furniture – or the furniture they happen to have
hired. It would seem very doubtful, I dare say, whether

man were not, after all, made for the Sabbath; and worse, for beds and dinner-tables and washstands, just to discharge the obligations all those have created.'

'I don't think I should ever believe that,' said Milton, amused.

'Well, just think of this,' she continued. 'Though it may have been an Idea in the first place that made churches be built, it was the churches already existing, with rows of pews for people to sit in and a pulpit and things all ready that had to be filled, that made you into a parson.'

'I'm afraid I don't agree with you at all,' said he with a finality that impressed her.

'It really isn't worth disagreeing with; I was only talking for the fun of the thing. Of course I don't believe that more than anything else.' They had been walking under the windows of their own Hotel, and she now paused in the gateway with the light from the Hotel door streaming out on to her, looking at him remotely, as a gipsy might look over the garden fence at a house-holder mowing his lawn. 'I dare say,' her look said, 'that in your encumbered kind of way you are happy. I am not, in any way, and I don't want to be.' It was with this air at once complacent and desolate that she seemed proposing to part from him, for she glanced at her wrist-watch, murmured something in the nature of a farewell and slipped ahead.

'Oh, I say!' exclaimed Milton helplessly, and racked his brains for something further to say to her.

'What?' asked Sydney, looking down from the steps and with faint impatience swinging her racquet.

'I hope you didn't think I was offended?' said he wildly.

'No. Why should you be?'

'What you said about churches . . . I was afraid you might have thought——'

'Well,' said Sydney, 'it's no use trying not to offend people, so I don't think I ever think much one way or the other. I've given up listening agonizedly for the possible reverberations of every remark which, if you'll forgive my saying so, I think you do.'

'I'm sorry,' said he, with the humility of twenty years' seniority.

'Oh, it doesn't matter a bit. Good night.' He had pulled open the swing-door for her and she passed through it ahead of him, trailing her cloak which had slipped away from her shoulders. He gathered up the fringe of this from the floor and handed it to her. 'Why good night?' said he, and several people sitting about the lounge looked up in astonishment. 'I mean, don't we see each other at dinner?'

'Oh well, of course we see each other at dinner.' Sydney glanced round the lounge, took note of the astonished faces and, after another slight bow to Milton, went upstairs slowly, humming a tune.

CHAPTER XI

THE DANCE

ON the night of Ronald's arrival a dance was taking place in the Hotel dining-room. Chairs and tables had been stacked away in a corner, the floor polished and the walls festooned with paper flags and specially illuminated. The music, audible in every part of the Hotel, though generally as a sustained thin humming with the pianist's undertone as an irregular and tuneless pulse-beat, had drawn everybody; lounge and drawing-room had been drained of their usual occupants. Dances at the Hotel were not usual and this was in the nature of a gala-night. The concierge's face was wreathed in smiles, but Ronald felt his manner lacked *empressement*. It was irritating, when one had inquired for one's mother, to be told with an appearance of indifference that she, too, would be, doubtless, at the ball. He had been sustained till now by the brilliant certainty of being expected and awaited, but he was tired after his journey and the lounge, from which the palms had all been taken away to decorate the dining-room, now seemed repellent, mean and artificial.

'Tell my mother I have come,' he said to the concierge, and sat down in a wicker chair while the dance music throbbed at him. The concierge went away, but nobody came, though he waited; so at last he walked over to the dining-room door and, unable to see anything through the blind but twirling forms and wavering shadows, opened the door sharply and surveyed the scene from the threshold.

It must be admitted that the impressions he received

were coloured for him by a prejudice against the Riviera which he had cultivated from his childhood and believed to be innate.

Veronica Lawrence was the first to remark and point out to her partner that a young man, probably Ronald Kerr, was standing in the doorway. She was wearing a tight green dress like a sheath, and every time she passed she looked thoughtfully at Ronald over her partner's shoulder and once even smiled. Girls and young men had been asked in from the other hotels and the floor was crowded, while a close-packed row of onlookers sat or stood along the walls, pressing up so near to the band that the red-coated fiddlers began to look desperate, having scarcely elbow-room. The sexes were unequally represented, several couples of girls were dancing together. Some of the elder ladies had also taken the floor and were spinning round at a high velocity in the arms of their usual bridge-partners, whose coat-tails whirled horizontally, to the constant danger of more modern dancers whose poised totterings, hesitations and smooth forward rushes they perpetually interrupted.

'He's rather decorative,' said Veronica. She had at last elicited a bow from Ronald, who felt convinced that the girl must know him.

'Oh well,' said Victor coldly, 'if you like 'em floppy——' He set his jaw again and silent as ever they flitted across a pool of floor that opened for them, light as moths above the shadows. The Lawrences were remarkable everywhere with their burnished hair brushed up into haloes; they trailed enormous feather fans across their partners' shoulders negligently and refused to waltz with elderly men, though they would make an exception in favour of Colonel Duperrier.

Mrs. Duperrier sat against one of the walls, following couple after couple round with her eyes. Now and again

she would smile metallically at a girl she knew and ask
her whether she were having a good time. Though she
never seemed to be watching Colonel Duperrier, she
knew where he was all the time and could have pointed
him out immediately. She had trained herself to
remember distinctly whichever scene from her past had
at the moment most torturous significance for her; now
she could see herself at nineteen, admired to satiation,
waltzing with Captain Duperrier at Darjeeling. A
French window stood open on to a balcony, from which
steps led down into the black-dark garden; couples dived
in and out of the window perpetually, and presently
Mrs. Duperrier, who had been expecting this the whole
evening, saw her husband disappear with one of the
Lawrences and waited in vain for him to come back.
Mr. Lee-Mittison, who had been working his way round
the room, bumped down beside her abruptly with his
hands on his parted knees.

'I hope you agree with me that our girls are doing us
credit? There isn't a girl in the room that can hold a
candle to one of the Lawrences; Sydney Warren's looking very distinguished (I can't honestly tell you I care
for this thing they're all dancing), and even the little
Bransomes light up well. Mark my word——'

Mrs. Duperrier suddenly felt she could not bear this,
made a queer little sound and shot up from her place.
After one last look through the window she pushed her
way between the dancers and out of the dining-room.
She passed Ronald Kerr in the doorway and looked at
him in amazement, then rushed past him and shut herself up in her room.

Sydney wore a scarlet dress and danced as though
she had for once forgotten herself. A young Italian
whose name she did not know had attached himself to
her; she divided her dances between him and Colonel

Duperrier and a gingery Captain Somebody-or-other from another hotel, who thought her conversation smart, and giggled ecstatically. The Italian danced, as Veronica afterwards said, 'like a seraphim'; he taught Sydney the tango as it is danced in Rome, and it was while she was standing balanced against him to the slow music that she looked sideways and saw or rather for the first time apprehended Ronald: she realized that he must have been there some time.

Cold all over and for a moment lost to the tango she thought: 'Ronald!' then returned her eyes to her partner's dispassionate face and slid her long step sideways across him; they both swung half round and balanced again at the conclusion of the bar. The floor was emptier; all but a few couples had been driven off it by the unnatural music; the remaining few were visible from every part of the room, and were reflected in the twirling mirror. Ronald was watching her, and before the end of the dance she excused herself to her partner and crossed the room to speak to him.

'I beg your pardon – aren't you Mr. Kerr?'

'I am,' said Ronald gloomily.

'Surely you have come early? Mrs. Kerr was not expecting you——'

'Oh, thanks, but I happen to know my mother *is* expecting me.'

' – not expecting you before half-past eleven,' said Sydney, finishing her sentence imperturbably. 'The Paris train——'

'Excuse me, but I didn't come from Paris. I've come from Genoa.'

'Really? You see you never said how you were coming, so we rather assumed——'

Ronald's long stare plainly inquired what right *she* had had to have 'rather assumed'; and more, what she could know about his mother's assumptions! It was diverted from Sydney by the arrival of Mr. Lee-Mittison, who hurried towards them, skidding slightly in his eagerness on the polished floor. 'Can I do anything for you, my boy?' said Mr. Lee-Mittison.

'Well, yes,' said Ronald, turning towards him. 'I am looking for Mrs. Kerr, who happens to be my mother. Perhaps you will be able to tell me where——'

'Mr. Lee-Mittison will certainly be able to help you,' said Sydney. She and Ronald bowed to one another and she walked away. 'To the knife,' she thought, surrendering herself to her next partner, the gingery captain, who had waited meanwhile in the offing. In the succession of broken glimpses she had of him subsequently she saw Ronald being led round the edge of the room by Mr. Lee-Mittison, who had laid a hand on his shoulder, with bowed head, but with every sign of complaisance to being Mr. Lee-Mittison's boy. After a few minutes' conversation they left the lounge together. Their exit was watched with an equal interest by James Milton, who thought: 'So that's what Ronald is going to be like.'

Milton had spent the evening propped against the empty fireplace wishing he could dance. The high mantelpiece caught him uncomfortably just between the shoulders, giving him a slight stoop forward. He was dissatisfied, but did not wish to take a seat along the walls among the women and the very old gentlemen. The men of his age were all dancing and his isolation irked him, yet he could not tear himself away from the music and the lit-up, hypnotizing circulation of the dancers. He had noticed Ronald at once and wondered whether he ought to go across and speak to him, but there was something about Ronald at once remote and ominous which forbade the hazards of so public an encounter. He resembled, in the cool, wide stare across which the dancers were allowed to sweep, while it never singled out or followed any of them, in the backward tilt of the head which sent the stare down over the protrusion of the cheekbones, and in a droop down at the corners of the mouth that lengthened the chin, a supercilious young Florentine among the retinue of the Magi standing apart and Gallio-like on its fringe, staring out of the picture. Ronald was not, however, at any one moment entirely superb; he could achieve a slouch in any attitude, and the lock of hair tumbling slantwise across his forehead towards one eyebrow broke up the design of his features into something irregular and rather baffled. There was a glitter about him which betrayed a cropping-out of the Shelley from behind the mask of Hellenic remoteness so carefully worn.

'Snubbed!' smiled James Milton, watching Sydney, with a swirl of the red skirts, turn on her heel and return to her partner. The only sentiments she did not at present arouse in him were those of protectiveness or of pity. His own sensitiveness, however, made him turn away from her at this crisis of discomfiture, and he caught instead the eye of Eileen Lawrence, who, disconcerted at finding herself without a partner, was advancing towards him with the undulation of a Spanish dancer. She looked in her bright black so very striking, so very unlike the sort of young woman over whom he had even permitted his imagination to linger, that he was gratified at her coming up to strike an attitude before him. She said with a glance which in spite of his armour of subtlety did elate and disturb him: 'Now then, Mr. Milton, you're very diffident: aren't you going to dance with me?'

'There's nothing I should like better, but I *don't*, unfortunately.'

'Oh, tut,' said Eileen. 'But what a relief – I had been

afraid we weren't beautiful enough for you. Very well, then, take me out for a stroll in the garden.'

'*Rather*,' said Mr. Milton, coming forward with alacrity. 'But won't you be cold?' Though he did not mind this at all he could not help noticing that she had less on than he could have imagined possible. She did not answer, only lashed her feather fan to and fro in a contemptuous gesture; so he said no more and followed her through the window.

The Hotel garden, though not large, had been so laid out with screens of trees and with circuitous paths as to afford visitors the maximum of variety and exercise. It had taken on this evening from the insistent music and from the light that splashed down on to the trees a character so unusual, so vivid yet unearthly, that James Milton could hardly recognize it for the place of gravel and thin foliage where some days ago he had been talking to Miss Fitzgerald on an iron chair. There was no moon, but the sky was pale with starshine. 'I suppose,' said Eileen Lawrence after a few moments, sniffing, 'that this is what they'd call in books a balmy and languorous Southern night.'

'It certainly smells good. Perhaps the lemon trees . . .'

'A night made for love, that's what they'd call it.'

'I suppose they would . . . I say, are you certain you're not cold?'

She had shivered, but at this delightful thought. 'A night when men go out with pistols and shoot themselves on the Casino terrace . . . Heavens, if this were Monte!'

'But it certainly *is* the Riviera,' said James Milton, and he thought of the whole band of white hotels like palaces along the line of coast into which their own seemed now to be knitted – hotels with light streaming out of them towards the tideless sea that, never advancing on the shore or receding from it, was like an inexorable unfailing Memory, not worked upon by thought or changed by sleep. 'The Church Militant,' he thought ridiculously; then stared back at a conviction which stared at him that there could be no closer oneness than in this community of desire however unworthy, of emotion however false, and that perhaps in just this consisted——

— Eileen Lawrence brushed against him as they turned a corner.

'What jolly arms you've got!' he, feeling still immensely far from her, was moved to exclaim.

They strolled together amicably, following the doublings and twists of the path, meeting or overtaking other couples and overhearing now some scrap of conversation, some interchange of personalities from behind a screen of trees or the depths of an occasional arbour. Their cigarette ends glowing and fading preceded them like a pair of luminous noses, and equidistant spots of fire advertised that other pairs of Dongs were promenading solemnly. 'How ridiculous!' laughed James Milton at the music, in sudden elation. He had not been to a dance for years, he had forsaken even Christmas parties because they made him feel avuncular: all this was new to him. Eileen, who thought this was the dreariest dance she had ever been at, a travesty of all that was highest in human enjoyment, was as near depression as the Lawrences ever descended, and replied: 'Yes, it's pretty futile, isn't it? I suppose the dowagers are enjoying it. Shall we go in?'

Milton, who had been taking a keener pleasure than she understood in her nearness in the intimacy of the darkness, actually laid a hand on her arm to detain her. He entreated, 'Not till the end of this dance!'

His unwillingness to give her up was not decreased by a sharp irritation that she with her white arms and her attractiveness – which he was conscious of as something as material as phosphorescence, in which he could have dipped a finger curiously – should have stopped short at being Eileen Lawrence. He was convinced that if she had been anybody else, say Sydney (now dancing, indifferent, in the room above), the situation would have had a key for him, and he chafed with indignant longing. 'I say, Eileen——' he began and, determined to understand himself, reached out a hand for her.

'Well?' challenged Eileen, and they stared at the greyish blots of one another's faces in the darkness. After a moment her expectancy broke into laughter. 'I really thought,' said she, 'that you were going to kiss me.'

'So did I,' said James Milton, and following her back to the ballroom he tried in vain to decide whether she and the mood to which she had given colour had been base or very admirable. He gave her up to her next partner and returned to the fireplace, but the dance became meaningless; he could not see Sydney anywhere. Once he thought she appeared beyond the window, half in the darkness, but she was shut away from him by the spinning barrier. He determined to find her, to allay the restlessness which was beginning to sap his benignity and make him look with contempt at the older people and at the young with resentment. If he did not find her soon he would begin to believe that there was not a place in the world for him – he started at a flash of red in one of the mirrors, but it was only the sweep of Eileen's crimson fan. He felt that he could no longer endure the ballroom, and that even if by leaving it he were to cut himself off for ever from all it contained, he must leave it to look for her.

He went out into the lounge with his heart in his mouth, but there was no one there but Mr. Lee-

Mittison, walking about and rubbing his hands, so happy that he had had to expand here in solitude.

'Charming boy, that,' said Mr. Lee-Mittison. 'Really an acquisition – charming boy.'

'Indeed?' said Milton, who had forgotten Ronald.

'Found his mother for him. Nice woman, very nice woman. Pretty to see 'em together.' He beamed at Milton as he had not beamed for days.

'Was it?' said Milton. He stared again round the emptiness of the lounge, went to the foot of the stairs and looked up, listened and with a last desperate inspiration looked into the drawing-room.

'Looking for anybody?' asked Mr. Lee-Mittison, observing this.

'No,' said Milton, and nodding good night to Mr. Lee-Mittison he went down the basement stairs into the smoking-room and out by a glass door into the garden again. Here he walked to and fro, repelled by the darkness, peering angrily into the arbours which were now all empty and silent and quickening his steps at every turn of a path. He looked at the great sheer façade springing upright above him with here and there a light coming out in a window, and thought, 'Of course, she is tired; she has gone up to bed.'

'But she was not tired at all: she did not look as though she would ever sleep again,' his memory told him.

'I suppose I must love her? – But I cannot, she is so erratic and cold——'

'It is because she's erratic and cold that you've been able to surprise your emotion.'

'Oh, rats!' said James Milton, kicking a stone. A figure that had come out on to one of the balconies started and peered down into the garden.

The quick movement betrayed some tension of fear or expectancy. *Mrs. Kerr*, he thought in surprise, as having counted the windows up from the ground and then along from left to right he located the balcony. Why should she still and in such wretchedness be waiting for Ronald? He listened and watched; the room behind her was empty. Then, as the figure still with its arms stretched out gripping the balcony turned her head sideways, he recognized Sydney. It was on the tip of his tongue to call to her, as though she were a child for whose conduct he was somehow responsible. She should have left them alone tonight, he thought, and flamed with disinterested anger. He took a few steps backwards, propped himself against a tree and remained looking up at the balcony. She shivered; he shivered in sympathy. How much (though how properly) Mrs. Kerr had found to say to her son. It was long past midnight now and very cold; the dance was over and the music silent some time ago. All the other lights were out except one at the very top left-hand corner, where Ronald and his mother must still be talking.

'Damn Ronald!' thought James Milton; 'she and I will be catching our deaths.' A clock down in the town struck the half-hour and a bell from a convent above them answered it. Emboldened by the breach these made in the silence he called, 'Good night, Miss Warren.'

Sydney started violently and after one more fierce glance on to the trees retreated from the balcony. He saw her pause a moment under the light and look round as though to take a farewell of her expectations; then the room was dashed from his sight by darkness. A panel of fresh light shone for a moment as the door on to the corridor opened and shut. Sighing, and with a sense of half-accomplishment, he too went in to bed.

CHAPTER XII

ANY HOPE?

'WELL?' Mrs. Kerr said expansively, meeting Sydney on the stairs next morning. 'Isn't it rather a nice puppy?'

She was dressed to go out, with a blue straw hat pulled down over her eyes. She had paused with a hand out to steady herself against the frame of the staircase window, and the north light defined the smiling curve of one cheek and drew prismatic colours out of an ear-ring. She was evidently very happy.

'What puppy?' Sydney said blankly, looking up from a few steps below her.

'My Ronald. Isn't it *rather* a nice——'

'Oh very, yes. I thought it seemed a rather severe puppy last night, but I dare say that was the journey.'

'Oh, severe?' said Mrs. Kerr delightedly. 'Was he really severe? Sydney, you must tell me; how fearfully funny!' She narrowed her eyes for a moment as though she were trying to picture the meeting of Sydney and Ronald. 'I don't believe,' she admitted, 'that he was pleased at finding everyone dancing. It didn't, somehow, seem right. But I dare say he thought *you* severe; I must ask him – you sometimes terrify me. He seemed rather dazed by you all.'

'I'm glad his first day is so fine,' said Sydney, and felt as though by this she were somehow including herself in the happiness of the Kerrs.

'Yes, I'm always lucky,' agreed Mrs. Kerr. 'Now we're going out together. You can't think what it is like to be going out with a son. It is ridiculously nice – I'd forgotten.'

'Well, goodbye,' said Sydney, standing back against the wall for her friend to pass. 'I don't suppose we shall see each other again today.'

'Oh, shan't we? What a pity!' Mrs. Kerr said vaguely. 'There's that unfortunate Ronald,' she cried, glancing out of the window, 'marching up and down out there – do look – in a panama hat. How horrid of me to dawdle!' She nodded to Sydney and went on smoothly downstairs leaving behind her faint perfume, a sensible backrush of eagerness, expectancy and delight.

Sydney stared out at the hills, then went on upstairs. She thought how ironic it was that a day made to order for two people's occasion must be at the same time dealt out as a background for everyone else. She felt she had no energy and could never get as far as her room, choose her gloves, find her parasol and put on her hat. At the thought of anything beyond this, her prospect for the day, she faltered. With a sense of reprieve she let herself be waylaid by Cordelia Barry, who was hanging about the stairs.

'I say, Miss Warren, it's Thursday.'

'Is it?'

'I don't go to the convent on Thursdays, I was wondering . . . I thought perhaps . . . No, but of course you wouldn't, would you? I don't suppose it would suit you at all . . .' Cordelia, with an air of infinite calculation looked sideways at Sydney under her lashes. Sydney remembering the promise Cordelia had extracted, had a pang of acute nostalgia for that afternoon of the carnations, sundered by the eternity of a different mood.

'I'm sorry, Cordelia: I'm going for a walk with Mr. Milton.'

'O-oh! That *is* a pity. I suppose I couldn't come, too? Oh no, but of course you wouldn't want me, would you?

But I don't mind Mr. Milton if he doesn't mind me, and I don't see really why I shouldn't come.'

'Neither do I. I suppose – you can come along if you want to,' said Sydney, denying a sense that this was mischievous on her part and a shade dishonourable. At all events, to annoy somebody in her turn surely was owed to her? 'He pretends,' she thought, 'he professes to be fond of children. And it's not as though we had anything to say to one another. We talk and talk and cancel out each other's ideas until it all comes down to what it was before: that we do not agree. At the end of it all it is as though nothing had been said. I do not even understand myself any better at the end of it, and if that fails what is the use of conversation? Nothing will ever crystallize out of our being together; not so much as a notion.'

She deliberated, however, for some moments over her hats and scarves and returned more than once to the looking-glass to review herself critically.

Milton was waiting below in the lounge and his face did fall perceptibly as Sydney at last appearing at the turn of the stairs indicated Cordelia, less in tow than towing, capering round possessively.

'Oh!' said he, and, looking down at their two pair of descending feet, could think of nothing better to say.

Sydney wondered if *her* face had looked like that to Mrs. Kerr some moments ago: the comparison was distasteful. 'This is Cordelia Barry,' she said with bright hardiness, 'the eldest of them. She would like to come with us; you don't mind, do you?' To her surprise, Milton turned away without a word to take his walking-stick from the rack behind him.

'You don't mind, do you?' echoed Cordelia shrilly.

'I'm very pleased, of course, if Miss Warren has invited you,' said Milton, holding open the door for them.

But as Cordelia passed out behind Sydney with the self-assurance of a pet monkey he looked daggers at her profile.

'I've just seen the Kerrs going off,' he said to Sydney as he came abreast with her. 'Ronald looks brighter this morning: indeed, decidedly pleased with himself.' His pale grey eyes encountered Sydney's thoughtfully.

'Yes,' she said, 'it's nice to see them together.' She could tell by his tone that he was angry with her and was vaguely brandishing a weapon which he understood to be deadly but did not quite know how to use. He was nice-looking and at the moment unapproachable; she felt too spiritless to spar with him, and said, to propitiate, 'It *is* a lovely day for a walk. I haven't been for a walk for ages,' and looked at him gently. He noticed that her eyes had dark circles round them which were unbecoming and pitiful.

Milton had woken up this morning with the determination to take Sydney for a walk. Nothing, in that moment of lucidity, had seemed simpler to arrange, and nothing could actually have been simpler, as things had turned out. He knew as well as she did, and would have been prepared to admit to her, that the time they had spent together up to now had been profitless and left them both sore. But he was convinced (the conviction emerged with what now seemed inevitability from the confusion and ill-spent emotion of last night) that a need corresponding to his must exist in her somewhere. A need, perhaps, less of each other exclusively than of something only attainable jointly, of something rooted in both. 'But I do not know how to begin,' he had complained to himself till this morning. Now he felt a mastery of the situation to be possible. 'If I could only make her understand,' he thought, 'there would be time enough for her to care for me. At any rate, here they were walking together. The presence of this confounded little girl he chose to discount.

He turned, however, to talk to Cordelia kindly. They had chosen a road above the town for the sake of the view, and meant to drop down through the fishermen's quarters and come home by the sea. Cordelia begged that she might be allowed to visit the graveyard. Milton observed conventionally that her taste seemed a little bit morbid.

'Oh no, Mr. Milton; you really ought to see the graveyard here; it's most uncommon and beautifully decorated. I suppose as a clergyman you've had so much experience of them that you get out of the way of noticing, but I am sure you'd be struck by the one here.. It's *most* blood-curdling.'

'If you like that sort of thing,' said Milton in the somewhat top-heavy manner in which he could not help talking to children, 'you should get your mother to take you to the Campo Santo at Pisa.' Cordelia evidently suspected from his tone that he did not think her taste sufficiently elevated, while Sydney remarked parenthetically that she did not see Mrs. Barry taking her children to Pisa.

'I might, of course,' suggested Cordelia, 'be sent to a convent there, to be taught to speak whatever they do speak. You see, my mother has got a perfect mania about languages. She would like me to be able to speak ninety-nine different ones even if I never learnt anything else. Though what, I should like to know, is the use of speaking ninety-nine languages if one has nothing to say? Now I think the nuns have no idea of teaching. I've never been so badly taught in my life. They flap about and go on and on at one, and half the time one can't understand what they're saying, and when one does it doesn't make sense. I don't wonder they got turned out of France – I'm not learning anything. However, the nuns think nothing matters so long as they go on being religious, and mother thinks nothing matters so long as they go on being French, so there you are.'

Sydney agreed that this was all very difficult. Milton, who wondered what would become of this little girl, was silent and looked so much depressed that Cordelia, to cheer him up, caught hold of his hand, and swinging herself along by it asked him whether he were fond of reading. 'I am,' said she. 'My two favourite authors are Rider Haggard and the Baroness von Hutten. Who are yours?'

Milton hesitated, and Sydney and Cordelia looked at him with curiosity. Conscious of Sydney's attention, he was still debating how to answer most fruitfully when she said to Cordelia across him: 'I don't think Mr. Milton ever reads at all. I never see him with a book.'

'That's not fair,' said Milton. 'I read too much, as a rule. I came out *here* for . . .'

'For what?' said Sydney, looking about her expressively.

'For people,' said Milton unwarily.

'Oh!' they both exclaimed. 'What an extraordinary thing to come for! – To come *here* for,' Sydney added.

'Don't you know any people? Do you like them so much?' Cordelia inquired. 'How funny! I only like people in books who only exist when they matter. I think it is being in danger or terribly in love, discovering treasure or revenging yourself that is thrilling and for that you have to have people. But people in hotels, hardly *alive* . . .!'

'Well, you don't know what may not be happening to them,' Sydney, emerging from her detachment, felt it necessary to point out instructively. The road, a favourite promenade of the natives and visitors, rounded the face of a high embankment; they could have been looked down upon from the terraces of villas on one hand, while

on the other they were level with the tree-tops: the roofs
of the town were below. Milton, distractingly engaged
in conversation by Cordelia, and Sydney, released but
not unfriendly, looking ahead of her, they emerged on
to a gravelled plateau overlooking the sea. Here some
seats had been placed, under umbrella pines forming a
kind of pergola, to promote contemplation of the bright
panorama of coast. Beyond, the remoter hills were still
snow-capped; others ran down to the sea in a succession
of fine blue noses; headland behind headland fading
towards France. The earth had this brilliant morning a
kind of independent luminousness; there were still no
shadows anywhere and the rocks, flat clustered roofs and
campanili seemed to shed light as well as to receive it.
For miles the bright-blue swelling glassiness of the sea
received the coast gracefully among ripples that frayed
continually into foam, slipped back into themselves, and
slid on again. When Sydney, Mr. Milton and Cordelia
had seated themselves on a bench, the fleshy spears of
some cacti fringing the plateau darkly occupied the fore-
ground of their vision. 'Ah!' said Milton, taking a deep
breath of the air which here seemed to him stronger and
fresher. Sydney was glad of his enjoyment of the day
which to herself still seemed to be spilt out wastefully.

'Doesn't everything look as though it was cut out and
painted?' exclaimed Cordelia, joyously swinging her
legs.

'Cordelia!' said Milton, looking at her with an air of
inspiration, 'do you like nuts?'

'Very much. But I get plenty of them.'

'Or figs?'

'The seeds are bad for any teeth.'

'Well, dates?'

'I adore dates. I'm not encouraged to eat them much
because they're stickies. But I do adore dates,' said

Cordelia thoughtfully. 'I wonder if I shall ever eat a date again?'

'You may at any moment,' said Milton, and he told her that there was a little fruit-shop that he knew of, just below, where she could buy for the three lire he proposed to give her enough dates for them all. 'I adore dates, too,' he added. 'The shop is on the left, by the tram-terminus, and they will talk any language you like.' He gave the child a slight push that was unnecessary, for she was already sliding off the bench. After a side-glance at Sydney, who had opened her mouth to protest, she fled to some concrete steps and with a yelp of excitement vanished down them.

'But she isn't allowed to run about the town by herself,' said Sydney, vexed, 'and she certainly isn't allowed to eat between meals – she's very much be-Nannied. Whatever made you do that?'

'She's not the sort of child to get talked to, and I'm sure she has an inside like an ostrich. If her people encourage her to attach herself to strangers like that, they'll have to take the consequences. I sent her off because she's been the most infernal nuisance all the morning.' He was crimson.

'You feel strongly about it,' said Sydney, laughing at him, bathed in sunshine and forgetful of perils to Cordelia. 'Moral indignation?'

He did not interrupt her, but something in his silence, his arrested consciousness of the gap Cordelia's disappearance left between them and the clear view they had of each other, made her interrupt herself.

'I'm sorry she has bored you,' she said nervously. 'I really ought not to have brought her.'

'No, I don't think you ought. I asked you to come for a walk; I didn't ask you to collect an expedition.'

'Well, you see——' she began, then stopped again.

Their conspicuous if isolated situation, the matter-of-fact sunshine and the sense that with all said and done they were English Visitors, he and she, sitting appropriately on a bench before a view designed for their admiration, had up to now kept her purely impersonal. So objective did she feel that she imagined a delighted Commune gazing down at the two of them: 'English Visitors'. In the expansion of the free air she had laughed and felt that neither of them were realler than the scenery. Now, at some tone in his voice she was surprised by a feeling that some new mood, not of her own, was coming down over them like a bell-glass. The bright reality of the view, the consciousness of their unimportant, safe little figures were shut away from her; they were always there but could no longer help. She felt the bell-glass finally descend as he, after a glance round at the other benches and over the edge of the plateau, said quickly, 'The thing is, Sydney, aren't I ever to know you?'

'I don't see what you mean,' she said, suffocated by his manner. 'Like everybody else, we see each other every day. Which was what, according to you, we are here for.'

Milton, losing touch with her, lost touch with himself and was terrified. He had said, 'Yes, but I was wondering if you would marry me,' before he had had time to think, on an instinct that he must get out something at any price and have it there to stand by. She had understood what he said before he did, and answered: 'You are very good, but no: I'm afraid it's impossible'; so that he had proposed and been rejected before he had entirely realized that they were not still quarrelling about Cordelia. When this did dawn on him he turned to her in dismay. 'I'm afraid,' he said with a return to his usual manner, 'that that was terribly awkward of me.'

'Oh no, not at all,' said Sydney, smiling shakily. 'It's supposed to be very gratifying.'

'I did not mean to have said that today, I need hardly explain. It was unforgivable of me. But I suppose while we are on the subject that there is no further harm in my asking you, whether you can – as I think they call it – give me any hope?'

'No, I'm afraid not,' said Sydney, feeling she had been asked something so preposterous that the answer was a matter for her common sense alone and that further inquiries need not be instituted.

'Very well,' said Milton and the bell-glass lifted, though it hung above them. She felt as though this image must have presented itself to him also, for he drew as though released from constriction another deep breath of air. After staring straight ahead at the sea for a moment he said, 'Thank you': she did not know for what, she supposed for her courtesy. This implied, she felt, a dismissal: a 'You may go now, I have done with you!'

CHAPTER XIII

CEMETERY

'BUT I thought he liked dates!' cried Cordelia. Panting at the top of the steps she stood clutching her package, appalled, to see Milton walk away rapidly in the direction from which they had come. She had run both ways so as to waste as little time as possible away from her friends, and she couldn't help feeling that the escape of Milton in so short an interval could not but be due to some mismanagement on the part of Miss Warren, who now alone on the bench sat staring before her, smiling uneasily. There had seemed no risk in leaving him for a moment; he had had an appearance of being rooted there, or better perhaps, tethered.

'But he *said* he liked dates,' she repeated, bringing up reason to support her astonishment.

The remark, which was not answered, seemed further to contribute to a gloom that had taken the place of the affable Mr. Milton and which, momentarily, to both their perceptions, darkened the sunshine. Miss Warren now rose abruptly, shook out her pleated skirts and for the first time unfurling her parasol tilted it from her shoulder at an angle with a concentration upon these details of her elegance which implied dismally to Cordelia the exclusion of Mr. Milton even from memory. With a renewed, more genuine smile to Cordelia she suggested that they should continue their walk. Except for a few arcs and triangles in the gravel before the bench the friendly clergyman might never have existed.

They followed the loops of the road in their gradual descent towards the cemetery. Sydney was talkative;

they discussed novels, the difficulties of arithmetic and the superiority of cats to dogs. Once she turned and looked back at the benches as though horrified by the thought that they would still be there. Cordelia asked, 'Have you forgotten something?' and she replied, 'Oh no,' in confusion. It transpired that Mr. Milton had been recalled by an engagement of some importance, till then forgotten. Cordelia, who was able to estimate the probable importance of any engagement locally, said nothing. She suspected him to be a feeble walker, and moreover a man of quick appetites as quickly forgotten. She ate his dates and ceased to regret him; allowing the stones to accumulate in one cheek and spitting them out by half-dozens with great force. She proceeded downhill beside Sydney with a hop-skip-and-a-jump, kicking up the powdery dust so that it swirled round her feet and, settling, iced the top of her shoes. She derived keen pleasure from this, also from a sense of the enviableness of walking with this appearance of intimacy with the distinguished Miss Warren. She hoped in vain they might be met by some of her friends.

'I do think two's better company,' she said at last, 'but I hope this hasn't been a disappointment to you?'

'It's a pity, of course,' said Sydney, who could not help feeling it would have been more vigorous, more admirable on Milton's part to have continued the walk with them. She believed herself able to recognize in what had occurred simply another of his nervous impulses; there had been, she was convinced, no impetus of emotion. In the unique encounter of eyes they had had, as with raised hat he was turning away from her, he had shown her nothing of what he felt but astonishment: a profound astonishment, at which of them she could not be sure. Those pale-grey eyes with their penetrating blankness were still vivid to her, but though she now

intensely desired to reproach herself she could not
wring from her memories any sense of his emotion. She
came to doubt that she had witnessed anything more
painful than the momentary topple of a shy but very
potent vanity that had over-reached itself. A suspicion
of having been casually snatched at hardened her towards
him. He had not hurt her, but he had set the pain
of the earlier morning free to renew itself; a nerve was
insistently throbbing. She became aware with the knife-
edge of a first realization, of each implication of the
words, expression, gesture with which Mrs. Kerr had
detached herself and in smiling expectation gone past her
downstairs.

In such a mood she was not proof against the ordinary
reflections on mortality as she looked with Cordelia
through the cemetery gates. To see better, they pressed
their faces up against the cold bars. Cordelia for the last
ten minutes had been hurrying, her whole self narrowed
down; she had become silent with apprehension. She
was tortured by an expectation that the cemetery with
its ornaments might have rolled itself up and vanished,
or worse, that it might fail in its pungent appeal, so that
she would not this time experience what she had learned
to describe as a *frisson* as she gazed through the gloom
of the trees down that distracting prospective of monu-
ments. Also, she had made herself responsible for the
reactions of Miss Warren from the moment they turned
down the suggestive cul-de-sac away from the sea, walled
in steeply and vanishing at a succession of angles round
the palm-tufted bases of the hills.

The cemetery seemed quite deserted. Gashes of overcharged daylight pressed in through the cypresses on to
the graves: a hard light bestowing no grace and exacting
each detail. In the shade of the pillared vaults round the
walls what already seemed the dusk of evening had begun

to thicken, but the rank and file of small crosses staggered arms wide in the arraignment of sunshine. In spite of the brooding repose of the trees a hundred little shrill draughts came between them, and spurting across the graves made the decorations beloved of Cordelia creak and glitter. A wreath of black tin pansies swung from the arm of a cross with a clatter of petals, trailing colour-less ribbons; a beaded garland had slipped down slant-wise across the foot of a grave. Candles for the peculiar glory of the lately dead had been stuck in the unhealed earth: here and there a flame in a glass shade writhed, opaque in the sunshine. Above all this uneasy rustle of remembrance, white angels poised forward to admonish. The superlatives crowding each epitaph hissed out their '*issimi*' and '*issime*' from under the millinery of death. Everywhere, in ribbons, marbles, porcelains was a suggestion of the *salon*, and nowhere could the signific-ance of death have been brought forward more startlingly.

'I must say,' remarked Cordelia, 'I do like Italian graves; they look so much more lived in.'

'They would certainly be more difficult than others to get clear of,' said Sydney; and quickly, in unthinking perturbation, she pushed open the cemetery gates, as though she were on a message to a friend's house, and hurried in. Once among the graves she stood with Cordelia behind her, looking round again. She was oppressed by the thought, less of death than of the treachery of a future that must give one to this ulti-mately. She was not accustomed to consider death as other than as a spontaneous fine gesture. Now it hinted itself as something to be imposed on one, the last and most humiliating of those deprivations she had begun to experience. She thought, 'It is all very well to escape to the future and think it will always be that; but this is the end of the future.' Looking up to watch a bird fly slowly across the sky, she realized that living as she had lived she had been investing the future with more and more of herself. The present, always slipping away, was ghostly, every moment spent itself in apprehension of the next, and these apprehensions, these faded expectancies cumbered her memory, crowded out her achievements and promised to make the past barren enough should she have to turn back to it.

James Milton's attempt to come farther into her life, to regions by his acquaintance of them surely sufficiently ice-bound, appeared in the light of present considerations heroic: he had been staking his future. But his future, she recollected, spun itself off into infinity. He did not acknowledge finality anywhere; this made him leisurely-seeming and easily generous. His impulses in any direction were not intensified by her own sense of urgency. In the light shed serenely down from that ultimate spaciousness he was covering life at an equable pace. He presented himself an undriven, a comforting figure. She saw him conducting a funeral: voluminous, fluttering, milk-white, leaning like one of these angels over the yawn of a grave to scatter his handful of earth, his tribute to mortality; with the expression, a sub-merged beam, of this having in a cognizant Mind its order. The word 'death' used in his presence would have a slow-dying ring to it, to which one would be able to feel him subconsciously listening. She contemplated with a faint inclination a life shared with someone for whom it would have this overtone of significance.

And to be wanted! She remembered in what a mood she had climbed the stairs that morning, and she looked round her at the now for ever undesired dead. She tried to recall the feel of his handclasp and to imagine the touch of his lips. With a sigh: 'I am very ordinary!'

she tried over any terms of endearment which seemed within the range of his manner, listening for the reverberation which, like the word death, she felt they would have for him.

Cordelia sat on the end of a grave among a little city of glass domes, looking up intelligently. The child had read so many novels that she might well have been expected to know what there was to be known about the affairs of the heart. Feeling the bright eyes of Cordelia fixed for some moments upon her, Sydney began to wonder whether her lips had been moving just now and, if so, what Cordelia had thought; she found that she might have gone so far as what in Cordelia's novels would be called murmuring. Of this the child would approve too readily. For the moment, however, her attention did not seem to have wandered from the graves, and she was determined not to allow Sydney's to do so either.

'Did you know,' she began, 'that it costs a great deal of money to be buried permanently?'

'It never occurred to me.'

'A girl at the convent had a grandmother who died and she told me that the grandmother's last request was to be buried permanently. If you aren't – and it is fearfully expensive – they come and dig you up again. Italians never think of this; they are most improvident. They spend a lot of money trimming up the graves – I must say, they do do it very nicely – and then after all their trouble the cemetery people come and dig their relation up again, because the cemetery is too small, and people keep on dying and dying, and they have to go in somewhere, if you see what I mean.'

'Oh!' said Sydney, and glanced behind as though she might expect to see the new dead jostling one another in the gate. She felt that it had been a mistake to have come here at all, even to recover herself. This high-walled place with its one gate might well be a trap for her, and she wondered what she should do if, instead of the dead, Mrs. Kerr and Ronald were to come in suddenly talking and laughing (she could see them) as they stepped over the graves. Why they should come to the cemetery she could not imagine, except that her dread of them, even in thought, might well prove a magnet to their unconsciousness.

'Of course, of course,' she said loudly, 'people must keep on dying. They should have made allowances for that.'

'There is a rubbish heap at the back of the chapel. If you'd come with me I could show you.'

'What a horrid little ghoul you are!' Sydney said mechanically. She found that in actually dealing with children theories collapse and one must retreat on the conventions. But when Cordelia in her reasonable little voice objected 'Why?' she could think of nothing to answer. There seemed no reason, even conventionally, why she should impose on Cordelia the adult idea of 'morbidity'.

'People wouldn't like you to talk about being dug up,' she said at last weakly, 'though it seems to me a very practical arrangement. The Italians are realists.'

'What is a realist?' asked Cordelia, while, having gathered up some china flowers lying about on the ground she stuck these by their wire stalks into the band of her hat. 'Haven't I made my hat smart? What *are* realists?'

'Ask Mr. Milton,' Sydney said promptly.

'Is he——'

'No, of course not. But he will tell you what unenlightened people they are.'

'He is a long-winded man,' said Cordelia, looking at her friend sideways.

'Not at all,' said Sydney irritably, 'and, anyway, what do you know about it?'

'Oh, nothing, nothing at all. I don't know what "long-winded" means, even.'

'Then you shouldn't——'

'It was a sporting risk, after all,' said Cordelia gravely, and Sydney, rebuked, wished that she could be so honest. 'Where,' she asked, 'do they put the English?'

'Over there; we have a very nice corner reserved. I'll show you, shan't I? There's a little girl of just my age – mustn't the people in her hotel have been upset about it? I often think——' she brooded.

'Yes, I dare say you do. I often used to. But it wouldn't be much fun, really, dying to impress other people, or to be picturesque or pitied.'

'I suppose not, really. But I couldn't help just imagining, that day they were so stuffy with us 'cause we broke the lift. I put my tongue out after Mrs. Hillier when she had stopped and been sarcastic at me in the passage, and I thought "Yah! if I liked you'd be sobbing and sniffing tomorrow and putting flowers – carnations – on my coffin and saying what a darling little girl I'd been!" '

They went on to look at the English end of the cemetery, where more discreet memorials had been hewn into shapes better suited to granite than to Carrara marble. All round the cypresses waited. How complete the Riviera was, thought Sydney, one could even die here. Birds were rare, she started as one dipped from a tree and flew zigzag with a shrill cry, skimming the gravestones. Like an echo of the bird's cry they heard the creak of a hinge, as the gate hidden by trees was pushed open decorously. Sydney could feel her heart thump as they listened and waited.

Presently Miss Pinkerton appeared between the cypresses, conscious even of the dead, her face composed into an expression of nobility. She looked to left and right of her through the graves, and though she saw Cordelia and Sydney she did not seem at first to recognize them. They might have been figures in a crowd. Did they intrude? . . . She was carrying narcissi. She approached: the path allowed her no alternative, but she approached serenely; the encounter did not seem distasteful. 'Good morning,' she returned in a low voice when Sydney bowed. They turned to leave her.

'Such a lovely spot,' remarked Miss Pinkerton, not unwilling to detain them.

'Lovely,' Sydney agreed, 'so peaceful!'

'A friend of mine,' said Miss Pinkerton, looking at them with her mild august eyes, 'has a cousin here.' She indicated the destination of the narcissi. Sydney stooped to read the inscription.

'He was an Admiral,' said Miss Pinkerton, and sighed again.

'Isn't he an Admiral still?' exclaimed Cordelia, whom Sydney, pulling by the hand abruptly, began to lead away.

'You shouldn't have asked that, Cordelia.'

'But why shouldn't I?—— Oh, Miss Warren, don't hurry so! One would think you were running away from the Admiral – why shouldn't I have asked that?'

'I suppose,' said Sydney after some reflection, 'because Miss Pinkerton doesn't know.'

CHAPTER XIV

MUSIC

SUDDENLY the group round the doors had dispersed and everybody was leaning over the drawing-room balcony. Above, all the way up the front of the Hotel, faces blossomed out unexpectedly, flinging away like veils the first oblivion of siesta. One would have thought a note of music had never been heard before or that the man into whose deep mouth they were all gazing down were himself Orpheus.

He plucked from his mandolin shaking notes which the tensity and blaze of noon and the gathered silence of his audience did invest with a strangeness, and sang while the whole of him quivered. He did not cease to parade beneath the balcony while maintaining fountain-wise the spout of song. The child with red skirts clutching his coat-tails echoed, with the addition here and there of skip or quaver, his strut and his song. Her face, with a smile's general glitter across it, was upturned to the balcony, eyes closed as though she could feel the benevolence of visitors descend upon the lids like rain.

The airs were not classical. He sang 'Funiculi-Funicula' and 'O Sole Mio', and presently (encouraging his little girl to dance for their English friends and quickening the measure till her brief skirts spun out into a disc) a song about the beauties of a doll.

Ladies on either side of him began pressing Ronald closer, and more and more people came out through the window behind and leaned across his shoulders. He could hear, when he kept his head low, quite an orchestra of excited breathing.

Ah ch'è bella la bambola mia
Quasi, quasi più bella di me
Un vestito di ràso celeste
Un cappello di——

'Splendid!' somebody cried out, and the wave of
admiration mounting behind Ronald broke into clapping
of hands and laughter. 'This balcony,' he remarked to
his mother under cover of this, 'is like a print of a public
execution.' He shone with an exhilaration induced by
the music in spite of himself, but preserved his expression
of disillusionment. 'It will bust in a minute or two, and
serve them all right for watching anything so beastly.'

'But, Ronald, *beastly*?' She turned to him in con-
sternation, innocent as never before of irony.

'The little devil's blind,' said Ronald, pointing down
and moving his shoulders angrily, for there were two
what he called great fat women leaning on his back.

The word spread somehow, and when the child's eyes
again dropped open, then lazily shut, several people
were alert to notice that the eyes were china-white. The
minstrel, appreciative of the interest thus created, pulled
his companion forward and stopped in his song to advertise her with a flourish. 'Cieca, cieca!' he exclaimed, and
straddled shining up at them, all teeth. The little girl,
in the ecstasy of this, flung her arms out and began to
dance again, whirling at such velocity that it was as
though she tore the music from the mandolin to follow
her. Ripples of 'Shame' and 'Cruel' crept down the
balcony, but from the windows above the first drops of a
shower of nickel were spinning already. The shower
thickened, and there was for a moment or two in the air
a continuous glitter. The little girl paused leaning
against the wind of her movement and seemed to listen
in ecstasy. She snatched up handfuls of air and surren-

dered them laughingly, then flung herself with cries of
delight to and fro on the gravel and, groping, gathered up
her harvest. There followed some heavier coins, the
escape of a sigh and a faint burst of horrified laughter.

'But she is happy,' maintained Sydney, standing back
against the frame of the window, and a voice she could
not trace but believed to be Milton's supported her with
'Yes, yes, she must be.'

Ronald wriggled beneath the weight of the two good
women, but could not extricate himself in time to see
who, on either occasion, had spoken. He would have
given much to do so. All today there had been phrases,
broken-off, exclamatory, rising stark like this out of a hush
or a hum with a significance for him foreign to their
context, with startling relevance to something in his
mind.

He pushed his way back into the drawing-room, now
quite vacant and in yellow shade from the awning. He
sat down on a sofa, leaned back, crossing his legs, and
waited for his mother to appear in the window, as she
almost immediately did, and after a moment's blank
stare into the dusk to perceive him and come over
royally. She did concede, and generously he could
approve the concession, a few words back over her
shoulder, perhaps to Miss Warren out there. Then she
sat beside him, most beautiful in the half-light, her
attitude settling into complete repose as silk settles into
its folds. She had still a little amusement, a faint
perturbation, but she was allowing these ripples to widen
and fade in her mind. It would be clear of them soon,
a smooth consciousness on to which he hoped to stream
like light.

They were still after this lifelong strangeness to one
another at a stage when the novelty of being together
made each seeking out of one another unique. A meeting

was in the nature of a rendezvous, and the *mise en scène*
queerly important. The isolation of rendezvous made
indifferent such publicity as that of a bench, a waiting-
room, or this rigid sofa pasted square to the wall of a
drawing-room. As they sat here, Ronald exulted.

'And now?' his mother said, after some moments in
which the music, having come to an end, the shoal swept
past from the balcony with a sympathetic aversion of
glances. A lust for spectacle which the little blind girl
had aroused was gratified by them passingly, and Ronald
knew that many people had considered them 'touching'.
The room empty once more, it was as though Mrs. Kerr
had had to expostulate with herself for being too happy.
'And now?' she resumed with an air of obligation.

'Why "now"?' said Ronald. 'Can't we stay here? I
mean, unless you want to sleep. What is this room,
anyway?' He looked round at the armchairs all facing
one way with awful intelligence.

'I think quite a number of women sit here.'

'Obviously. But I'm not afraid of an atmosphere.'

'Dear Ronald, you seem to be thickening. I was
always alarmed and impressed by the idea that you were
afraid of atmospheres: that they were dangerous.'

He had been alarmed and impressed by the idea that
she had not an inkling of his subleties; or rather, would
not exert herself to perceive them. But since his arrival
at this hotel, he had been amazed by the fineness of her
perceptions, not only from moment to moment but by
a sudden vista of them along the past, perceptions so
delicate, appreciations so faultless that it could only have
been some lack of an equal fineness that had made him
suffer an infinite deprivation. Now when she said that
he was thickening he was able to smile at her.

'I suppose I must have amused my mother?'

'Ronald, you were so subtle. I was inadequate.'

'*I* was inadequate. Shut up!' He shook her arm gently.

'I can't help laughing. Do you know, I – I respect you? Why should I have to confess this instead of announcing it? I do respect you,' she repeated, saying the word diffidently and looking back on what she had said with apparent misgiving.

'As a matter of fact,' said Ronald gravely, 'I don't think *we* mind being respected. I think, Mother, if you don't mind my saying so, that it is a mistake ever to confuse us with your *fin-de-siècle* friends. Of course a remark like that would have a thousand satirical reverberations in – say – a Wilde play. But really, one is able to take it quite simply.'

'That's where you all are so wonderful,' said Mrs. Kerr, with the deep thoughtfulness she brought to bear on his every remark. 'Of course, I do date hopelessly, as Sydney says.'

'Sydney? Oh, the girl, yes. Was she asked?'

'Ronald, you're unkind. Don't say "gurl!" like that. I thought you'd like her; she's immensely clever.'

Ronald was surprised to realize that the fact that he did not like Sydney, of which he was himself only now aware, must long have been obvious to his mother. 'If she were not a "gurl", she wouldn't be here. Anyway, isn't she rather unnatural? The young Lawrences have at least a certain crude attractiveness.'

'She's been crude enough to care for me.'

'I thought you couldn't tolerate schärmerie.'

'Oh, but that suggests the backfisch. Could one be ungenerous enough not to take what is offered one finely? Don't be tiresome to her; do justify yourself. She's prepared to find you *rather* tiresome.'

'Was she asked?'

'She thinks twenty is a tiresome age. She's twenty-two, you see. Anyway, don't let's bother about her now. This "respect" that I've just discovered and you've authorized is so very comfortable to me. It does please me so – you may have felt this, but I haven't put it into words because these large admissions are embarrassing – that you've come down to me from Germany, given up Germany. I hope it didn't cost a lot?'

Ronald looked embarrassed.

'I meant in *development*. Pictures. Music.'

'Oh, those, no. Anyway, Mother, as I should have explained' (an irritated consciousness of having already done so at great length brought a note into his voice) 'those were a purely secondary——'

'Of course they were. How dense I've been again, I *mean*: the Rentenmark.' She laid a hand on his knee, leaned back her head against the wall and, he believed, even blushed her contrition; yet this was all said with such a vivid disclosure, such a flash of her personality, that he was overwhelmed. In spite of a convinced Femininism which should have armoured him, Ronald never failed to be overwhelmed by sheer femininity. Not since little boyhood did he remember such flashes from her; she had seemed for those middle years rather withdrawn and perverse; in her very elegance, abstract.

He stuttered his reasons for coming from Germany, sadly abashed. He told her how she had distracted him by a letter now and then, or a memory, from his regard of the economic confusion upon which he had so admirably concentrated himself. Her reprehensible undistress had been a constant temptation. Also he had not been able to see when else in the press of the next two years he could be with her for long. Also, he admitted scrupulously, it did happen to fit in very well with his project of meeting the Byngs in Sicily.

He did not, however, admit to a childish feeling of

homelessness or to having been lonely in Munich and
bored in Dresden, while several people had been rude
to him in Berlin. He did just glance for a moment
tentatively at his mother, then he gulped the admission
down; he drew in his feet and stared a little haggardly
round the drawing-room. He may have guessed they
were not likely to come nearer to each other than these
precipitate little plunges into intimacy, this succession of
rendezvous, would bring them.

Round him stripes prevailed, on the tight brocades of
the upholstery, on the mats methodically diamond-wise
on the polish; stripes were repeated innumerably in the
satiny wallpaper and the lace blinds over the door. One
had a sense of being caged into this crowded emptiness.
This seemed the strangest place to sit and make demands
on motherhood, the strangest place for motherhood,
answering, to make itself palpable. He felt impelled
to ask his mother some fantastic question: 'What do I
mean to you?' or 'What part do I play in your life?' or
even (a final outrage), 'Do you care for me?' (This he
could not remember that she had ever avowed.) Even
were the putting of such questions conceivable, a direct
reply from her here was not; there must ensue some
cataclysm, the stretched brocades would rip audibly, the
potbellied vases crack. His most daring conception of an
intimacy was that there would be freedom to ask or to
answer such questions; though he also conceived that in
such an intimacy the reserves would have trebly their
value.

'It will be dull for you here,' said his mother, inter-
preting his vague scrutiny. 'I do nothing at all all day
long, so I haven't had time for a feeling of rootlessness,
but if I'd known you were coming out I'd have taken a
villino. Sydney found me the nicest little villino stuck
to the side of a rock and wanted to take it for both of us,

but it would have meant the dear muzzy cousin with the inside coming too, and that Sydney wouldn't consider; though she couldn't for a moment, either, consider leaving the cousin. So the idea dropped. A pity, I think now,' Mrs. Kerr said reflectively.

'A disappointment for Sydney.'

'I'm afraid they seem inevitable. She is a very disappointable girl. But it really is a pity from our point of view, because she'd be moving out now and you would be moving in. How long is it, I wonder, since you and I have kept house? Perhaps I have deprived you of something? — I cannot feel that I have.'

'The idea that you should what is called "live for me" is quite barbarous,' said Ronald reassuringly.

'Yet I cannot disentangle myself from the idea that it isn't right for a woman not to be a little barbarous.'

'Being rational,' Ronald considered, 'should take them as far. You see, they can . . . they can *canal* the natural forces——'

'Oh! But I don't feel as if I had got any natural forces,' said Mrs. Kerr, alarmed. 'And — you know, Ronald, you would hate me to be rational. It's forbidding and horrible in a woman, I think.'

'But one does want them to understand themselves.'

'Oh, you know you wouldn't be attracted by a woman who did!'

'Do attractions really matter so much?' asked Ronald in the strained voice of one in whom a whole torrent of convictions banks itself up behind the narrow escape of speech, impeding its own exit.

'My darling . . . Shall we have to be so very hygienic and bald?'

He could put nothing he felt into words.

His mother took up one of his hands, turned it over thoughtfully, then laying it down on her knee pulled each

148

finger gently, spreading each out and feeling the tip with her own. 'Nice hands,' she said with a sigh. 'I do wish you hadn't had to go to Germany.'

That 'hygienic' had stung Ronald. It was like getting a splash in the eye from a disinfectant. 'I suppose,' he said, as though he were speaking to her in the dark and had to guess her position, 'that you, think I don't like things to be beautiful.'

'Don't be chilly with me – I didn't mean that. I'm frivolous, you see, and I can't express myself. I only do mean that I think you and Sydney are a little inclined to over-estimate the value of what you call "truth" (though I do agree it is very important), and that this does tend to produce in your conversation rather an atmosphere of white tiles.'

'It must be depressing for you to have a son like an operating-theatre,' said Ronald with bitter mirth, and amended, more fatally apt, 'or a bathroom.'

Mrs. Kerr leaned her head against the wall again and shut her eyes; her lids remained closed as though she already were sleeping, and a faint and very mysterious smile suggested to him for some seconds a profound slumber. With an idea that it might be forbidden to sleep in the drawing-room (could one have imagined it possible to do so) he got protestingly up and stood over her.

'*May* I go to sleep?' she said without moving. 'Even for you, darling, I can't do without my siesta.'

'Tell me before you go quite away,' he exclaimed, 'if I've been boorish and horrible?'

'You've been lovely,' breathed out Mrs. Kerr on a sigh, and behind the mask of her face she perceptibly retreated from consciousness, in the attitude of the Beata Beatrix. Looking down at her he went back through his memory, past his admiration for Rossetti, to the day when at six years old he had called his mother 'My Beautiful'. As she did not stir and, the Hotel being absolutely silent, there seemed no danger of anybody coming in to disturb her, he sat down again silently on a small chair. From here he could see, to the left of her sofa, the long strip of awning, orange against the sun, and, under it, the blue line of sea, with clotted geraniums swinging down from their boxes. Across his panel of sea a fishing-boat made a slow progress; this had vanished behind the window-frame and another had followed it before Mrs. Kerr opened her eyes again or Ronald stirred from the profound meditation into which, with folded legs and limply hanging arms, he had relapsed.

CHAPTER XV

LUCID

VERONICA was in despair. She slipped, after a doubtful tap, round Sydney's door and, professing an acute desire for sympathy and consolation, sank without further explanation into the billows of plump eiderdown on Sydney's bed, kicked her white suede shoes across the room and flung her hat after them.

'The floor hasn't been swept,' said Sydney, looking up from her book. Notwithstanding the slight sense of degeneracy induced by reading novels before luncheon she had been enjoying *Jude the Obscure*. She did not mind Veronica coming in, but wished she did not have to talk to her.

'I don't care if I don't put any of them on again,' announced Veronica in the toneless accents of sincerity. 'They are abominable.'

'*I* think the clothes you wear are nice,' said Sydney. 'Have you got a pain?'

'As a matter of fact, I hate all my clothes. And I don't know what is to become of me. Does it ever occur to you that being alive is a mistake?' She swung a stockinged foot and sighed. 'I do wish,' she said, 'that I had brought my knitting. I do think conversation when one hasn't got anything to do with one's hands feels fearfully awkward, don't you? And I really should like to talk, if you don't mind. You're not doing anything – I mean, only reading?'

'Why don't you go out?'

Veronica explained that she was sick of other people's faces, and was certain, comfortably, that Sydney would understand what she meant. Sitting here in Sydney's room, to which she hadn't yet been invited, among Sydney's possessions, gave her a feeling of being listened to which she would never have had on neutral ground. Ordinarily, this would not have affected her one way or the other; she herself never listened very attentively to what other people were saying. The gist of their remarks was enough for her. This was a north room; the morning's sun was reflected back to it faintly from the face of the hill. Veronica preferred her own room, and thought that it was just like Sydney to be at the back of the first floor instead of the front of the fourth, with a balcony and sunshine. She, Joan and Eileen shared a room with sloping ceilings that resembled a rabbit-hutch. This, she thought, looking round her, was rarefied but rather depressing.

'Does it seem to you,' she said weightily, 'that this world is entirely divided into rather stupid men and very silly women? And that the stupid are all one will ever have to hope for and that the silly are all one can ever become?'

Sydney, thoughtful over this, was certain that there must be other variations.

'There aren't,' said Veronica defiantly. 'I think you are usually fairly lucid, and at present I am; I have absolutely no illusions about anyone. Look at the things people say to you and the things they expect you to do, and the ridiculous way people don't know what they want and the fuss they make when they can't get it. Look at the sort of way people go on if you ask them for any opinion about anything you've done.'

'I never ask anybody else their opinion,' said Sydney (she felt odiously).

'One must have something to go by.'

'Go by yourself.'

'As a matter of fact,' said Veronica, rolling sideways on to her elbow to pluck a long white feather out of the eiderdown, 'I suppose I'm rather humble, really. By the way,' she added after a pause in which two more feathers had been extracted, 'what is your absolutely candid opinion of the man Victor?'

'*How* absolutely candid? – I mean, would anything hurt?'

'Nothing, thanks. Do I look it?'

'Well, candidly, I do think he's rather a dreary young man.'

'I thought you did,' said Veronica briskly; 'everybody seems to. Of course, I know him fairly well.'

'And isn't he?'

'Oh, not more than others.' Veronica slipped off the bed and began to walk round the room thoughtfully. Hands on hips she paused a moment to look at herself in the wardrobe from every angle. 'One might be led to expect,' she said with obvious relevance, 'something better than all that, you know.' It did seem that for all she had been designed for she was tragically more than adequate. She remained staring at Sydney with a fated air while Sydney said: 'He seems attached to you.'

'Of course,' said Veronica, matter-of-factly but without complacency.

'Do you want to get rid of him?'

'Yes – no. What would be the good? Everybody's the same and I must have somebody.'

'Oh, well,' said Sydney, withdrawing. A moment's rather fine light had played on Veronica, but now Sydney felt, in revulsion, a kind of contempt. Women, she thought, are all tentacles: this last remark suggested a wide but horribly purposeful groping about.

'And if you come to think of it,' said Veronica, 'people who are fond of one may be damned dull, and absolutely monotonous, but they are rather touching. I hate pitying people, but I can't help it. Fancy feeling like that! I do think men are pathetic, don't you? If only they were more interesting.'

'I should have said they were interesting.'

'You wouldn't if you'd had as many as I have,' said Veronica gloomily. 'I do envy you being so fearfully clever, Sydney: it's kept you young for your age. I dare say I thought men were interesting when I was about seventeen. Now I can see they're all exactly the same.'

'If that's the effect you produce on them,' said Sydney, 'I should let them be. And it would be fairer. After all, as one was told when one wouldn't finish up one's dinner, there are many poor girls——'

'Oh, I dare say. But what am *I* to do? I don't want to *be* anything. I'm not modern. I'd be perfectly happy the way I am if only other people weren't exactly like they are. Sydney, you give me the creeps sitting there like an idol. Do say something. Tell me what you think will become of me.'

'Why do you ask me? I'm the last person in the world to be able to understand you. It would be better, even, to ask Victor.'

'I never talk to him. But you're so *lucid*.'

'Who said that?' asked Sydney at once, pouncing on an adjective which did not seem to have its place in Veronica's vocabulary.

'Mr. Milton,' said Veronica unabashed. 'We think "lucid" is a good word: we've taken it up. You should hear Eileen! *He's* got a tremendous vocabulary: he said you were "clear-cut".'

'Oh! How amusing. Does he talk about me?'

'Of course he does; he's fearfully keen on you.'

'Oh! How amusing. . . .'

Veronica laughed tolerantly. 'In love, if you prefer it,' she continued. 'I suppose as he's middle-aged that that is rather more expressive.'

Sydney, feeling as though she had caught Milton unawares, felt rather ashamed of herself. The realization that came as those awkward-sounding words left Veronica's lips was as sudden as though that scene on the plateau (which had disconnected itself from the rest of her memories) had not occurred. She had so entirely divested that ill-staged proposal of all the traditional trappings that she had come to account for it merely as a more blatant of his occasional solecisms. They had frequently met since then without awkwardness, without the ghost of an echo.

Sydney could never hear any mention of love without an envious pang for its object, and now, as though feeling came quicker than thought, she felt this pang sharply before she had had time to say to herself, 'He is in love with *me*.'

'I dare say he may propose, you know,' said Veronica maternally, with an air of having their situation well in hand. 'That will be awful for you: he's a darling old thing – not so very old, either,' she amended politely – so politely that Sydney realized she must have transgressed an etiquette in depreciating Victor. 'He is one of the few men,' said Veronica with a sigh, 'who can talk intellectually to me and make me talk intellectually without feeling a fool.'

Sydney longed to overhear them. 'He and I,' she said, 'can't talk to one another. He keeps tripping up and tripping me up like a bad dancer.'

'Oh, *well*,' said Veronica, 'under the circumstances what can you expect?' And Sydney shrugged her impatience at this conception of things. Veronica sitting down at the dressing-table leant on her elbows, curling her feet round the rungs of the chair. She amused herself for some moments by squinting horribly at her own reflection, then she took up Sydney's puff and began thoughtfully to powder her face. 'Talking of types,' said she, 'none of us seem to be making much impression on young Ronald, do we? Did you ever see such a Mummy's boy! Oh, I beg your pardon, Sydney, I was forgetting Mrs. Kerr was a friend of yours.'

'It doesn't matter.'

'I must say, I do think she's odd about Ronald. She doesn't seem to have taken any notice of him for years, and now they go about all over the place like Romeo and Juliet. Of course, I dare say he makes a fearful fuss of her. These selfish mothers get the best of it all the way. I shall be a selfish mother.'

'As a matter of fact, you won't,' Sydney said with a flash of insight.

'Well, I should never have the nerve to be as blatantly selfish as she is. I think she's treated you very badly, too: that makes me furious—— I say, Sydney, your powder doesn't suit my face! Look, it makes me pale blue. You have got a skin, you lucky devil! *I* always use *basanée*.'

'Why do you think she has treated me badly?' asked Sydney dispassionately. She waited for Veronica to continue, and her expectations of what was coming raced ahead.

'Well, she has so absolutely given you the go-by, hasn't she?' said Veronica, replacing the alabaster lid of the powder-bowl, then looking down to blow some powder off her dress. 'It was "Sydney this" and "Sydney darling that" and "Where's Sydney?" and "Sydney and I are going together," and now he's come she simply doesn't see you.'

Sydney, after an interval, leant sideways to push the window farther open. She seemed to have forgotten

Veronica, who energetically continued: 'Of course I'm
sorry for you. Everybody's sorry for you.'

'Oh,' said Sydney.

'Do you *mind* the way she's going on?' asked Veronica
curiously.

'It hadn't occurred to me that there was anything to
mind,' said Sydney with a high-pitched little laugh and
a sensation of pushing off something that was coming
down on her like the ceiling in one of her dreams. It
seemed incredible that the words Veronica had just made
use of should ever have been spoken.

'Well, it has occurred to everybody else, you know,'
said Veronica, and picking up a string of amber she held
it against her dress and leant back to admire the reflection. 'Take a word of advice from one who knows, my
dear,' said Veronica sagely, 'and never trust any woman
an inch. They're all alike, cats every one of them.'

'I thought there was something special you wanted to
talk about,' Sydney broke in eagerly, making a dart for
this way of escape from herself. For very nervousness
she could not stop talking, and Veronica's affairs now
offered themselves gratefully as a kind of jungle in
which her own values could be obscured and forgotten.
'You were in despair, Veronica,' she insisted more
eagerly; 'you said just now you were in despair.'

'I know,' said Veronica willingly. 'I did feel like
nothing on earth. But you've cheered me up immensely. It's queer how the most ridiculous little worry
of somebody else's will often take one's mind off one's
own. But there really was something I wanted to ask
you about. I'm engaged to Victor – would you advise
me to be?'

Sydney could not help feeling that any matron in the
Hotel could have done as much for Veronica while she
pronounced wisely: 'Not if you're not happy, of course.'

'Well, I feel in a kind of way happy,' said Veronica, wriggling her shoulders. 'You see, I do like Victor, and we do seem to be rather involved – which comes, of course, from having nothing to do here. Oh, don't look so grim, Sydney, you look fearfully grim. I mean, you might say the usual sort of thing even if you don't mean them; you give me the creeps.'

'My dear,' said Sydney more warmly, 'you must marry him if you care to. And I hope you'll be fearfully happy.'

'You know I really don't see why one shouldn't be,' said Veronica, brightening, as though the possibility had only now presented itself. 'Of course, he's got no money and no work and nothing *you'd* call ability; but that makes me feel less of a mean pig.'

' "Pig", Veronica?'

'For not feeling more thrilled. And he and I've got rather the same sense of humour. Of course, there are people at home I could marry, but there's not really much to choose between any of them. You see, I've got absolutely no illusions. I do feel I might have been terribly fond of somebody; I don't think I'm really hard or anything – do you? Do you think perhaps men aren't what they used to be? . . . It's all very well to say, "Don't marry!" ' cried Veronica, throwing both her hands up to forbid interruption and raising her voice, 'but I must marry somebody. You see, I must have some children.'

'Well, you needn't necessarily marry——'

'My dear Sydney!' exclaimed Veronica, horrified and scarlet. Her changes of mood, definite as the slipping-along of lantern slides, expressed themselves in changes of attitude, so that all unconsciously she was dramatic. Dejection once again drew out each line of her; she exclaimed: 'But I've *kicked* Victor: what is the use of a man one can kick?'

The problem seemed likely to be one which she would be called upon to consider in its length and breadth repeatedly; she at once accepted the likelihood and turned away from it with a nod of admirable philosophy. 'God knows!' sighed she not irreverently. The problem would be dismissed at its every reappearance with this undefeated gracefulness. Sydney had a return of her earlier admiration. Veronica had taken up a sound position midway between defiance and resignation and seemed likely to achieve serenity.

'And what shall you do?' asked Veronica, as though they had been talking over their plans for the day. 'I mean, when you get back to England?'

Sydney was blank for a moment – back to *where?* 'Oh, go on where I left off,' said she; 'try and pass my next exam!'

'Oh! Why?'

'Well, I really——'

' – I don't suppose I should understand, should I? Funny how well we know each other – I've never given myself away like this before – and yet how little we *know*. In an ordinary way, in London, we should run miles, I dare say, rather than meet. Of course, I should have met Victor anywhere. I say, I hope I haven't made your bed uncomfy, rolling about. I really can't sit on foreign armchairs: they're so steep.' She picked her hat up from the floor, brushed the dust off it tenderly and put it on. 'As you say, this is not such a bad hat.' She heaved a deep sigh. 'I feel ever so much happier; you are wonderful. Have you got a shoe-horn? These shoes are so tight, really that's why I dislike them. I say, will you come to tea with me and Victor at the Pâtisserie and look at him again? He's sensitive really; if you were nice to him he'd buck up tremendously – you'd be surprised. We eat a tremendous amount of pâtisserie; we adore it, and it doesn't seem worth while beginning to economize until there is some remote prospect of our getting married. And if we don't get married – I mean, to each other – there will always be this to look back on. That's what we feel.'

Sighing and talking, vaguely she drifted towards the door. There she turned back and brilliantly nodded.

A suspicion that this mood of lucidity had, after all, been induced by an over-indulgence in pastry cast a slight shadow on Sydney's farewell. 'I should be careful said she, 'or you'll both get most fearfully spotty. Look at those little Italians! Can't you try some other narcotic?'

'You should be thankful we don't drink,' said Veronica, and shut the door after her – not satisfactorily, for it clicked open again and began to creak on its hinges in the manner of hotel doors all over the world.

Sydney heard her quickening footsteps retreat; she listened forlornly, straining her ears for the last of them. Then she got up and tidied the bed; smoothed out the eiderdown, picked up the amber beads and hanging them round her neck stood telling them off like a rosary. Some premonition, such as that with which a recurring physical pain announces itself, made her snatch up *Jude the Obscure* quickly and stare at the pages, but there she found nothing but print. She looked up for a moment and – 'She has so absolutely given you the go-by,' the room repeated, catching her unawares. The shapes of the furniture, everything that she looked at, said it again.

CHAPTER XVI

VILLA

THE Villa Tre Cipressi concealed itself to the last, blotted out among the trees of its hillside; a long lane with broken-down walls led circuitously to its gates through olive gardens. Since the last date of the Villa's habitation the surface of the lane must have deteriorated; it was impossible now to imagine the burnished, sleek rushing down it of cars or the thin-shod delicate stepping of the Russian ladies. Miss Fitzgerald's party going forward in the leisurely and spread-out manner called in Ireland 'strealing' had begun to feel a profound disbelief in the existence of the Villa. Miss Fitzgerald had, however, in doing them the honours of what had been a private experience, constituted herself their hostess, and they hesitated to suggest this disbelief to her otherwise than obliquely, by a disposition to linger, sweep the hill with a glance then gaze back through the olive trees, or to seat themselves at intervals, with some obvious thought of encampment, along the smoother parts of the walls. In the selection of them for a social bouquet there had been nothing striking except in a last addition – Mr. Milton went on nearly everybody's picnics (it seemed a destiny beyond his influence); Miss Pym, as half of a duality, had been inevitable; Mrs. Hillier had been led to tolerate these two good women who did not know India and this parson who did not play bridge by her passion for villa gardens. It was Ronald who had been the master-stroke; he redeemed the bunch of them and made their grouping together seem superbly conscious and studied, suggesting depths of art behind its effect of naivety. So at least Mr. Milton felt that Ronald must be thinking, and he did not doubt that Ronald was right.

After a series of sharp turns the Villa gates stared down on them, aware, one might have supposed, by their triumphant whorls and scrolls of painted ironwork, of all they gained by presenting themselves so suddenly. A mild ascent led up to them, and the three cypresses, which had an air of drawing together in council, dominated the approach. They came up rather breathlessly and stood behind Miss Fitzgerald in silence, as though they were prepared to rush the opening, while she sent the great key she had produced beforehand screeching round in the lock. Then they pressed in behind her, looking to left and right of them up at the palm trees or between the boles which had an exotic, rather horrible fatness. The tangled gloom and the expanse of silence swallowed up their cries of admiration. Miss Fitzgerald, after checking off with nods of satisfaction all she still found here, invited Ronald to tell her whether this was not all he had hoped.

Ronald had hoped nothing; he had not wished to accompany her. They misunderstood one another (though she didn't suspect this); she had marked him down from the first as being of that delightful age which expects to be taken seriously and which to one's ardent gravity will make shy, delicious disclosures. Ronald preferred in any encounter with women of a no longer redeemable age that might be forced on him to retreat behind an impassible whimsicality which amounted to archness. Thus there had been a conflict in their methods of approach, the equal determinations of each of them to 'take' the other rather than 'be taken'. She had plumped down beside him that morning with her invitation at an instant of such crisis in his thoughts that

VILLA

he could have murdered her for the interruption. In
Germany he had found he could not think; there had
been too much time, some element of condensation had
been lacking; here there had been nothing but a series of
agonizing ruptures; the very fact of sitting down alone on
bench or sofa seemed to be provocative, and Ronald
could not think properly standing up. 'Your mother,'
she had begun, 'wanted me to ask you if you'd come
with us to the Russian Villa – I have been lent the key.
She is sure you will be delighted with it.' There had
been nothing left for Ronald to say.

A number of disappearing pathways darted off from
the avenue; Corinthian pillars suggested themselves
through a net of undergrowth, and the arch of a stone
bridge let one suppose water. The party hung fire, embarrassed by this choice of attractions, then continued to
move slowly up the avenue in a close formation. This
was more than a villa, it was a country-house, with, for
the moment, nothing but the distinct shadows and an
irregular splash of water to give away its foreignness.
Then Miss Fitzgerald caught Ronald by the arm and
pulled him sideways, pointing excitedly as though they
were to surprise some living thing. 'Look,' she cried, 'up
there – the Villa!' They all had a glimpse of it and were
repelled, forty supercilious white windows, blankly
shuttered, a vacillating shabbiness across its grey face
that was neither old nor new. It had a solidity that was
not local, an assured air of having been finally answered
for; but it was as disappointing as one's first princess.

'Of course it isn't like a *cinque cento* villa,' said Miss
Pym, anxious to make all allowances.

'It is amusingly suggestive, isn't it,' Ronald said to
Milton, 'of the "Nuit de Portofino Kulm"?' and was
made to feel himself utterly isolated by Milton's kind,
blank stare. 'I'm afraid I haven't read——' said Milton.

163

Ronald felt with complacency. '*Oh ...*' said Ronald. He would have liked to discuss also, in the light of his own recent observations in Germany, that mild baron of Charlottenburg who kept snakes in his parlour behind violet silk curtains. He sighed as though a door had been slammed in front of him. Perished civilizations interested Ronald, who had come too late to share a mild distress at their demise. Soon he was thinking fruitfully about Russia, and was glad when Milton again gave him another opening by saying to Mrs. Hillier: 'I often wonder whether the Russians weren't, after all, the only people with any real notion of aristocracy.'

'Does that mean you did or didn't like Russians?' said Mrs. Hillier, looking at him cautiously; while Ronald, almost simultaneously, exclaimed, 'So real it was that this world was no place for them!'

'Do you at all mean to suggest,' asked Milton, giving full attention to this last remark, 'that they have simply been translated? Because I think that's very tenable. It strikes me more and more as I live that this world's no place for anyone with any real notion of anything, and that its expulsion of them must be almost automatic.'

'Their type was very refined,' said Mrs. Hillier, 'lovely creatures – but one can never altogether like them.' She looked about at the garden which, with its profound and hidden hollows around them, seemed to be waiting. 'I must say,' she confessed, 'this is delightful. Shall we go over that bridge? The garden must go on indefinitely—— Look, there's a seat with steps up to it right on the hill!' She made for the bridge, appearing, so abrupt was the turn of the path, to have plunged waist-deep into the shiny dark leaves that flopped back, heavy as fishes, from the sweep of her skirts. These plants with their overpowering glossiness must have sprung from wet soil. Milton and Miss Pym went after her; Ronald and

Miss Fitzgerald seemed to have been delayed by a short argument – perhaps as to the nature of aristocracy. The garden gave Milton a distinct feeling of nervousness, as though he were being scornfully watched. To allow this was to underrate oneself, so he asked abruptly, 'If one comes to think of it, what was the good of them?' There was a pause filled in by the agitation of leaves; then Miss Pym, upon whom an ever-deeper despondency must have been working, replied, 'If you come to think of it, what is the good of *us?*'

'Well, really . . .' said Mrs. Hillier.

'Us *three?*' asked Milton, in an attempt to evade the issue. He could tell from the set of Mrs. Hillier's back that in another minute or two they might be at grips with the problem of Empire.

'No,' said Miss Pym, still more wildly, 'I mean us all, our class. . . .'

Mrs. Hillier stared at her, then decided to laugh. 'I didn't know you were a Socialist!'

'But must one be a Socialist,' went on Miss Pym defiantly, 'to wonder sometimes what is the good of us? Because one can't help it (without wishing to attach oneself to any party) these days, when so much is in the melting-pot.'

'It's hardly easy to talk about, is it?' said Mrs. Hillier lightly, with the same well-bred instinct to cover this that she had when anybody tried to discuss religious experiences (though at present, with the excuse of a specialist, *that* would have been more permissible). 'I suppose,' she elected to say, 'it's a matter of example, really, isn't it? I mean, giving the others something to go by. I mean, people do notice. Why, one feels it even out here – Italians *notice*.'

'But don't you wonder if they don't just think we're lazy?' Miss Pym exploded. 'I do: when my friend and I have been walking or reading and one feels them up on those terraces looking down on one and working away. Why, even in the Hotel, you know, one does wonder if the waiters——'

'You're just getting acutely self-conscious, Miss Pym, that's what's the matter with you,' laughed Mrs. Hillier, bluntly and kindly. 'The creatures are positive parasites. If you'd lived out of England as long as I have, and seen how——'

'– I've lived all over the Continent——'

' – Oh, but that's different. I mean, that just tends to make one cosmopolitan.'

'Yes, but that's just it——' cried Miss Pym, then subsided, thoroughly confused.

This engagement left Milton free to escape from them, which, while walking decorously enough alongside and keeping back here and there a branch with his walking-stick, it is to be feared that he did. The path, by going up steeply for short distances and only gradually coming down again, presented a clever effect of being Alpine: one felt one must have climbed to a great height. One was humoured in this by being railed away solicitously from small precipices, and by being made to walk dizzily over the arch of bridges from which ravines with water seemed to drop away. Every now and then an artful perspective would be offered, to be veiled once more by trees. Once, in a Corinthian arbour that seemed balanced on the top of a tree like a ball upon a jet of water, he had a glimpse of Miss Fitzgerald talking to Ronald ... 'And I expect,' she said, after a prolonged and breathless inspection of all the profile he vouchsafed her, 'that you write poetry, too, don't you?' Before his path dipped again he heard Ronald reply in a very nearly extinguished voice, 'Well, as I said before, you see, my subject is economics.' Milton, whose sym-

pathies were all with Miss Fitzgerald, ground his teeth.
He considered Ronald definitely disobliging in his refusal
to give hostages anywhere. He had been prepared for
clever indolence or for a cool kind of wantonness in Mrs.
Kerr's son, or for polite nullity or resentful dullness in
the son of Mrs. Kerr's husband; he had begun to build,
successively, on each of these probabilities. But he had
not foreseen this refusal to emerge from behind a non-
committal mannerliness, or the long ray to be directed
upon them that showed them all up, even Sydney, in the
maze of a gnat's dance, an aimless passionate jiggle apart
and together. It had not been in Ronald to precipitate a
crisis on any plane: he was not, thought Milton, either
vivid or generous enough. He had come to stare, one
could only imagine, and Milton had a view of him
lounging along a row of cages. He wondered how much
Ronald had hurt Sydney, whether she had been able to
make her hurt him at all; though she had been so visibly
'out' from the earliest word of his coming, to make a
juggernaut of her friend's son. Milton did not know
whether, except for that brief encounter in the ballroom,
they had ever exchanged a word. The reservation would
be enough to engage this perverse girl in still deeper
designs on him and to make her, to merely a lover, more
inaccessible than before.

They climbed up to the skeleton of a summer-house;
the walls might have blown away or might simply have
rotted. Miss Pym began to search about diligently,
looking under the seat and into the corners and running
the point of her walking-stick along the cracks of the
pavement. She explained that 'they' might have dropped
something. This for a moment seemed so probable that
Milton went just as eagerly down on one knee. 'Think,'
said she, 'if one were to find a little purse, or a bangle
that had slipped off, or even a button! I can't believe

they wouldn't have left something; they must have come here day after day.' Milton laughed at her tolerantly, getting up again and dusting his knee. She didn't explain why she should have concentrated her hopes on this arbour; she perhaps left the arbour to do so, for perched out over the garden it was as intimate as a nest. Mrs. Hillier, sitting down dreamily, said, 'It would have been a nice place for a proposal or something.'

Another allusion to a technique he had disregarded! Milton said quickly, 'But we wouldn't understand – do you realize? – a word that has ever been said here!'

'But people in the better-class Russian stories always seem to talk French or English.'

'I can't imagine anybody who wasn't obliged to making love in English.'

'I suppose,' said Mrs. Hillier, looking at him thoughtfully, 'that one only feels one's own language a limitation if one is not sufficiently carried away.'

'Oh!' cried Miss Pym, waving, 'here is Eleanor coming up!'

Mrs. Hillier said she did hope that she really were coming alone. 'Though, of course,' she added, 'I should be sorry if Ronald had actually fallen into a tank or anything. Though one can't say that it might not be for the best. For I can't think what is going to become of him!'

'I will go and look,' said Milton and, full of determination, left the arbour.

Descending, he called Ronald everywhere: the silence that received his voice gave him back an infuriating sensation, less of being unheard than of not being answered. The boy might be round any corner listening compassionately, telling himself that there went poor old Milton hollering away. So he pressed on in a shut-down kind of silence, and was surprised and aggrieved as at each turn the emptiness renewed itself down

pergola, lawn or glade. A flitting echo of Mrs. Hillier's remark sent him suddenly towards the gleam of water.
There was no path: he had to push his way out through
some bushes to the rim of a larger tank that had been cut
out, a square of vivid green water, under the jut of a
cliff. The tank had a kerb of yellow marble, and he saw,
looking across it, that the smooth streaked sides went
down about three feet before they came to the water,
which might be lower than usual but gave some suggestion by its unmuddied yet complete opaqueness of
being very deep. The water looked solid; if a body
disappeared through the surface it might leave a dint,
perhaps, a gash which would slowly heal, but never a
ripple. He could not imagine the green line swelling up
or fretted for even a moment against the face of the
marble. He leant farther over it, after a glance up of
instinctive watchfulness at the cliff which, like a lid on a
hinge, had seemed at that very moment to lean farther
over him, and inwardly smiled at a picture, a fanciful
composition to which his attitude and manner con-
sciously leant themselves, that could be called 'Temptation to Murder'. He saw his own head and shoulders
reflected, and the cliff and sky (though none of these
impinged on the greenness), and presently, after some
recorded disturbance of branches, the figure of Ronald
which, coming out from under the cliff, stood on the kerb
of the tank nonchalantly, then sat down, dangling it legs.
'He might say something,' Milton thought resentfully;
but after some seconds of silence, whose duration seemed
insulting and ludicrous, he had to throw a 'Well, hullo!'
across the water in impatient concession.

'Hallo,' answered Ronald. 'Exploring on your own?'

'Yes – you, too?'

'Not quite,' said Ronald politely. 'I've been exploring
with Miss Fitzgerald.'

'Biggest tank I've seen,' said Milton, nodding down.

'Yes, isn't it? More of a swimming-bath.'

'What on earth – it's like talking to about ten people!'

'Yes, it's this cliff.'

'Can't you come round?' said Milton impatiently.

'Beg your pardon?' asked Ronald, and when the invitation had been repeated conveyed by an instant's pause some surprise at it. He looked round the tank carefully, but had to point out, with regret, that this seemed quite impossible owing to the way the bushes hung over. 'But I dare say we'll meet farther on,' he said; 'these curly paths are wonderfully good for meeting people. At least, so one would expect, but Miss Fitzgerald and I didn't meet anybody. Not a ghost, even, though we were sure we could and were very anxious to.'

'What have you done with Miss Fitzgerald?'

'I think she went to find Miss Pym. I think perhaps she was lonely. You don't believe, I hope, that I've dropped her into the tank?'

'The way you haunt it does seem suspicious!'

'But she'd have come to the surface again: if I *had*, you know, I shouldn't dare come back. No, I came back for the tank; itself – I like water.' Ronald, gripping the edge of the tank, leaned forward to watch with a smile the reflection of his dangling feet. Milton, sitting down opposite him, took out his pipe and lit it. He observed, 'You ought to have brought your mother – she would have liked this.'

'She's a bad walker – don't mean she's got corns or a heart or anything; she's just lazy.'

'Or was not sorry, quite possibly, to get you off her hands for the morning,' laughed Milton with the bluff and stunning impertinence of which only the nervous are capable, and by which no one can be more appalled than themselves.

'I dare say,' said Ronald. 'One does get tired of people.' He gazed across thoughtfully, not at Milton but at Milton's reflection, which he was able to watch without raising his eyes, while remaining as impenetrable to his *vis-à-vis* as the water below him. 'Such an intelligent girl,' he remarked – 'that Miss Warren.'

'Oh, you think so? Have you been talking?'

'No,' said Ronald, 'she is one of the few people in this caravanserai who have nothing to say to me. I would not say, you know, that she was one of those casual talkers. She would have, I imagine, her moments that she saves herself up for.'

'She's considered unfriendly.'

'Oh! But would you want her to be friendly?'

'It scarcely affects me – I have known her some time,' said Milton, making the slight reservation that Hotel time was reckoned differently.

'Oh, really?' said Ronald respectfully. 'You see, where I am concerned she doesn't appeal as an enterprise. She is already in the family.'

'Like a disease or a ghost?' suggested Milton, with a smile that must have been lost on Ronald since his faint image did not reproduce it.

'More like a ghost, I think. She is to be seen on the stairs – still, I dare say, if my mother hasn't already gone out with her.'

'An hotel, you know, is a great place for friendships.'

'Mustn't that be,' said Ronald, 'what people come out for?'

'Perhaps some——'

'But are there really people who would do that?' asked Ronald sharply, in a tone of revulsion, as though he had brought himself up more squarely than he had anticipated to the edge of some kind of abyss. 'You mean women?'

'Yes, I suppose so,' said Milton, smiling across at the agitation of Ronald, very secure and avuncular.

'There is nothing now to prevent women being different,' said Ronald despondently, 'and yet they seem to go on being just the same. What is the good of a new world if nobody can be got to come and live in it?' Sitting above his impassive and pale reflection, crumpled forward on his folded arms, he remained immobile while the echoes of his last exclamation still seemed palpably to hang about under the slant of rock that roofed him into a cave. The decay of the garden must have seemed to him for a dark instant to have profited nothing. Such a collapse at a mere glance at feminine frailty into the most profound despair suggested, more than loss of balance, a sharp assault from the rear by some exterior, malignant force. Milton justified his own silence, his unwillingness to go to the rescue of Ronald, by a feeling that this collapse had its austere fitness and that the garden had been, after all, fully entitled to revenge itself.

CHAPTER XVII

PATISSERIE

THE Pâtisserie had a dozen little blue tin tables dotted about under a happy-looking striped awning. Hither many people gravitated early in the day. Mrs. Kerr, who had insisted they should visit the shops, had for the last half-hour's slow parade of the plate-glass given her companion about a quarter of her attention and a little less than her quarter-face. She had meanwhile chosen for Sydney and presented charmingly a string of dull amethysts, saying it seemed too good to be believable that they should be together again. When she saw the little tables and the English people round them sitting sideways and eating pâtisserie off the tips of their forks with an amused air of concession, she exclaimed with pleasure and her attention became entirely distracted. The scene appeared to delight her and she concentrated her delight into each of the smiling nods she sent across to acquaintances.

'Do look, Sydney – how civilized!'

'How greedy!' said Sydney, who was trying to direct her friend to the older end of the town, where she would at least find nothing but fruit shops.

'Yes, that's just what I mean – how civilized! Anybody can eat at meal-times. Come over – oh, Sydney, we must!'

'But we're not hungry!'

'No, of course we're not.' Mrs. Kerr, propping up her parasol against a table, positively beamed. The table was as small as a mushroom between them; she looked helplessly at her handbag, then passed it over to Sydney to be disposed of, and drawing off her gloves eagerly looked round to see what other people were eating. 'I'm so seldom allowed to do this. Ronald is spending his own sort of morning – a very genuine dead villa – the Riviera, you see, is so tinny' – she tapped the table – 'so why shouldn't I?'

'I never knew this *was* your sort of morning. We might often have come here.'

'I suppose,' said Mrs. Kerr, 'that I hardly liked to suggest it. I could never, of course, suggest it to Ronald ... Oh, vermouth? You are ascetic! I should like some chocolate. Will you drink very slowly, then we shan't have to go?'

'Oh! But weren't we——?'

'But where is there to go? And I mean, why should we? But of course, my dear, I will go anywhere. This is really your morning. If I didn't spoil you, you would never come near me now. I don't know what you've been doing; I never see you—— Oh, look, there's Veronica Lawrence with that dreadful young man. What unnatural tastes she's got; why doesn't she run after Ronald?'

'It would be very discouraging.'

'I don't see why it should be; Ronald's rather susceptible.' Mrs. Kerr, her folded hands on the table, sat looking sideways, absorbed. 'He is looking at her with the most awful expression, with cream on his chin. Isn't passion debasing? Tell me, Sydney, are that couple engaged?'

'Oh, probably.' Sydney looked conscious.

'Oh, does she tell *you* these things?' asked Mrs. Kerr curiously. 'What a queer friendship! Does she show how tremendously sorry she is for you, or is she too deep? What does she say about me? It would amuse me to know.'

'But why should we discuss you?'

'I can't think. But you must talk personalities, surely
... Isn't she really rather a common little thing?'

'She rather attracts me.'

'Oh, if she only *attracts* you ... It matters much more
whom one likes. Will you look for a plate and choose us
both some pâtisserie – nothing too sweet?' Sydney with
a dazzled blank feeling got up indecisively. 'You know
what I like – you've an instinct.' Mrs. Kerr, looking up
for a moment, let her general vague smile quickly be
personal, and gave Sydney a glimpse of her old mood,
fleetingly, yet so that to turn away was an agony. 'Do
go, won't you?' she urged, with such a promise implicit
that the coming back would be memorable that Sydney
left her forthwith, slipping between the chair-backs to
the shop door and the crowded counter.

Here, moving up and down thoughtfully, she found
herself elbow to elbow with Victor, who, fork in one
hand and plate in the other, was also selecting, and in a
practised manner spearing, pâtisserie.

'Oh, hullo!' said he as she hesitated. 'Can I help you
in any way? I know all these pretty well. Don't go for
the coffee kind, they look first-rate but they're hollow.
Do you mind if I take the last green one? Veronica's
fearfully keen on them. We come here a lot.'

'So Veronica told me.'

'Yes, by Jove, she did, didn't she?' said Victor,
remembering. 'I say, look here, don't wish me the
usual – I feel perfectly rotten.'

'Oh, I'm sorry,' said Sydney. Her sympathy necessarily lacked directness, because Victor was the sort of
young man who continues to move about uneasily while
talking and to talk for a long time without looking
straight at one.

'Still, one's only young once,' remarked Victor, and
roamed away down the counter. Later on, she followed

him out through the door, which he blocked for her by a moment's misgiving as to the ultimate excellence of his choice.

Mrs. Kerr had discovered herself back to back with a friend and had turned to converse with her. The friend was animated, Mrs. Kerr sympathetic. Sydney stood a moment to watch them.

'*Delicious!*' exclaimed the friend, a dark lady from another hotel, whose party, a broken-up circle, sat listening all at a loss and turned now and then a long stare of timid resentment on the brilliant intruder.

'*Absolutely* delicious!' agreed Mrs. Kerr; then, catching sight of Sydney, broke off, still laughing, and faced round once more to her table. 'You've been ages, my darling,' she cried. 'Have you brought the whole shop?'

Sydney put down her plate on the table, showed with a gesture what exactly she had brought and silently began sipping her vermouth. 'That "darling" must have been Ronald,' she thought; 'what a habit of mind he is! . . . Do relations become a habit?' she asked. 'I have so few.'

'I dare say they might,' said Mrs. Kerr, very kind but abstracted. 'What a pity you've got so few' – she sampled the pâtisserie. 'I mean after all, home life—— Why don't you marry, Sydney?'

'I thought we'd been into that.'

'Yes, but it does worry me rather,' said Mrs. Kerr, and turned upon her friend's downcast pallor a profound, limpid, yet prettily conventional stare.

A sharp movement of Sydney's foot shook the table, the china leaped on the tin. 'Well, if you'll keep Ronald a year or two——'

'Sydney!' exclaimed Mrs. Kerr in a low voice, paused a moment and put down her fork. 'Don't be so – so ugly! It's like – I don't know what it's like; it's not like

you. I wish you hadn't made these common friends;
I wish there'd been more girls of your own sort. When
the very essence of you is delicacy and fineness and, well,
breeding, this horrible veneer that you've affected lately
seems so . . . well, it may be what you'd call "in a grim
kind of way funny", but——'

'*This* seems in a grim kind of way funny,' said
Sydney. 'It's like being given tea by an aunt at the Zoo.'

'I only wish you had been taken more to the Zoo! It
seems from the way you sometimes talk that your
friends must be common in the worst kind of way –
exotic! You've distressed even Ronald, though he is as
a rule neither observant nor critical; he said you were so
unnatural, and though at the time I was angry with
him, I must say that when you talk in that tone I should
find you difficult to defend to anybody.'

'I'm sorry Ronald can't like me.'

'Oh, I think that's putting it too strongly,' Mrs. Kerr
said gently. 'Perhaps I have put everything too
strongly—— Sydney darling, don't sit there in that
queer stiff way as though you had swallowed something:
people will notice . . . You know how reprehensible I
am, how I do like my friends to be pleasant. I would
never have said anything if you hadn't shown your
teeth at me; I wouldn't for worlds have spoilt our morning. But we won't let it, will we? . . . Look, eat one of
those little flaky things you've brought, they look
delicious.'

Sydney, trying to get down a mouthful of pastry that
became like sawdust, had a sense of being widely yet
concentratedly glared at, though whether she had really
attracted attention or this were merely the sun striking
down through the awning she did not dare to determine.
Certainly the conversations around had subsided, and
the general turning away of eyes from their table, the

fixed stares – across the street or back into the shop or down on to plates – of which, with a glance round, she assured herself, were elaborate enough to be studied. Little staccato remarks here and there seemed to prick up through a tensity. She suspected that Mrs. Kerr, by her unusually bland expression of basking in reverie, the unconcern of her movements and her solicitude that Sydney should finish her pastry, must be 'passing off' something. Sydney in an effort to further this continued to eat pastry quickly, in spite of a frightened feeling each time that she might not be able to swallow. She could not help a shaken kind of exaltedness such as a child feels when it has upset a table of china.

Presently she let herself fall back on an outside consciousness of their both being well-dressed, distinguished-looking and leisurely, and thought how plainly this must appear from the other side of the street and how, if she were someone else, she would stand on the pavement and look at them. She would admire their graceful air of being friends, of being completed by one another, and go away distracted by a memory of them both sitting there in the temperate shade of the awning. 'I think,' she said conversationally, affected by the thought of this admiration, 'that this is very good way of filling up a morning abroad.'

'*I* think so . . . shall we look for carnations? Shall I buy some for you?'

'Shall I buy some for Ronald?' Sydney looked into Mrs. Kerr's face with a smile, but impersonally, as though it were a picture. Mrs. Kerr seemed to meet something hard in her eyes, for she raised an eyebrow infinitesimally.

'He would love that, it would be quite new to him. I don't think people like to give him things usually. He doesn't, I dare say, give the impression of being in any sense very receptive. Poor Ronald, I wish he could learn to be likeable. I thought once that you might have done something for him, but I don't see now that you very well can.'

This little dead maternal design she laid out before Sydney with naivety and appeared to consider forlornly but with beautiful resignation. Sydney, startled by its appearance, sat speechless and looked at her friend, whose unreproachfulness quietly accused her. 'I know,' said Mrs. Kerr, apparently going off at a tangent and looking down so that there was nothing but the movement of her eyelids and the modulations of her light voice to show or give point to what she was saying, 'that I haven't professed to believe a word of all you have, both of you, so expansively and delightfully told me about life. I haven't a grasp of abstractions, and life, when you mean the theory of living, is an abstraction, surely. You know I've been flippant and difficult, but at least I did try to be honest – I didn't believe. But, my dear, I have so intensely wanted to: I could have prayed (if ever one did) for either of you to justify yourselves, or, best of all, both of you. I've never professed that anything could transcend the conventions; you have. Well, you've insisted passionately that an understanding is possible between a young man and young woman that can remain quite un-bothered, without electricity or diffidence. Ronald insisted, too. When I've said "Well then?" at intervals, you've both waved your arms and declared that you couldn't produce at the moment the right kind of person to demonstrate with. Well, here you both are, and I'm waiting. Has it been too matter-of-fact of me? Possibilities burgeoned, and I'm here waiting for the most idyllic relationship to spring into flower. Can you wonder I'm disappointed and cynical – it's been a poor kind of triumph – at having had to watch you two resolving yourselves into just such an ordinary state of suspicion and watchfulness and antipathy as might precede the most normal attraction in which the heart of a biologist could rejoice?' She laughed deprecatingly; the whole idea of such attraction seemed to be distasteful to her. 'I've talked a long time,' she said, 'rather confusedly, and had to use several words that I rather dislike. What I might have asked shortly – since it's all really that I wanted to know – is: Why ever can't you and Ronald be friends?'

Mrs. Kerr's hand, that lay with casually spread-out fingers under Sydney's eyes along the edge of the table, had some vague connection with her personality, but neither seemed to have anything to do with what had been said. The amazed Sydney could not reconcile them. 'Do you mean what you've just been saying?' she said doubtfully. 'Do you really believe what you've just said? Did much really stand or fall on our making a success of things – I and Ronald?'

'So it did seem to me,' said Mrs. Kerr, also looking slightly bewildered, as though by all these questions Sydney were confusing the issue.

'Did you think you had helped us?'

'Only by . . . valuing both of you.'

'I suppose,' said Sydney, struck by this, 'you do in a kind of way value us?'

'Yes,' said Mrs. Kerr, 'and I've missed you very much. When I had to throw away your carnations this morning I was sorry; I didn't a bit want to.'

'Only this morning? Carnations do last a long time,' said Sydney, and considered the phenomenon gravely. 'One didn't want to intrude, you see,' she added.

'Intrude?' said Mrs. Kerr, repeating the rather middle-class word wonderingly. Her gentle, mystified air was not sympathetic. 'I think,' she said slowly, as though trying how best to express herself to an almost strange young woman, the school friend, as it might be, of a daughter, 'that you've been a little . . . over-important about it, perhaps, haven't you? I mean, how could your coming or not coming make any difference between me and Ronald? He would have been pleased, he was ready to be friendly; he knows just what you've been to me, and in his own tied-up sort of way he is ever so grateful. He likes me to have friends wherever I am. I don't think,' she concluded, with a smile of pity for the girl's inevitable incomprehension, 'that anybody could put things wrong between me and Ronald.'

'In fact, one seems to have taken too much for granted. Funny!' said Sydney and laughed.

'Oh, Sydney dear, no. Why? Don't be so bitter.'

'Why bitter? I see how tiresome a girl can be.'

'Never tiresome; you've been charming; more than unselfish – giving up so much of your time to me, giving me so much – I've accepted too much, I'm afraid.' Mrs. Kerr broke off with compunction.

'Why reproach yourself? Don't you find all your friends are the same?'

Mrs. Kerr sighed and looked down at her hands, allowing this to pass for an admission. With a smile of particular ruefulness that drew up the eyebrows tragically and brought the face to its fullest, profoundest expression of all of her, she confessed: 'But in your case I've been specially guilty. I begin now to guess you've expected much more of me, and that I've been taking and taking without so much as a glance ahead or a single suspicion of what you would want to have back. I'm afraid we've gone wrong through your not quite understanding. You see, I'm so fond of you, but———'

'But?'

'Well, simply but! I mean, there is nothing else there.

It had always seemed to me simple to like people and
right to be liked, but I never can feel that much more is
involved – is it? I have a horror, I think, of not being,
and of my friends not being, quite perfectly balanced.
I think moderation in everything – but perhaps I am
cold . . . Will you take my purse now – if you won't
eat any more – and go in and pay for the cakes?'

To Sydney the cumulative effect of this succession of
touches (especially the last: herself brandishing with
commercial insistence a long bill that her bewildered
debtor felt unable to meet) was of vulgarity. The
attribution to herself of an irritable sex-consciousness
vis-à-vis to Ronald did not hurt, but sharply offended.
Mrs. Kerr, however, sitting there with her half-smile,
her evident deprecation of the interlude, her invincible
air of fastidiousness, had maintained her own plane,
whereon 'vulgarity' would be meaningless. Sydney
could only suppose that cruelty as supremely disinterested
as art had, like art, its own purity, which could transcend
anything and consecrate the nearest material to its uses.

The friend sitting back to back with Mrs. Kerr had
gone away minutes ago; the little blue tables one by one
were deserted. The business of the Pâtisserie wilted
temporarily before the approach of lunch-time. Surprised by this isolation, as though the trees of a wood
had melted away from around them, the two left the
shade of the awning and stood dazzled for a moment,
looking vaguely up and down the street.

'Where now?' said Mrs. Kerr, and laid a hand on
Sydney's sleeve in her anxiety to be directed.

Sydney could make no suggestion; she remembered
they were on an edge of Europe and had an impulse in
the still active top of her mind to suggest Prague, the
Hook, or Rouen. The facility with which it would
be possible for her to cover larger distances and her

present complete inability to move from the kerbstone presented themselves simultaneously. She could not command the few words, the few movements which should take her away from Mrs. Kerr, or imagine where, having escaped, she would find a mood, room, place, even country, to offer her sanctuary. Her own background, apart from which the crisis of today, of these last weeks, had produced itself, was seen very clearly at this distance away from it, but presented an impenetrable façade with no ingress. She could see her life very plainly, but there seemed no way into it; the whole thing might have been painted on canvas with a clever enough but not convincing appearance of reality.

She thought, 'So there is really nothing to go back to,' and said, gently drawing her arm away from Mrs. Kerr: 'I think, if you don't mind, I'll go back to the Hotel.'

CHAPTER XVIII

I DO WANT TO

MRS. LEE-MITTISON brought their Continental *Daily Mail* down to the lounge with her and sat on it. She did not wish to read it herself, but did not dare put it down beside her because she knew that someone would come up and ask just to glance at it – people so soon lose their delicacy in these little matters. They would rumple it up and take the creases out: Mrs. Lee-Mittison knew so few people who could look at a paper without rumpling it. Whenever anybody strolled through the lounge with the air of exhausted resources peculiar to this half-hour before lunch-time, she knitted faster than ever and looked unconscious. Life had developed in Mrs. Lee-Mittison a fine set of jungle instincts; she could apprehend and be rigid before, looking over her glasses, she had actually discerned with her usual mildness the approach of the predatory.

'I do wonder if there is any news this morning,' said somebody (one of the talkers), drifting about with her wool-work and looking distastefully at each of the chairs. 'There seems to me to have been no news for a long time.'

'I *do* wonder,' said Mrs. Lee-Mittison truthfully. She did not so much as glance at a headline before Herbert had done so – Herbert was upstairs taking off his boots.

'It's very odd, nothing definite seems to happen at all – I mean, of course, there is always Politics, but that goes on and on and on, so one begins to lose interest.

184

Especially out here where one cannot see what effect they are having, though one does doubt really whether they do have any effect.'

'There's been the pit disaster.'

'Miners,' said the lady distastefully, 'always seem to be getting into trouble. One is so sorry, but it is difficult to go on and on sympathizing, especially out here where one gets on just as well without them – they burn wood, you know, and do everything else by electricity.'

Mrs. Lee-Mittison began to count her stitches audibly. 'Do excuse me,' she said, 'but I am turning the heel—— Oh, good morning, Mr. Milton. Back from the Villa?'

Mr. Milton, looking nicer, more unconcerned than when he had first come out, and burnt to a pleasant brick-colour, bowed and sat down at one of the writing-tables. 'Letters to write before lunch,' he explained politely, unscrewing the top of his pen. It did not yet seem to him courteous to ignore the ladies he found in the lounge without making some excuse for himself; life, however, had to be lived somewhere, so he had acquired the trick of explaining parenthetically. 'Chapter to finish.' 'Must keep up one's philosophy.' 'Ever read Jacks?' 'Working out this beastly acrostic,' or (showing a bundle of letters) 'Must just see what my friends 've got to say. . . .'

For a moment or two his pen worked slowly, conscious of the formation of each letter, as though the two ladies had been leaning over his shoulder; then he settled himself down on his elbows and his pen flew. He stuck out his long legs at either side of the writing-table, which was small and rickety, a rubber-shod heel tapped the the floor noiselessly; he gave both ladies the impression of being a person of affairs.

'I do wonder,' thought Mrs. Lee-Mittison, 'whether he will ever be a bishop . . . I do wish he would cut off his moustache; I'm sure it gives people the wrong impression. If he were a bishop he would have to. Perhaps if he were married he would, too. If I were married to him. . . .'

Mrs. Lee-Mittison, who was not otherwise immodest, often married herself imaginatively to men she took an interest in, then reviewed the possibilities of such a union. 'I would do something for his hair at the back,' she thought. 'I am certain that is accidental baldness, not hereditary. If only it were to be taken in time. . . .' The lady with the wool embroidery opened her mouth: a torrent of conversation seemed to be coming. Mrs Lee-Mittison held up an admonitory knitting-needle. 'Hsssh,' said she, and the lady with the embroidery moved off haughtily to the other end of the lounge. Milton, towards whom she glanced solicitously, made no sign; he had missed this by-play. He blotted one sheet with such force that the writing-table trembled and began another.

Mr. Lee-Mittison came downstairs and, sitting down carefully, reached out for the newspaper. Its folds were by now so immaculate that it undid with the suddenness of a pocket-map. Every time a door opened and shut he looked over the top of the paper; he did not say anything, but always stared in the same way, quite impartially. Nobody was allowed to feel that their coming in and out did not matter; he did not challenge what they were doing, but liked to be sure that they had some good reason for doing it and were not entirely irresponsible.

'Here,' he said to his wife, 'is Miss Sydney. Good morning, Miss Sydney.'

'Good morning, Miss Warren,' said Mrs. Lee-Mittison, who was at pains to waylay anybody in whom Herbert might be interested.

'Good morning,' said Sydney, startled, looking as

though she had expected to find the lounge crowded and to push her way through it.

'You're in early, you know,' said Mr. Lee-Mittison; 'you must have miscalculated. It's seven minutes past twelve. What have you done with Mrs. Kerr and the boy?'

'Ronald has been with our party,' said Milton, 'up at the Villa.' Sydney, standing on the mat vaguely, was looking towards him as though she had something to ask. He had an instinct to go over to her, with an urgent feeling that it lay with him to do something he could not at the moment recall. The glass doors behind and beside her flashing as they opened and shut, the staircase going up and down and doubling off at angles into oblivion, and the way the lift came sliding down the shaft to wait behind the latticed gates were all like so much expressionist scenery, emphasizing the effect she gave of being distracted, mechanical and at a standstill.

He did not like the Lee-Mittisons to see her so much at a loss, and even hoped that he might distract their attention by his own awkwardness, which he felt to be palpable, as he towered, his hands on a chair-back, over the writing-table, not quite liking to sit down again. The Lee-Mittisons were startled, obviously, by her so uncharacteristic willingness – it seemed eagerness – to linger there and to bestow herself upon them; she was known to proceed from point to point in her days with impatience and without hesitancy. They repeated that she had come back very early and asked her to sit down with them. She came over, smiling.

'Look,' she cried, 'at my beautiful new beads! They were a present this morning – Mrs. Kerr gave them to me.' She took off the beads and passed them round to her friends, who held them up to the light and exclaimed at the colour. '*Aren't* they beautiful?' she repeated, as though she could not be satisfied with everybody's praise.

'Beautiful,' Milton said obediently, weighing the beads in his hand and hating them, hating the amethysts. He gave them back with an appearance of reluctance and thought she had been valued at so much; just these were what she was worth. He watched her slip them over her head again and turn in a kind of glittering animation, like a poplar in a gale, to Mrs. Lee-Mittison.

'I have always wanted amethysts, dreamed of them!' she declared, and fingered the beads restlessly.

'Very nice of your friend Mrs. Kerr,' said Mrs. Lee-Mittison, thinking nothing or everything, watching the heel carefully, knitting away.

Mr. Lee-Mittison, who had never given Sydney credit for being so good-looking, decided to have a good look at her; turned half round in his chair and crossed his legs comfortably in order to do so. 'Who's a lucky girl?' said he, and wagged a forefinger. 'Won't this be a day to remember?'

Her poise, her air of being caught up, admitted this: she laughed and looked over at Milton. 'Don't go,' said she as, with a keen sense of humiliation on her behalf and an instinct to escape from all this, he was gathering up his papers. 'Stay and tell us about the Villa – do stay!'

He was to be haunted – during an afternoon in which he avoided her sedulously – by this ineffaceable new impression of her making a free presentation of herself to all comers. Heaven forbid, he thought, she should be 'charming'! Her lack of 'charm' had from the first been distinct to him; it was a quality more than negative; she had a kind of starkness that enforced itself on his judgment as 'good', like the starkness of Norman architecture. It pleased him – he was frank enough to admit this as vanity – to hear her spoken of as ungracious, un-

forthcoming, frigid, even as repellent. He was accustomed to let himself in alone, as it were, to his large, dark,
lofty conception of her with a strong sense, to forbid a
possible oppression, of his own singularity as well as of
hers. 'I don't want her like that,' he thought angrily as,
looking down from his window about three o'clock, he
watched her in her noisy setting-out for the tennis-courts
with a party of the Lawrences and their friends. 'That's
not the girl who wouldn't marry me,' he thought, and
it was his sharpest criticism of her; for it was that passage
by the town bench high up in the sunshine which had
given him till now his pang of pride in her, his clearest
feeling of her being incomplete and so beyond the doom
of limitation. She had offered herself as a break in what
seemed, as he was growing older, a general closing-down
of horizons. 'She mustn't be like this,' he said in his
desperation, and to hide her clattered the shutters
together and turned away. He felt that most profound
concern possible for another human being, when it
becomes a question no longer of the extent of one's own
possession of them, but, transcending this, of what in
their untouchable selves they *are*.

He went for a walk up the hill at the back of the villas,
along the precarious terraces from which the town looked
small and the coast, in spite of its uniform blueness,
disordered and desolate. Having stared for some time at
all this, and at the unshadowed horizon with never a
boat, without any sense of having been enlarged or
inspirited, he came down again hurriedly by a steep
direct way, slithering on the baked earth and sending
stone after stone from beneath him bounding and crash-
ing to what seemed the imminent peril of the colony
below. In such a manner he descended to the tennis-
courts and, exceedingly loath to go in, stood staring
through the wire-netting and dusting the earth from

his hands. To his relief and chagrin he could not see
Sydney anywhere; his day bade fair to have simplified
itself and he contemplated his future, over which an
afternoon still to be filled up seemed to extend enor-
mously, with a proper sense of reprieve but without
appetite. One had to amuse oneself, but he did not see
the necessity.

At a point in his reflections she must have come up
behind him inaudibly, for her voice said abruptly, 'Do
you never play nowadays?' He faced round guiltily and
saw her, buttoned to the chin in a blazer stridently flame
colour, with hands deep in the pockets, less like herself
of the morning than a rather aggrieved little boy.

'I never see *you* here when I do.'

'I used to play once,' said Sydney. 'I could play – I
can't any more. Shall we walk somewhere?' With an
expression of being still, though with even greater
indifference, at anybody's disposal, she nodded backward
indefinitely in the direction of the hills.

A silence, descending on them abruptly, protracted
itself from minute to minute as he followed her up the
path. She felt herself taut upright nervously, her racquet
sticking out from under her arm. Her vivid blazer hurt
his eyes in the glare, he had always to be looking away
from her. She was not like the woman in the swinging
white cloak with whom he had come this way in the
advancing twilight on an evening when there had been
some kind of a shock, when he had been startled –
perhaps by a wild gash of light on some rocks. He recalled
his own shiver, the shiver about him in the very dark
trees; something must have been immanent. The path,
their very contiguity seemed to be haunted; he wanted
to catch up the girl ahead and put out a hand to her for
comfort at this crisis of regret and nostalgia.

'Where shall we go?' he asked, and she cried without

turning round, without, clearly, a thought for him: 'Oh, anywhere; just down the road. Not far or I'll die!'

They went forward more hurriedly till, with a sense of escape from a funnel, they came out into the road. Here, pausing, she looked up and down; nothing beckoned in either direction, though she stood expect- antly as though a paradisial perspective should have opened up for them. It was the same road, not to be changed for her, with its double rank of trees, its villa gates somnolently ajar and its same air of stretching mildly ahead to be sauntered on. The chestnuts already were budding; soon, sign that the visitors must be gone, they would roof the road over with their interknit fingery leaves. The air about them was gummy, smelling faintly of spring. He caught his breath sharply – was this moment also, like that other, slipping away to torment him?

'I shall be sorry,' he said, 'when we've gone. One might easily be so happy here. It can't, while one's here, be impossible. It will be fatal to go. The thought of those leaves coming out has a kind of taint about it, like autumn.'

She looked at him doubtfully, with a twitch of the lips at the thought that might well have been scorn. 'Mr. Milton,' she asked, 'do you still want to marry me?'

'Let's walk on,' he said quickly; 'don't let's just – just stand here . . . Either way – this way, then. *Oughtn't* we, don't you think, to walk on?'

'Do please try and answer,' said she; 'you embarrass me fearfully.'

An instinct made him catch at her elbow and guide her, as they walked, as though between puddles. He felt her elbow shake.

'You know I love you,' he said, and was startled by the ring of this avowal, the certainty. 'Sydney, Sydney,' he sighed, and felt at the back of closed eyes her white face and dark eyes looking up.

He looked at her again and for a moment she was nothing but a girl talking. 'I will marry you,' she was saying then; 'I do want to.'

Why was she quick to assure him of this? He met her eyes, straight, searching up for him, eyes nearly black, overcharged, impenetrable, crying out to be read. 'You don't love me?' he said – 'I mean, do you?'

'Oh, no.' She seemed appalled at the misapprehension, but her elbow, rigid in his slackening grasp, asked not to be relinquished. 'But you know, I do want to,' she said.

'My dear Sydney . . .' Saying this, he turned to look instinctively up and down the empty road.

'Yes, you could kiss me here,' she said, 'if there's nobody coming.' He stooped quickly and kissed her.

'I think there *was* somebody' – she laughed a moment afterwards, with embarrassment – 'looking through the gate of that villa. Shall we walk on, looking rather ordinary?' After a little of this 'ordinary' walking on she asked with anxiety, 'You did *really* want to marry me, didn't you?'

'How can you ask me that, can't you see?' he exclaimed in torture.

'Anyhow,' she said, 'even if I couldn't see, it wouldn't, would it – now I have accepted you – be really a fair thing to ask?'

Mrs. Lee-Mittison, coming out cautiously through the garden gate of the villa where she (such a pleasant introduction!) had been calling, stood back a long time between the gate-posts, a corner of her card-case pressed against her lips, to watch them down the road.

'Such a little slip of a thing . . . I don't think she *understands*,' said Mrs. Lee-Mittison.

CHAPTER XIX

TEA-GARDEN

D R. LAWRENCE talked of taking his daughters away from the Hotel. 'I quite agree,' he had said, looking at Victor distastefully, 'that my daughter Veronica must marry somebody; but I fail to see any reason why she should marry you.' This had seemed an unnecessarily disagreeable way of putting things. Dr. Lawrence wore yellow spectacles out of doors, where the interview had taken place; these gave him the advantage of looking sinister. An abrupt man, Victor thought, not at all the sort of person one would care to consult if one needed to visit a heart specialist. In spite of all the tennis and dancing Victor was beginning to put on flesh out here; he felt that Dr. Lawrence had noticed this; he had just borrowed twenty pounds from his father and this he felt that Dr. Lawrence knew. It had all been rather awkward. Veronica did what she could; she admitted to Victor that her father was a bit of a beast, and to her father that Victor was a bit of an idiot, then retired to bed for two days, announcing that she had a headache. Dr. Lawrence entered into correspondence with some hotels on the French Riviera, but they were full up: the affair hung fire.

'Our father,' Eileen Lawrence told Colonel Duperrier, 'has got a devastating way of taking the starch out of things for us. We often fear that we shall die unmarried.'

'Oh . . . surely?' Colonel Duperrier was much concerned. 'I thought,' he said, 'that girls could do pretty much what they want to nowadays. I should have thought any of you could.' He was entertaining

Veronica's sisters, after tennis, at the English tea-gardens; they sat together in a triangle round a small expectant table under a lemon tree. The declining sun made the girls' arms and faces coral-pink and their dresses gold; Colonel Duperrier regretted more than ever that he had no nieces.

'We could,' said Eileen, 'if we ever really wanted to do anything for long enough. But everything is undermined by other people's damned subtleties – especially father's. "Oh, of course, do it if you like, my dear," he says, and looks at one as though one were diseased. "If you are so very keen to, if you really think it is worth while." You see, one's put at once in such an impossible position, having to be "very keen". It makes one so inferior to father, who is never keen on anything, especially when it is a question of any of us marrying any of these young men – though it is the same thing with any career any of us ever want to take up; we do feel it must be an advantage to a girl to have some kind of career, though she might not want to stick to it. And no young man, if one comes to look at it dispassionately, is worth all the fuss father expects us to make about him. Then father sighs and says, "Well, I'm afraid if you don't feel more strongly than *that* about it——" and one looks so feeble. Our father,' said Eileen, 'is most fearfully subtle. No wonder he's a specialist.'

'But I don't think specialists need be subtle in that way,' said Joan, with an eye on Colonel Duperrier, who appeared surprised.

'One is tempted to wish,' observed Eileen, 'that, for purposes of marriage at least, one hadn't got a father at all, like Sydney Warren. Though in her case, anyway, it would be difficult to kick up a fuss. I must say, if Sydney really did want to get married – and she never gave me a bit that impression – it was very business-like of her to pick out anybody as eligible as dear old Milton. But then, Sydney is a very precise sort of business-like girl. She was going, you know, to have been a doctor.'

'I had no idea,' said Colonel Duperrier.

'*I* think she's cold-blooded,' said Joan; 'she gives me the creeps rather. And I don't think she's a bit suitable for a clergyman's wife: I can just see her looking disdainfully at the churchwardens and people.'

'She'll make an excellent bishop's wife,' said Colonel Duperrier. 'All the bishops' wives I have met were very disdainful. She'll look very handsome, too, in kind of black satiny garments, twenty or thirty years hence.'

'The Honourable Mrs. Pinkerton would prevent his ever being a bishop,' said Eileen. 'How she does hate him! She would bring it up against him just when he was going to be elected that he had once taken somebody else's bath. It's a pity, because Sydney would look very well in black, rather hard satin when she's about forty-five, much more herself than she does now, here. Isn't it funny that for everybody there seems to be just one age at which they are *really* themselves? I mean, there are women you meet who were obviously born to be twenty (and pretty at that) and who seem to have lost their way since, and men you do wish you'd known when they were, say, thirty, or twenty-four, or feel sorry you mayn't come across them when they're forty or fifty-five, and children like that horrid little Cordelia who are simply shaping up to be pale, sarcastic women of twenty-nine, who won't, once they're that, ever grow any older.'

Joan Lawrence looked dreamy; when the tray was set down and Colonel Duperrier asked her to pour out tea and do hostess, she blushed and looked very much startled. She had a glimpse of herself and Colonel

Duperrier having breakfast together on some veranda out in the Tropics, face to face with one another over a dish of some very large futurist-looking fruit. She was not sure of her tropical background; she did not travel or read much, so it was sketched in vaguely: there was, as here, a profusion of heliotrope that coloured the scene and their silence, for they did not seem to be moving or saying anything. She was being looked at . . . he had taken off his topee. She was wearing white muslin; embroidered, beribboned, diaphanous; she did not think she was wearing what was strictly speaking a *frock* . . . What a thing to imagine; what an unspeakable liberty to have taken with Colonel Duperrier! She clattered the lid of the teapot, poured boiling water over her fingers, did not dare think any longer and did not know where to look.

'You don't like sugar, do you, Colonel Duperrier?'

'Thank you, no sugar, and I don't like very much milk.'

She had guessed this, she had known instinctively that he would not take very much milk.

'This Hotel,' said Eileen, 'seems to be producing brides in very large quantities. What a pity we have used up all the men! Do you think any others are likely to come out, Colonel Duperrier?'

'I can't think.' He was wishing it were not impossible to take the Lawrences out separately. This would be all very well if he were simply taking out Eileen. But Joan had withdrawn from the tea-party, she sat and looked a long way away; he felt cheated of her. 'I must say,' he went on with an effort, smiling round affably, 'I think this would be an excellent place to be in love, engaged and so on. It's a pity we don't most of us come out here till we're elderly.' The tea-garden did for an instant flash on him a something half-remembered or never quite

visualized, with its lit-up lawns, its bulging gold lemons
and oranges hanging down in the sun. His companions
smiled. 'All this,' he said, 'would be ever so jolly.'

'Where were you in love?' asked Joan. 'I mean, what
was the scenery?' Tilting back her head, her hands
clasped under her chin, she gazed with a limpidity that
might well have been mischievous beyond him and into
the sunshine.

'What a thing to ask!' Eileen cried saucily. 'Colonel
Duperrier's travelled a lot.'

Colonel Duperrier at this moment of nervousness and
surprise did seem to himself to have travelled a long way.
His thoughts went back through the conversation to look
for something they had shied away from: what had somebody said about women born to be twenty and what they
became? Someone had lost herself, been lost to one,
vanished . . . He knew that all women were born to be
twenty – twenty-two, twenty-five possibly: the thing
seemed obvious, looking at Joan. Something, however,
had become of a Miss Macklean he had met at Darjeeling,
and of a subsequent lovely Mrs. Duperrier of whom he
had asked no more than all she triumphantly promised,
to be twenty at any age; he would not have counted the
years. Perhaps, in spite of herself, she had eluded him.
Lost her way? She was lying alone now up there, up in
her room, waiting angrily for the sun to go down and
the light to go quite out and the darkness to stifle her,
lying with the window thrown open expectantly on to
the void of sky, waiting to shiver, tossing to and fro in
her poor mind while her body lay rigid, silent though
she was so pent up, storing up her cries for him: 'Oh, *here*
you are, Alec . . . No, I didn't really expect you to come
in. Why should you have come in? I dare say you were
happy down there. . . .'

Mrs. Kerr and a party of friends who must have been

having tea together farther down the garden passed by
and went out talking and laughing, and Ronald strayed
after them, looking slightly disorientated. His panama
was folded under his arm; he glanced sidelong at each
of the tables under his lashes, prepared to swerve wide
of them if anyone hailed him or put out a hand. Colonel
Duperrier, though he did not take to the youth, was
vaguely sorry for him; he wasn't, like Master Ammering,
either plump, complacent, or noisy, and his idleness
might well be a phase and had (like Colonel Duperrier's
own) the grace of dejection. He made, therefore, an
encouraging sound in his throat and pulled back a chair
from the table invitingly, while Eileen, who seemed to
find Ronald's manner of going by them provocative,
shouted, 'Hi, Ronald!' so sharply that everyone jumped.

Having affected their capture, they all three smiled at
Ronald with the anxious benevolence, the slightly
embarrassed solicitude which it seemed a gift of his own
to inspire in all circles, and which had made, for some
reason, his company out here particularly sought after.
He was asked everywhere, to bridge, to dinner at other
hotels, to the Lee-Mittisons' coffee-parties, and went,
under some delicate indirect maternal compulsion, with
always the same air of being strung up for martyrdom
to the occasion as the young Sebastian of painters is
strung to a tree. He did not look at present a happy boy
as, leaning forward, slack wrists crossed on a knee, he
gazed with an unreserved attentiveness which they
found still further embarrassing from one Lawrence's
face to the other.

'It is neither of you, I think, that I am to congratulate
on an engagement to Mr. Ammering?'

'No, thank Heaven!' said Eileen emphatically.

'Oh!' said Ronald, surprised, 'but *wouldn't* you like
to marry him? I thought he seemed so popular here.'

'He is an exceedingly lucky young man,' pronounced Colonel Duperrier.

'Of course,' agreed Ronald politely. 'I have just congratulated Miss Warren, too,' he added, 'and Mr. Milton, whom I met out walking together. They both looked very much surprised and rather offended. Surely I haven't done the wrong thing, have I – they are engaged?'

'Everyone knows,' said Eileen, 'and I don't suppose Sydney likes that; it isn't select. But *you* ought to know something about it, anyway; she will have told your mother.'

'I don't think she has,' said Ronald vaguely. 'I'm afraid not. I suppose my mother's not the proper sort of matron. She would hardly, I suppose, provide the bosom that young women on these occasions are supposed to require. I'm afraid she may perhaps feel like I do, that one's friends, however various and delightful they may be at other times, are least interesting – while of course deserving all respect – at these moments when they approximate most closely to the normal. What people call life's larger experiences,' said Ronald, 'are so very narrowing.'

'What a vocabulary you've got, Kerr,' said Colonel Duperrier, respectfully offering his cigarette-case. 'I've never heard such a flow of language. Write?'

'I try not to,' said Ronald, looking ruefully at a cigarette as though he wished he had not taken it; he inclined with a sign to Colonel Duperrier's lighted match.

It was another of these idyllic evenings, agonizingly meaningless; the evening air brought out the scent of the lemons. The Lawrences, shrugging up their wraps round their shoulders, slid forward in their chairs luxuriously and sank down into themselves like cats into

their fur. Thin blue smoke drifted away through the
clearness. Joan said thoughtfully: 'I don't suppose it
matters – talking, I mean – so long as you know exactly
what you mean yourself. I don't, because I never do.'

'You may think all the more,' said Colonel Duperrier,
knocking the ash of his cigarette off, not quite looking
at her.

'Oh yes, I do think a good deal,' said Joan, swinging
one foot and watching it, very mysterious.

'Do you really?' said Ronald with interest, coming
wide awake. 'What do you think about?'

'Well, really . . .' interposed Eileen, after a hard stare.
'Well, really, Ronald, you *are* cool!'

To Colonel Duperrier's embarrassment, Ronald
reddened and stuttered. Ronald was thinner-skinned
than one thought, he hated offending people and making
them angry. But he couldn't imagine, obviously, what
he had done. 'I – I'm most awfully sorry. But why . . .'

'Well, I mean,' said Eileen, 'really, if a person's own
thoughts aren't their own . . . I mean, if a person's going
to be expected to say what they feel about everything——'

'I didn't say "feel," I said "think".'

'Well, it's the same thing,' said Eileen. They stared
at one another.

'Oh,' said Ronald. 'I'm very sorry. You see, what I
think is so public, if anyone's interested.'

'Well, it would be – you're only a boy.'

'Oh, look here, Eileen; don't bullyrag Ronald——'

'It's all right, thank you,' said Ronald, still rather
pink. 'I am very much interested in your sister's point
of view.'

'I haven't got a point of view,' said Eileen indignantly.
'I'm simply talking plain sense. Look here: if you look
at a bun you don't just think about its being a bun, do

you? You wonder what you feel about it and whether it would be nice to eat, and whether it is somebody else's bun and there would be a row if you did. And with a person or anything else it's the same thing.'

'Ah well,' said Ronald, 'if that's what you call think-ing, I dare say it may be private, very private indeed. You see, I don't know anybody else who thinks like that; I had no idea——'

'I don't suppose many people would take the trouble to explain to you how they do think. They'd just let you run on with your own ideas and nod and smile and say, "How lovely!" and think about something else all the time.'

Joan, while the privacy of her thoughts was being battled for, had remained since her one intervention abstracted, her gold hair spread out scroll-wise over the mounting folds of her scarf. 'Feel my wrist, it's like ice,' she said suddenly. 'It must be awfully cold.'

'My dear child!'

'Oh! I don't suppose it is cold really.' Joan felt as though of her own accord she had dropped a crystal and smashed it. '*Don't* let's go,' she begged with pathetic eyes of Colonel Duperrier. 'I don't know why I said that at all – it was only my wrist.'

'*I* don't want to, I'm sure.' He looked around the garden regretfully, as though they were not to come here again; it seemed a better garden than he had realized, more friendly and intimate. 'But we can't have you frozen,' he said, and looked at Joan helplessly, because it would be ultimately beyond his province whether she were frozen or not.

'Idiot!' cried her sister. 'Where are your gloves?'

'These evenings,' explained Ronald, 'come down like the knife of a guillotine. I must be getting on anyway after my mother.' He rose and looked down at them thoughtfully: a queer (he seemed to think) and never entirely satisfactory group. 'Are you coming my way?' he asked Eileen.

Her mind leapt forward immediately to telling Veronica that Ronald ('Yes, my dear, I swear he did actually——!') had asked her to come for a walk. 'One to me,' she reckoned; 'there's nothing like being crisp with these slithery, day-after-to-morrow people who only half see you. He'd eat out of my hand, I'll swear he would. I shall keep him out for an hour, take him round by the town.' Smiling, she said to the others: 'Do you mind if Ronald and I move along?' Her only doubt, as coming out of the gate she turned the head of Ronald resolutely townwards, was whether she could postpone for so long the ecstasy of telling Veronica, who should be now, she knew, curled up in her bed by the window, reading a magazine and eating peppermints, and regretting more and more, as the interval of solitude prolonged itself, that the affair Victor should ever have occurred.

The other two were left in a solitude which, quite unprecedented, they felt to be exigent and a little singular. 'I expect,' Joan said with a little stiff movement that did not do much for her, 'that we had better be getting along, too.'

'I expect we had,' said Colonel Duperrier. It was half-past five, he discovered; up there she would be half insane with speculation; by this hour he had till now never failed to present himself. He looked about him at the other tables distant between the trees where couples in rather forced and conscious intimacy still lingered, the evening before them, gazing a shade owlishly less at than around each other, weighed down by their leisure. Odd, thought Colonel Duperrier; queer, following his look, thought Joan. She propped her chin on her chilly hand

and sighed a melancholy, unresentful sigh. 'Cheer up!'
her friend said solemnly.

'I haven't got such a cheerful disposition as you have,'
she stated.

'I suppose I have got rather a cheerful disposition,'
said Colonel Duperrier, glancing reluctantly at himself
and looking away again.

'Of course,' she said in her matter-of-fact little voice,
'you are wonderful.' She leant back to grope behind her
chair for her racquet and repeated 'Wonderful!' in a
tone of indignation, perhaps because the racquet wasn't
there. 'I expect,' she began again, 'we ought to be——'

'I know. I really think we ought to be coming in.
If you catch cold, you know, I should never forgive
myself.'

'I promise I won't catch cold,' poor Joan said faith-
fully, and getting up looked round distractedly, huntedly,
for the racquet propped against the side of her chair.

'Thank you very much,' she said, 'for our nice tea.'

'It has been a pleasure to me,' said Colonel Duperrier.

CHAPTER XX

MRS. KERR

DEAR Mr. Milton,' exclaimed Mrs. Kerr, 'is this true? Because if so, it's wonderful!'
He remained standing; she, propped reposefully among cushions, sat looking up at him. 'Yes, you are charming,' he doubtfully thought, 'you injurious woman.' He tried to look straight, as though dropping a plummet, into those profound brimming eyes, but the light from the ceiling invaded them; raw, hard-edged light, as though cut out of tinfoil, that touching them softened, swam down through them, melted, so that he could read nothing, looking down into luminousness. He had to surrender to her effect of mild brilliancy, of being serious, eager, friendly. 'Yes, it's true,' he said. 'Didn't you know?'

After dinner, since Ronald's arrival, she no longer went straight to her room, but would sit with him on a sofa backed by a palm at the quieter end of the lounge. Here they looked, thought James Milton, approaching, like a fancy of Omar Khayyam's, with a small tray of coffee beside them, a stack of serious periodicals (presumably Ronald's), and a basket of crystallized fruit which Ronald advanced to their guests with a deprecating, vague liberality, as though he did not really care for this sort of thing himself. Their guest one did definitely constitute oneself, Milton felt, by coming over to them; her graceful delighted reception of one confirmed this, also the punctilious uprising of Ronald, who would continue to tower, prolonged by his shirt-front, indefinitely tall, crumpling gradually till asked to sit down again. Milton was not uninvited; he had insinuated himself down the lounge between eager conversationalists and touching chair-backs in response to a direct glance, a concentration upon himself of her general smile round as she looked at him.

Ronald pulled a chair forward at right angles; Milton sat down with them.

'Then, of course,' Mrs. Kerr said, summing up, 'you are happy.'

One is not, at such moments, expected to show oneself adequate; his smile and his gesture acknowledged becoming inadequacy. She nodded her womanly comprehension. 'Quite,' said she.

'Excellent,' said Ronald with an air of seniority to both of them. He recrossed his legs and bit into a crystallized tangerine.

'I suppose,' said Mrs. Kerr thoughtfully, 'I do perhaps understand a little of what this means to her.'

'She told you, of course.' Milton had presence of mind enough to make a startled gesture into a statement.

She nodded. 'A little,' she said. 'You know – well, of *course* you know – she is a very quiet person. She didn't say much, but she shone. She has the strangest possibilities of shining.' Mrs. Kerr seemed to have, as she spoke, a glimpse of Sydney from which he was excluded. 'Of course,' she added in the perfunctory quiet voice in which perfect taste demands the making of certain statements, 'she is very happy . . . I have wanted so much for her and expected, really, so little that seeing her so, so lit-up, so certain, has meant a great deal to me. You've done – do you really understand? – a great deal.'

'Thank you,' Milton said helplessly.

'There is no reason to thank *me*,' said Mrs. Kerr, looking at him very straight with her wide-opened eyes. 'What is there to thank me for?'

Milton, abashed by this parade of innocence, looked

at Ronald, wishing that he were not there. Mrs. Kerr, however, seemed determined to keep him.

'Now, Ronald,' she said with amusement, laying a hand on her son's knee, looking down at it thoughtfully and drawing it away again, 'feels sorry for people who are going to be married. He cannot believe (isn't it so?) "in any satisfactory *modus vivendi* between two people that's based on an attraction"!'

'I remain perfectly open-minded,' said Ronald, biting the stalk off a pear.

'About love itself,' said Mrs. Kerr, looking respectfully at her son, 'he is profoundly sceptical. There is a part of life, Mr. Milton, that I should be very glad if you could explain to my poor Ronald.'

'It's not a part of life,' said Ronald, 'it may be a streak in it. People talk as though it were a transverse section.'

'You see?' said his mother. 'But Sydney used to be a sceptic too, you know. I should rather like Ronald to talk to her now.'

'I don't think Sydney would like that at all,' said Milton, and was made to feel he had transgressed some delicate code by this hint of the proprietary.

'I had an impression,' said Mrs. Kerr diffidently, 'that Sydney always liked talking about anything she was perfectly sure of.'

'In spite of being rather a quiet person?'

'Quite compatibly with being rather a quiet person,' said Mrs. Kerr, illuminating, showing up his petty irritation with her lovely smile. 'I didn't, you know, propose that poor Sydney, who has so very lately, as one might say, graduated, should deliver to Ronald a kind of extension lecture. I just vaguely conceived that she might make him feel what a silly, immature little gander he still is.'

'I wish she would,' said Ronald, 'it would be so *cinque*

cento; a disquisition on Amor by an inspired young woman.' He looked carefully at Milton, trying, evidently, to consider him in the role of an inspiration.

'You have picked up *"cinque cento"* from Miss Fitz-gerald. It becomes a rather silly expression, Ronald dear, when it's used so often and so indiscriminately. But "an inspired young woman",' she decided, turning to Milton, 'is good. Don't you find your inspired young woman rather lovely?'

'Rather lovely,' echoed Milton, as though learning a lesson.

'Sydney in love . . .' mused Mrs. Kerr, and as though stepping back from the brink of some profound experience not her own, she said, 'I envy you!'

Milton encountered Ronald's clear, rather curious eye; they stared at one another profoundly. 'One is fortunate,' Milton said, and a stabbing sense of this irony made him shut his eyes sharply for a moment, as though the light were too much. When he looked up again Mrs. Kerr's son was still searching him, and put forward in explanation of this: 'Do excuse me, please, staring so awfully, but I've never heard anyone point-blank profess themselves happy before.' It was on the tip of the clergy-man's tongue to protest that he hadn't; however, he merely said blandly: 'Oh, indeed? If you care to, do certainly look!'

'You ought,' Ronald said, 'to feel very responsible.'

'– Ronald *darling*, you're not Mr. Milton's father.'

'But I didn't propose,' said her son, flushing hotly, 'to apply the remark to Miss Warren. I merely meant he must feel very responsible for *himself*. A state of mind——'

'Exactly,' said Mrs. Kerr briskly and waved him aside. She appeared to be rather oppressed by her Ronald; the boy became pompous. She looked at his overcast face in perplexity, puzzling herself again, it appeared, over some ancient error. Far back in the far-away history of Ronald – possibly in the espousal of Ronald's father – there had been a mistake. She looked down the lounge. 'Look, Ronald,' she cried with a happy inspiration, 'there is one of your Lawrences, one of your curious girls. She is standing and looking too languishing, down by the door. She has seen you, and worse, she has seen you have something to eat. It would be nice to go over and talk to her, if you don't mind. I don't like to *look* selfish, you know.'

She watched her son threading his way down the lounge, however, with such wistfulness, such an air of bereavement, and returned her attention to Milton with so courageous a smile, and with eyes for an instant so vacant, that he could not but believe that she had made a real sacrifice in sending Ronald away. He reproached himself for a suspicion of being closed in on, and of their oasis of silence, light and solitude having become for him a rather remote and dangerous island. Her personality had a curious way of negativing her surroundings, so that unless one made instant resort to one's senses the background faded for one and one conjured up in one's half-consciousness another that expressed her better, that was half an exhalation from herself. The crude and vivid glitter of the lounge, the hard light striking with an impact almost audible on glazed stuffs, noisy colours, reddened skins, the urgent hum of talk, all these relaxed their grip on Milton's consciousness, subsided. A feeling was produced in him of tempered light and clear gloom and of window open on profoundly dark and rather restless trees as Mrs. Kerr said thoughtfully: 'Religion, I suppose, is an immense outlet for gratitude.'

'One would be sorry to make use of one's religion as an outlet for anything.'

She retracted. 'The psychologists have led one so astray.'

'The fallacy's older than they are.'

'I suppose so,' agreed Mrs. Kerr. She went on with an effort, going against, obviously, all the fine instincts she had for reserve. 'You have felt, I dare say, that force of – of religion in Sydney. I've had to draw back there, because I don't, as you see, understand. One never would hold her, lacking that.'

'I don't see her ever as a person to be absolutely held.'

She was moved by a deep-down amazement, caught a breath as though she must have misheard him and lifted her eyebrows. 'Not held? You forget,' she said, 'I've been her friend.' She reflected: 'Does new power bring with it, perhaps, its own disabilities? You are, aren't you, quite newly her lover? You mayn't see yet, may not admit intellectually, but you must surely *feel* that.'

'You don't think I quite understand what I've got.'

'I don't think you can trust yourself yet to look down very deep. But you ought – she is yours; absolutely. We have all of us fallen away.' There was not a note in her voice of anything but triumph; she smiled at him like a priestess.

'You feel I need to be told this?' he said, and felt his own smile twist his face awkwardly.

'There is no need,' she said with a penetrating, long look. 'You do know.' He felt again, through that window behind her, that dark garden distressed by the wind; around her those undisturbed shadows, that never-ebbing, mild light.

'Suppose,' he began uneasily, 'suppose I were less fortunate. Suppose – you see, I am secure enough to indulge myself with these curiosities – she had simply caught at my hand, were gripping it desperately because she was frightened, or had been misdirected, say, and lost her way – I would be right, knowing that, to keep hold of her, for her protection?'

'– A protection!' interposed Mrs. Kerr, 'that you think with most innocent cynicism she would be capable of accepting? But go on, please, I won't interrupt you.'

'That was all.' He laughed. 'Vague curiosity. Should I be right?'

'If you cared to be just a convenience,' said Mrs. Kerr thoughtfully, 'it wouldn't be *wrong*. But can you believe she'd – make use of you? Would it be, in the most ordinary woman, pretty or admirable? · Could you reconcile that with the only Sydney possible for either of us? For our two Sydneys, I'm sure, are the same.'

'But there's panic. . . .'

'Panic doesn't last more than its moment. Of course, there's opportunism.' She caught Milton looking at her haggardly. 'You didn't think,' she said gently, 'that I thought you meant *that*?'

He gave, to express scorn, a rather ghastly little monosyllabic laugh.

'It does sound silly,' agreed Mrs. Kerr. 'It is silly, I think, to let oneself play, just because of one's sense of absolute security, with even the most far-fetched idea of her doing anything so careful and mean. An idea,' she said, shivering slightly, 'has a curious power; it preys on one. Oh, you must promise me that you won't,' she cried. 'It frightens me – you could send yourself mad!'

'It's nice of you to care,' said Milton.

'Do you think I don't value *my* Sydney?' she exclaimed and stared darkly at something, then brushed it away with her hand and smiled with a return of tranquillity. 'One's idea of a person,' she told him, 'refuses to take certain possibilities, like a material refusing to take certain dyes. Don't you feel so? For instance: for

anyone else, any woman, as angry and hurt in her
pride, and as disappointed as I'm afraid Sydney's
been with me lately, to have taken you up with the
strong position you've given her would have been the
inevitable, rather sordid, perhaps, but effective, complete little gesture. One would have looked for it,
wouldn't one? and – taking the thing at its own valua-
tion – rather applauded. One can't help applauding the
score-off, the adequate pat little retaliation, all the more
perhaps because, oneself, one could never achieve it.
And we both of us know,' said Mrs. Kerr radiantly, 'that
for you it would never be possible either. And even sup-
posing we didn't, that we weren't so exclusive on her
behalf, hasn't she given us proof?'

'If it were needed,' said Milton, and began chafing
his hands together as though they were cold. He was
silent a moment, staring down at the edge of her skirts,
at the ground. He dragged himself back to consider
something. 'What did you, by the way, mean by a
proof?'

'But her loving you,' exclaimed Mrs. Kerr, wide-
eyed, 'her loving you absolutely! Mr. Milton, do try
and make her less hurt with me. Surely you can, can't
you? Make her happy enough to come back.' Mrs. Kerr,
with her eyes and a gesture, gave herself away to him in
perfect humility. 'I do miss the child so!'

'But how'm I to know she's still hurt?' her lover said
dully, and looking at Mrs. Kerr in remote admiration had
a quick sense of being identified with Sydney.

'Perhaps,' said Mrs. Kerr, recollecting Sydney's
change of position, 'she's not. But I was impatient and
clumsy; I think she was hurt in her pride.'

'I cannot believe, Mrs. Kerr,' said Milton in a tone of
such infinite irony that his voice sounded gentler than
ever, 'I can't really believe that you've ever been clumsy.

I should say that your patience was infinite. But she has this queer appetite for pain: it brings with it its own ingenuity, against which one can't be defended at all points.'

With a sigh, with raised eyebrows, she allowed herself to accept this as possible. 'Thank you, you're generous,' she said and examined him. '*You*, if you like, would have infinite patience. You two can't, I think, fail to be happy together. I'm so happy about you' – she looked round with relief as though rising again to the surface and by taking everything in with such eagerness re-admitted the lounge to his consciousness – 'and, as middle-aged women do feel, quite important; as though I were standing, like your good Moses, at some kind of vantage-point and seeing ahead of both of you plainer than you can. It would be equally nice, I believe,' she concluded, swimming back to the plane she had come from, kind superficiality, 'to be married to either of you.'

He was dismissed; she appeared to have done with him. The laughter and voices packed round them between the four looking-glassed walls seemed to rise to a climax, a positive shout. The lounge seemed for a moment to mean something – he glanced for a hint of the revelation at some of the faces, but whatever it was had escaped him; the faces were shut-up and blank.

'If you will,' said Mrs. Kerr, 'can you look out for Ronald? I don't want him disturbed if he's happy – just tell him I'm going to bed. It's been so nice of you to talk to me about this, Mr. Milton. I've always felt that we knew each other and yet, do you realize? we've not spoken for more than a moment before. If I've kept you from Sydney, forgive me. You must go now and find her. Good night.'

When she had gone he sat down on the rather hard sofa, across which the cushions had, as she got up, tumbled down into disorder. He felt the light slanting down on him stupefyingly from the mirrors and ceiling a protection from feeling, a barrier, like an orchestra above which one could not, even if one had wanted to, make oneself heard.

CHAPTER XXI

VALLEY

FOR two days the sun had been cut away by an opaque, pale-grey, absolutely cloudless sky; this made the shapes of hills and houses more important; an ascent of the heights became arduous in the cool, close air and one was loath to go far up any one of the valleys because one felt it shutting on one like a book. The disappearance of sunlight from the flowers deadened the colours of them; from being like flames, spontaneous, they became tawdry and adventitious; bougainvillæa traced a heavy pattern on the walls, geraniums were the flat stale pink of old confectionery, and the mimosa blotched the faces of the hills as monotone and pale as mustard. The distances were pellucid; one would see for miles every detail of the coast, every ripple of the light sea, and these became important and a little ominous; one felt weighed down by them and half uneasy. Ronald, going alone up a river-bed in one of the valleys, found himself hurrying.

The river had once been expansive and impetuous, it had carried some of the hills along with it and flowed widely; at some points it had taken up the whole floor of the valley, leaping past the foot of the rocks hilariously or, dividing, made a long string of lemon-shaped islands. Now its wide bed lay parched, a petrified torrent up which Ronald, taking some pleasure in the performance, walked painfully with a sharp, continuous, loudly-echoed clattering together of stones. The river was young no longer; it had made an end of its variations and detours and had worn away for itself a very deep channel down which it flowed swiftly, with a sinister effect of purpose; steel-smooth, impenetrable to the eye of Ronald, to whom it was no longer a companion. They should have known one another centuries before.

The margins of land on either side, before the walls of the valley went up, were under cultivation; they were divided cross-wise, and when Ronald scrambled up out of the river-bed to sit down on a sagging lip of turf and nurse a barked ankle or extract a stone from his shoe it is more than probable that he was trespassing. In such a country, however, one is bound to trespass everywhere; much is forgiven if one be sufficiently beautiful, have an innocent expression and do not seem to understand Italian shouted from above. Ronald's expression, ingenuous and nervous as a foal's, would have disarmed the angriest proprietor, but for this there was no occasion; the valley seemed to be quite empty. Since he had left behind the three young women, the goats, the staring man, there had been nobody. Perhaps, he thought, the valley was today just *too* narrow, too clothed in the echo of water, too deep beneath the tension of the sky from hill to hill, and they had all turned back instinctively. He wondered at himself for going on.

The three young women leaning over the gate had admired Ronald, loudly and in every detail. They had spoken so very distinctly he could only suppose that they meant him to understand; he had slowed down in an effort not to seem to be trying to escape them; his ears changed colour, they remarked on this — it had been quite appalling. Their eyes had licked him up and down like the eyes of the American lady at Württemberg, who had compared him to a Donatello, and he could not revenge himself on *them* by making out a kind of mental chart of their repressions because one couldn't well suppose that girls who behaved in this way had any repressions. Which, of course, as Ronald told himself without enthusiasm, was excellent. They gave him, quite disinterestedly, all sorts of encouragement and good advice.

The man who stared also had shouted a word of encouragement, the same mystifying reference to some 'bellissima'. Then the solitude had come slowly to grips with him: there was nothing but the deserted bed of the river, the vague disorderly gardens like some half-memory and, now and then, a bird flying slowly across the sky. Ronald had nothing but a little lonely gleam of intellectual pride to sustain him; he felt that it must be good for him to be here, but he was very depressed. He felt trapped; if he turned to run back down the valley there would be nothing but valley to run to. 'O Solitude,' he exclaimed in a thin voice, 'ton sein vigoreux et morne déjà j'ai pu l'adorer . . .' He could not remember the rest of the paragraph, and besides, had not Barrès lapsed from this to the excesses of nationalism? What unaccountable lapses, thought Ronald, precede maturity which they are even believed to constitute. He suddenly gave up clattering among the stones, did not speak any more, and hugging the side of the valley away from the river walked on the turf quietly, because it appeared to him that one could best enforce oneself on this noisy solitude, not by more noise, but by silence. So quite quietly he rounded the turn of the valley and came in sight of the rock where Sydney was sitting looking up the valley away from him. After gazing for some moments at her apparent unconsciousness, he said slowly, 'Oh . . . you?'

'Oh, *you?*' she exclaimed, mystified, but not startled.

'I hope I didn't alarm you!'

'No. I heard you coming, but I didn't turn round because I thought I knew who it was. Were you expecting to find anybody in particular?'

'Well, no, not really anybody. They all told me to hurry up because there was a bellissima Inglese, but I imagined that that, you know, was just a general allusion to the "not impossible She" and thought nothing more of it.'

'They?'

'Some girls at a gate and a man doing nothing particular.'

'Whenever anybody just says "they",' said Sydney, who showed signs of being pleased to see him, 'one thinks of Lear, doesn't one? and an infinite perspective of long noses. "They" watched me, too, coming up here, but they didn't say anything. I am glad to know they were impressed.'

'They are impressionable,' said Ronald. 'If it is Mr. Milton you're expecting, he won't like those girls a bit. They are a positive barrage. Their conversation was very free.'

'I expect they liked you,' said Sydney, glancing at him with indifferent admiration. 'Also, of course, they wouldn't be able to imagine why you should want to walk up a valley alone unless there were a woman at the end of it. Unless, of course, you had carried a long gun and wore tight green velvet knickerbockers and showed every sign of going out to shoot linnets.'

'I'm afraid,' said Ronald, 'that's very English of you.'

'I'm afraid I don't like these people at all. I cannot see why they should ever have been born, or why, at least, they should need to go on being born over and over again so frequently.'

'I dare say,' said Ronald, 'they enrich the soil.'

'I dare say,' said Sydney. She was sitting on a rock that jutted up sharply out of the river-bed; it would once have been a perilous, amusing place to sit. At present it complicated his position rather; if he stayed where he was, they would have to talk in high-pitched voices to be heard above the noise of the water that hurried behind him; whereas if he came across the stones and sat beside her he would be made to feel himself rather tiresomely confidential and forthcoming. The rock, however, was large enough for both of them, and she settled the question by saying matter-of-factly, 'Here, come and sit down,' and twisting round so that her legs, which had been stretched out in front of her, could leave more room for him by dangling over the edge. 'What a lot of energy is wasted,' she observed, 'in replacing one lot of people by another exactly the same.'

She remarked this distantly, as though the indirectedness of the stream of things had been brought to her notice passingly but did not concern her. Her attitude seemed to Ronald deplorable; leaning back on his elbow he subjected her profile, covertly, to a perplexed and grieved scrutiny. 'And does this worry you at all?' he asked, in the hope that, while preserving an equal detachment, he might make her at least aware of her strange anaesthesia. An intelligent person, Ronald thought, should never be entirely unperturbed. She turned to look at him with the dark attention of wandering thoughts.

'*Worry?*' she said slowly, and tried to recall herself. 'Why should I worry? I can't do anything about it all, can I?'

'My mother, you know, describes you as independent and vigorous.'

'I had no idea,' said Sydney thoughtfully, and longed to know exactly how his mother had described her. Ronald might have been a key to a great deal; instead, he had his own obscure preoccupations. Except for his eyes and forehead and a few of her gestures and mannerisms which cropped up over-importantly in his conversation, out of tone with the rest of him, he in no way resembled his mother. Mrs. Kerr, at least, had not cared to replace herself. What qualities he had of hers had been given over to him unreservedly; they did not seem in any way to be shared or to bring the two into closer community. He, like the rest, revolved round his mother inquiringly with a perhaps more intimate but with the same exterior curiosity. He was at most two or three steps higher up the base of the monument: from here he said wisely to Sydney: 'My mother, you know, is intelligent. She understands, or she wouldn't admire.'

'I suppose she wouldn't,' said Sydney, and let the thing drop. But though Mrs. Kerr's son did not interest her she felt drawn towards him as though he were part of her youth, and she asked, looking back for a landmark to measure how far she had travelled, 'And *you* really do mean, I suppose, to make rather a difference?'

'Well, one can't help hoping one may,' said Ronald, smiling at himself, very elderly and indulgent. 'Usen't you, too?'

'*Usen't?*' said Sydney, aggrieved at being so taken up.

'Oh, I suppose you still may; but you can't overlook Mr. Milton.' Saying this, he tried vainly to reconcile the importance and solitariness in which she had just now been discovered with his idea of her as the engaged girl. She sat looking down, with a faint droop (he thought he detected), a hint of contrition, an acquiescence to being set aside, of which she seemed to be making a rather too sardonic and cool exhibition. She felt this and said deferentially:

'Of course *you*'ve got no patience with this sort of thing?'

'I may be young,' said Ronald, 'but I'm never so grossly ingenuous as downright to commit myself.' He began kicking the rock with his heel and, with pursed mouth and a gleam of amusement she was not intended to share, withheld his opinion.

'Why,' she asked in surprise, 'who said you were young?'

'Oh, I understand you did. But of course,' he said lightly, anxious that they should neither of them be embarrassed, 'it seems an impression one's bound to create. Would you ever have minded – why should one?' He looked serenely past her down the valley – a little, she thought, too serenely. Evidently he did mind. If he had not been likely to mind why should his mother have told him? 'Of course,' he vouchsafed, 'it is in a general way a mistake to involve oneself anywhere.'

Sydney felt wise, but it is poor satisfaction to be wise with the masses. She asked, 'Do you never mean to involve yourself?' Perhaps he never would, perhaps it was possible not to – a chilly suspicion.

'Oh, I just mean to live in a rather simplified way and not to leave off being reasonable. Now it's a mistake, I'm quite sure, to deny an attraction. One should cultivate it and be amused at oneself. Then one would be civilized.'

'And what about other people?' said Sydney; 'what about your mother, for instance?'

'My mother? She is very civilized.' Puckering their lids up in the sunless glare his eyes gazed past her, pale with a reflection of the sky.

'I know, that is her great advantage. But don't you think wherever she was she'd be civilized *alone*? Do you think she would promote your kind of civilization?'

'I don't know what you mean,' said Ronald. 'She is not an *earnest* woman. I can't imagine her "promoting" anything.'

'She wouldn't promote *that*, she wouldn't want to. She isn't at all modern, like you and me, you see. It isn't necessary for her.'

VALLEY

Ronald remembered what his mother had said about
'white tiles'. He felt annoyed with Sydney and rounded
on her: 'I say, you don't dislike my mother, do you?'

'No, you know I don't.'

'I wondered – people do, you know. Does Mr. Milton?'

'Why ever should he? I – I've never asked him.'

'He looks at her so – carefully.' Quite without malice
Ronald imitated Milton's expression. 'Of course, I think
he seems a most discriminating man,' he concluded
politely. He had been gathering together, while he spoke,
small pebbles and fragments which had accumulated on
the top of the rock, reaching out for them negligently in
all directions and heaping them up beside him. Now,
suddenly, he sat bolt upright and began to hurl them
one after another down the valley with a great effect of
muscularity and science. The pebbles skipped, the
fragments of rock rebounded on the boulders of the river-
bed with little sharp distinct sounds, pin-pricks above the
sound of the water. The hills seemed to peer forward.
This little tempest of exertion on Ronald's part, into
which he seemed to have been surprised in spite of himself, dishevelled the stillness of the valley, which un-
stressed by lights and shadows and unstirred by wind
hung gravely round them like a curtain.

'Oh, do look out,' cried Sydney angrily. 'You may hit
James; he may be coming up.'

'I suppose he may,' admitted Ronald, but could not
keep himself from sending off his last three stones. 'Then
why doesn't he come?' he said, relapsing on to his elbow
again. 'What is the matter?'

'I can't think. I cut out lunch and came up here this
morning because I had a headache, and I left word that
I'd be here if he cared to come up afterwards. I said the
third valley to the right, behind the convent. He may
have miscounted. Or he may not want to come.'

'But he must want to. After all, it would be only reasonable.'

'You mean, consistently *un*reasonable?'

'No, if I were in love at all I should expect to be with you all day,' said Ronald masterfully.

'Ah, to be in love *at all*'s the initial mistake!'

'More, really, of a misapprehension.'

While Ronald talked she often had a giddy sense of watching all she had ever said being wound off from a spool again backwards. Now and then came a truth that she had let slip away; she received this last one back again ice-cold. It went too deep and she wasn't grateful to Ronald.

'Well, don't you, my dear Ronald, ever misapprehend!'

'And don't you be maternal!'

Catching some idea of a sound or a voice from one another they began to listen, as though the very mention of Milton's name must have cast out a line to his consciousness and be drawing him up the valley towards them. For a moment or two they felt he was to appear immediately. Sydney leant forward expectantly, but nobody came into sight at the turn of the valley. She felt cold, and bitterly reproached herself for not having turned to smile sooner when she had been so sure she heard him coming before, when it had only been Ronald. She did not look at her watch, but knew that she had reached that psychological moment, that turning-point of any long wait when the likelihood of a friend's arrival instead of increasing with the advance of time begins to diminish. She feared that through some intervention of a too far-seeing Providence on Milton's behalf she might never see him again. She prayed that this might not be so: she felt sure that she loved him. Ronald, half aware of all this, felt a long way away from her, and began to wonder whether after all from the first he had not intruded.

He said (to observe the effect), 'I'll be going, I think. I may meet him – I'll hurry him on. Anyhow, he wouldn't want to find me here.'

The effect was a panic. 'No, don't, please don't go,' she exclaimed. 'I can't bear this valley alone: it's so empty.'

'You might have noticed that before,' he observed, warming in spite of himself at this display of femininity. 'Nervy?'

'Yes, nervy,' she agreed with a little boy's grin.

He sat down beside her again with mixed feelings of constraint and gratification, and began, while their silence relaxed again, from an alert, constricting consciousness of each other's proximity into a benign and restful indifference, to kick with swinging heels the side of the rock.

CHAPTER XXII

RATHER AFRAID

UNWILLING to go farther, distrustful of himself and of the valley, Milton leant against a tree at the mouth of it and looked disparagingly up the the river-bed. He wished Sydney had not asked him to meet her here.

He had spent the morning writing to his brother and sister to tell them about his engagement, and it worried him that he had forgotten to post the letters and was still carrying them round in his pocket. He knew them to be lively and expressive and likely to do him credit on their arrival in England, having just enough manly glow about them and just enough boyish reticence. His flair for a right note was a perpetual temptation to cynicism, and his consciousness that these letters, so bound to strike a note of sincerity, were in intention sincere, and had been written face to face with himself with a zealous effort to avoid misrepresentation, did not make him any better at ease about them. He wondered if anyone ever tried to describe the experience of love without a bottomless suspicion of imposing upon themselves, of falsity. Momentous letters should be posted white-hot; they impinge too much on the memory, are weighed over and over again by the conscience. He felt an indecorum in going to meet Sydney with these in his pocket, these meanly adequate little summings-up of his position *vis-à-vis* with herself, his praises of her already qualified by a faint possessiveness. So at least he assured himself; it was a pretty enough scruple for a leisurely lover in this little world of suspended activity, where there was time for the finest of shades. But he pressed on it rather too eagerly. Deeper than this, beyond the domain of scruple, he was not at ease.

Their meetings, since the night of his conversation with Mrs. Kerr, had been of the type disturbed and momentary, whose sum total is an effect of separation. Was he apprehensive of meeting her again in this bare narrow place, the stage for a crisis, where no side-issue could offer itself to be grasped at, and there would be nowhere to escape from Mrs. Kerr and all she had said? Since their talk in the lounge Mrs. Kerr had been with him unceasingly; his thoughts even in sleep were full of anguished reasonings with her. He did not cease to bitter crying, 'No, no, no!' against the shut doors of her eloquent reserve. The more clearly he remembered how little Sydney's infinitely loyal friend had actually said the more did he despair of Sydney's lover for having understood so much. The thought of Sydney waiting for him now (if she had not been impatient and gone away) in all good faith at the top of the valley, of the all-assuming confidence she had in him, which seemed the curiously simple and yet perfect flowering of her strange nature, like flowers springing out on a bare almond tree, destroyed his confidence in himself.

Next week Milton would go back to England. He had written this to his brother, taking some pleasure in committing himself definitely to the arrangement, but the fate of the good resolution lay with the unposted letters, still in his own control. He would go back, and she a little later would follow him; or she might even prefer to come back with him now. Could she wish to stay longer? Her tie with the Hotel that still exerted, he was aware, an agonizing restraint, had better be broken off summarily at the cost he could not tell of how much damage to her integrity – without help from him, with-

out a word from him that her confidence did not invite.
They had mentioned Mrs. Kerr frequently, but there
had never been more than a little head of her stamped
as it were for circulation on a conversational coin. They
had not yet talked of her, she had not in person entered
their field.

In a week, perhaps, the coast and hills would have
vanished for ever for both of them: he did not think that
either he or she would return. A year from now it
would need an effort of memory to bring the place to life
again for a moment; he would start at its name and
realize that it had without them both, after all, some
shadowy continuity. If an earthquake were to ruin the
town, or a landslide demolish the whole coast, he thought
he would be left with hardly a pang once horror subsided. The place would persist unimpaired in his memory, not much loved, scarcely thought of, but queerly
complete if he happened to turn to it – as the least loved,
most rarely revisited places often remain. The momentary impacts of colour and smells and light in his senses
that had built up the place for him would be forgotten,
only the sum of them, that he might have received in an
idle half-day, would remain. A thousand hours super-
imposed on each other would melt into one; a thousand
that had in turn been unique, coloured differently each
from the others by mood or circumstance.

'Will she ever,' he wondered, 'be so complete to me;
not a succession of moments but one? Will these evenings,
mornings, lights, memories, shadows, half-apprehen-
sions, glimpses, ever fall away or run together and be
merged in the whole of her? Could I love her so well if
they were? Is there a human being any more than a
Godhead with which one could bear to be face to face?'

He left the tree and started at a good pace up the
valley. A stone which somebody might have thrown

RATHER AFRAID

came bounding down from the heights and struck the
river-bed; later on a couple of goats, following one another
across an almost perpendicular piece of hill, looked down
at him sardonically. 'So much for you,' they intimated,
and blinked their onyx eyes. Presently he met Sydney
and Ronald coming to meet him at a swinging pace down
the river-bed. They were so deep in conversation and
were making such a noise among the stones that for a
minute or two they neither heard nor noticed him.
Ronald was flushed and looked interested; the inequali-
ties of the ground shook his words, which came at a
great rate, out of him, and kept the lock of hair flopping
up and down on his forehead. His arms swung loose, and
were flung out sideways occasionally to help maintain,
when a stone rolled sharply from under him, a precarious
balance. Milton noticed that the two were like each
other; they had the same build and the same carriage
and might have been brother and sister – to, he believed,
the advantage of both. He realized that this was the
first time he had ever seen them together. It would be
the last time, also, perhaps. They had been foredoomed
in the very nature of things to miss one another. Biting
a lip he looked back – had he been instrumental? There
was pathos for him in this ghost of a contact, well-timed
in this drained-out, colourless ghost of a day. Angrily,
with a sense of destruction, he put up his hands and
shouted.

Sydney started, her lit-up face turned vividly towards
him, and she waved her walking-stick, then came
hurrying down the river-bed, springing for speed's sake
from boulder to boulder clear of the loose stones.
'Slacker!' she exclaimed. 'Rotter, James!' Her soft hat-
brim flapped back in the wind of her motion, the ends
of her bright scarf fled through the air behind her. She
was radiant and boisterous. Ronald, who had been

227

making a good point, remained in mid-stream behind
her, shutting his mouth reluctantly.

'Where have you been?' she cried breathlessly. 'If
I'd the slightest grain of proper female pride I shouldn't
look at you . . . I told Ronald hours ago that you'd be
coming any minute; that if you didn't mountains would
have slid on you. And here we find you hardly even
hurrying!' She scrambled up the bank and took his arm.

'I had no idea – I didn't mean to delay.'

'You must have been thinking,' said Sydney. 'It's
really too bad of you.' With animation she waved
Ronald forward and Ronald, coming up after her, made
a benevolent third till they came to a point where a
parting of ways became possible. Here he nodded goodbye and made off by a steep track that doubled back up
the side of the hill. Going up he whistled, turned once or
twice to stare out over their heads at the sea, and showed
plainly that he had forgotten or at least was no longer
concerned with them. It was Milton, not Sydney, who
kept looking after him rather uncertainly as though he
had half a mind to call him back, until Ronald disappeared into a fold of the hill. Too light-heartedly Ronald
had shaken them off.

'Do let's not think about Ronald,' Sydney said,
recalling him with a sigh. 'I should like us just to be
together.'

'But, my dear . . .'

'Aren't we happy?' she rather fiercely exclaimed.

He nodded. 'And you know,' he said, and pressed her
arm gently, 'that silences me.'

'I can't see anything to be silent about,' said she, and
smiled crookedly. 'Kiss me!'

'How horribly quiet it is,' she said, still with a hand
on his arm, as he let her go again. 'Don't remind me I
came here: I won't ever again – an experiment's failed.

228

James, I won't let you be happy if you mean to surround me with silences – sinister silences that bulge like a bubble and never quite burst.'

He laughed. 'You don't like the ineffable.'

'Nothing's ineffable.'

'You are.'

'No, I'm not. I am not elemental and dumb. If you like I'll explain myself perfectly. Now be practical: talk about plans. Have you written those letters?'

'I wrote them this morning.'

'That is splendid. I do want to feel we've some sort of attachment outside this improbable place. I wrote last night and slipped down last thing, when the lounge was quite empty, to put them into the concierge's box. It was locked, so I couldn't take them out again, and I went to bed hugging myself. When did you post yours?'

'I haven't posted them yet,' he said ruefully.

'Oh, why didn't you?' she exclaimed, then recovered herself confusedly. 'I mean, doesn't that make me seem horribly eager? But I had to, I couldn't resist it; I couldn't go on carrying this bomb about. They'll all say, at home, "Well, what *has* she done now?" They'll be quite sure that there must be something wrong some-where, because I somehow always just manage not to do anything right. All the people I like are rotters. I can't pay my bills. If I don't use my brains I get dissipated, and if I do use my brains I get ill. I wonder if you've any idea what I'm like – well, I don't mean that exactly, I'm sure you've got heaps of ideas about me. But I don't think you're much good at outlines – you see a kind of haze of possibilities with a very faint nucleus. It's a fatal combination, I'm sure, to be clever and kind; you can never see clear: it's a sort of a squint. The stupidest person out here could describe me immediately.'

'I tell you one thing we have in common,' said

Milton – 'we do both like running ourselves down. I shall never tell you what I've thought about myself – I couldn't bear you to agree with me.'

'I should hate you to believe all I've said. You never would, James, would you?'

'Not while you look with those eyes——'

'Oh, yes, yes, yes,' she said, and, sighing and shutting her eyes, leaned her head on his shoulder. 'I do love you.' With his arms round her he began to speak impetuously, but she pressed a hand over his mouth to silence him, and kept it there while she went on: 'There is nobody else in the world now, nobody else in the world. I've thought so much about you. I must be with you always. You're so kind.'

He felt the hand tremble and drew it away to say: 'Kind?'

'Yes, kind. Do you think that is ordinary? Do you know, I thought you were never coming. I was so afraid, up here this afternoon, that you wouldn't come at all. I thought you'd been sent away from me. I thought Some One knew better.'

'Who could know better?' he said, with a cold feeling.

'Oh, *I* don't know,' she said, beginning to laugh. 'I am an idiot. Come on, let's walk faster; it's beginning to be chilly. One loses one's way in the day here when there's no sun.'

They went quietly on in the direction of the convent, anxious to be clear of the valley; discussing as they walked their plans for the immediate future. Sydney promised that if Tessa could spare her she would go back with Milton to England; though if Tessa seemed at all reluctant she should feel obliged to stay on another three or four weeks. They agreed to be married in June. 'I do hope,' she said, smiling doubtfully, 'that I shan't be utterly useless to you.' Before they came out on to the

road she stopped him again and said she was hungry and
wanted to eat some more nuts. She took a handful of
walnuts and almonds out of her pocket and he cracked
them by twos for her, one against the other, between
the palms of his hands.

'I wonder why I can't do that,' she exclaimed; 'my
hands are really like iron! . . . I've been eating these on
and off all today – they are better than lunch.'

'Extraordinary idea!' he exclaimed, and threw up his
hands expressively. She replied that her day appeared
to her to have been spent intelligently, and that she was
not yet incapable of planning out a day for herself,
though she could not answer for what might become of
her after marriage.

He suggested that if she were not by now too tired
and hungry they should, instead of returning tamely to
the Hotel by the road, strike out across the base of the
next two hills and drop down on the Hotel through the
olive trees. The alacrity with which she jumped at this
made him suspect her of flagging inwardly, but he did
not dare to withdraw his suggestion. Seen again from
the mouth of the valley the horizon, the suddenly
revealed expanse of sky, appeared beyond all memory to
have enlarged themselves. He could not have believed
in such clear air. The afternoon was yet more coldly
grey; the trees stood out from one another in the absolute
distinctness of this hour before they should begin to run
together into dusk. Under the opaque sky the sea was
white, glassy except where now and then a hundred
ripples gave the effect of a shiver. Here and there a
cypress waited, dark among the olives. The evening had
an ache about it, a hush of timelessness, and Milton
wondered if he should forget this, too. They walked in
the half-light of the olive trees, as thought deep down
under water; Sydney's face was pale, and some deception

of shadow made it look melancholy, but the colours of
her scarf burnt. 'This is a wonderful thing,' he said, and
caught at the end of the scarf. 'I love it. I like all the
colours you wear, especially white——'

'That's not——'

'Yes, it is. It's the clearest and brightest. Don't ever
be frightened and muddled and dark, my dear, even in
clothes.'

'But, James, for a clergyman's wife – I can't wear
scarlet and flame colour. Your life——'

'Do you think of that as muddled and dark?' he said,
realizing how little they knew each other, and how
difficult it would be for her ever to know him.

'I don't think of it, I think of you. I confess I don't
half like the sound of it.'

'But, Sydney——' He glanced round a moment as
though Mrs. Kerr were behind him, smiling at Sydney.

'But we're going to live it. Any life would look bad
from the brink; if we had to make the decision we'd
probably never be born. But most lives are the same,
I'm sure once one's in mid-stream. Ours will be lovely.
But you won't see me often again in a Roman scarf.'

'Don't change, don't be different,' he cried. 'I love
you so much as you are.' She looked at him in reproach:
at that moment he loved her as sharply as though she
already were lost to him. He snatched at the moment,
and letting go of everything asked to be carried away by
it; shutting his eyes to be nearer and holding her close.
They were both blotted out, himself and herself were
forgotten: he came to a brink.

Time carried him on again after he could not say how
long a cessation of being. He knew that through all this
the hill had been waiting with their two figures upon it
framed in solitude. Coming back to her there in his
arms at a sound or a movement she made, he did not

dare to ask her where she had been. Eye to eye they looked at each other questioningly, as though trying to learn from one another if they had been together; then each looked away, as though afraid to read they had been forgotten.

'I'm rather afraid,' she said, making a movement to break away from him, and in answer to all his questions kept repeating, 'I *am* rather afraid.' He could smile at this, feeling exalted; he let her go, but later drew an arm of hers through his own, and made her walk on again. Her air was irresolute; she seemed to be trying to shape her thoughts into words. She said at last, having looked again at him solemnly as though enjoining him to understand this better than she could, 'Haven't we – or I, at least, for my part – undertaken rather too much?'

He saw some shadow of what she meant but nothing more than a shadow. He was inclined to take her gesture as traditional, her mood as generic; she was a young woman – very young as a woman. With compressed lips she withdrew her arm. 'Oh no,' she said, 'why should I ask you? The difficulty is my own.'

'No, look here, Sydney . . . why should we be afraid? It's a way out for us both – can't you see it so? – a way out of ourselves. Don't you remember the boy – Curdie – in the fairy tale, who opened a door straight on to the sky and was told to walk through it? He didn't like it at all – naturally – there was just the sky there and some of the stars were under him. However, he went forward, and just found himself walking – he had no idea how. If we go straight ahead——'

'I'd have gone back through the door. I'm not the stuff for a fairy tale. I've no faculty of wonder, James. Nothing is new to me.'

He didn't like to say, 'Do I offer you nothing, then?' He found himself guilty of having supposed that he did.

She was new to him in every aspect, in all that she was and meant. He could not imagine a time when he would not take a stranger's pleasure in looking at her across a room. He could not imagine a time when her movements would be calculable to him, or when she would cease to reappear just as he had not expected from behind the veil of his thought.

'I think you're wrong there,' he said gently. 'After all, you haven't lived so very long. You may be surprised——'

She interrupted him here, not by saying anything, but by an odd silence. Her face had a strained kind of still-ness as though it might at any moment break up into tears. She tramped beside him doggedly, as though she were really very tired, along the rough track, ducking her head mechanically now and then to avoid the branches. She seemed so drawn away from him that he could not realize his arms had been round her a moment ago. He cried, 'Sydney, you're not happy!' The exclamation was torn from him; he would have given much to recall it.

'I tell you I am,' she said obstinately and coldly; 'if you're happy, I'm happy.' She managed to make him feel he had blustered at her, and he said with less warmth, 'Oh, very well, my darling, I don't want to bully you.' He had never been in love before and he had never quarrelled with anybody. This, he supposed, was now (or would soon be) a 'lovers' quarrel', coming with a too-obliging promptness to link up for him the two experiences. Was this, then, a glimpse of their composite temper – irrational, touchy and vain? He longed to ask her this – he believed her to be saner than he was. His face, bright with an incommunicable glow of speculation, suddenly angered her.

'Anyhow – *happy*!' she cried. 'What *is* happiness? –

what comes out of it? Why must we always be feeling
each other's pulses to see if we're happy?' She flung the
word at him distastefully. It had evidently nothing to
do, where she was concerned, with the purest, most
exhausting kind of nervous exaltation, and she could
make no use of it. He could have wept for her, and
longed to say, 'Can't you be more of a woman?' Instead,
he smiled with an effect of tolerance and said, 'You are
very impatient.'

'Oh, really,' said she.

'You jump on your feelings and put a pistol up to their
heads to make the poor creatures explain themselves.
You don't give them a chance. You don't, honestly,
Sydney, give them a chance.' He spoke with some
energy.

'Oh, all right, all right,' said Sydney. 'Don't shout at
me, James! The wood is quite quiet: I hear – I hear you
quite well.'

She did not, after all, make him angry by this; he
looked round through the trees in surprise, seemed to
accept a reproof from the quiet line of the sea, and agreed
with her. 'Yes, the wood is quiet. I've been making a
horrible noise. I'll——'

'Now *don't* make a silence——'

'Yes, I'm going to – listen——'

She clutched at his arm with elaborate manifestations
of terror. They listened.

'I won't let you,' she cried, 'you shan't – it's as bad
as the valley. How we ever sleep at the Hotel with all
this saving itself up behind us, and that idiotic little
tame sea slipping up and down, up and down the beach,
I can't think.' She stamped her foot and shouted again
and again; an echo woke up in the hills. 'Now we've
got a noise again, now we're at home, James, now we're
perfectly at home.'

'Sydney——' Something had caught his attention; he looked speechlessly at her; there was something he wanted to ask. She went ahead of him, her bright scarf flickered ahead like a flame through the olives. He took some long strides to catch up with her. 'Sydney——' he said.

'James?'

'You won't mind coming home with me. You've *no* qualms about leaving this place?'

All her high spirits came back to her. 'Never a qualm,' she said loudly and cheerfully, and looked at him with a bright eye. 'Never a qualm. . . .'

CHAPTER XXIII

NEXT CORNER

TESSA was so happy about Sydney's engagement. She wrote long letters about it to her
husband Anthony out in Malay; she spent less
time upstairs with Baudouin lying down on the sofa and
more time sitting alertly in the drawing-room, glowing
at friends. She laid aside her air of a devotee and put
on all the dignity of matronhood: one could never have
guessed how well this would become her. The effect on
her digestion was extraordinary. She smiled indefatig-
ably and followed Sydney about with her eyes, and
remained on behalf of the abstracted Milton and the less
than ever approachable Sydney a shining testimony to
the efficacy for all ills of Love. For the unconscious
pair her confidence, had they taken their stand on it,
might have been as a rock among the tangled under-
currents of criticism, of amusement, of pity, of speculation as to whether it would 'last'. The thing was more
than suitable; it was a coming together for which Time
itself might have laboured to shape the couple; one
could not look in her face and deny the possibility. Her
friends sighed out that they at least were glad *she* was
glad. Mrs. Kerr remarked: 'That dear little woman looks
positively bridal.'

Everybody, Tessa thought, was being so nice to her
Sydney; charming things were said to the girl in her
presence, and many others that she happened to miss
were reported. She glowed for her brilliant Sydney,
loved her better than ever and became speechlessly shy
of her. Of Milton she was not shy at all; she could talk

to him by the hour about Elective Affinities, and about Health, which she said was very important. 'You know there is no need,' she would say, looking at him reproachfully, 'for any of us to be ill at all.' And Milton, who had scarcely ever been ill in his life, would nod back at her wisely. He had a particular softness for Sydney's dear little cousin. She told him how wonderful it would be to her to see Sydney in a home of her own and with children, who would be, she was sure, the supreme children. 'And I'm sure,' she would add, 'that you'll both be so wise and bring them up right, quite right from the very beginning. Our health, you know, has to be built up from the very foundations. Our health——' He began to recognize this as the recurring decimal point in her conversation.

Tessa thought that it would be so nice for James to get to know Sydney's great friend Mrs. Kerr really well before they all went back to England, so she planned a surprise on her own account, hired a car for the afternoon and invited Mrs. Kerr and Milton to drive with herself and Sydney up to a village high in the hills; from which, she had heard, one could look right over a ridge and see a quite unbelievable number of other hills whose similarity to one another made one surprised at the size of the world. There would be also a church with a very dark, old-looking painting, and a pâtisserie kept by a lady from Nice where they gave you an excellent tea. The weather never let Tessa down; the afternoon was delicious. Milton sat in front with the driver, Mrs. Kerr and Sydney behind with Tessa, protesting that this was ideally comfortable, wedged in tightly between them. The old Fiat rushed up the valley with a loud rattling sound, screeched at a change of gear and took the ascent laboriously. The hill leaned forward over a void, and the hundred hairpin corners they bumped round negligently made Tessa catch her breath. 'We would be killed at any moment,' said Mrs. Kerr, 'if Mrs. Bellamy were not too valuable.' When they came to the top they got out painfully, looked at the view at the other side then walked out two by two to the monastery, followed by all the little boys of the town. Tessa every now and then whispered to Sydney that Mrs. Kerr and James seemed to be making such friends – didn't they? – and getting on excellently. 'I was sure they would, they are both so clever. I think we'll keep a little farther behind them, Sydney, they may be wanting to talk about you.'

The painting in the church was so dark that it might have been anything; Tessa could not help wondering why no connoisseur had already discovered it. The idea of this possible beauty stored up in secrecy made her quite dumb; she gripped Milton and Sydney each by an arm and forced them to stand and look up at it. She hoped that they might understand the picture better than she did and say what she felt about it, but when after a moment or two of attention they simply turned to smile at one another across her she felt constrained to put forward: 'There's something *about* that face . . . I know there's something about the expression. If only it could be cleaned a little without destroying the value . . . I should never feel the same, you know, about any picture in Florence; they are so *known*.' The air of the church was stale with the incense of years, the breath of long-dead congregations had not been disturbed; it was cold with the exhalations of stone for ever in darkness. Mrs. Kerr wandered off by herself and stood in abstraction in front of the altar; a shaft of light from a window above her leant solid across the gloom. 'I expect,' thought Tessa, 'she is really very religious,' and she felt stirred again, as she had been by the picture. She kept the others waiting about because she did not like to interrupt

Mrs. Kerr – she had always known that there was something *in* Mrs. Kerr, and at the moment perhaps it was
near them. 'I can't stand this air any longer, I shall be
sick,' exclaimed Sydney suddenly, and after a last glance
towards the altar pushed aside the leather curtain on the
door and went out hurriedly. The church stood on the
rim of hill between the known and unknown landscapes,
a melancholy outpost, and it would be pleasant for Sydney
to wait outside, though not, Milton seemed to think, to
wait alone: he went out after her. Tessa sat down by herself at the end of the church and presently, after one or
two uncertain glances round her, knelt.

Milton managed to dispel the swarm of little boys who,
having presented a bunch of flowers to Sydney with a
complimentary address, demanded to be paid for them.

The three now intimate friends of the happy Tessa
walked back with her to the village unaccompanied,
talking and laughing in the manner of excursionists
between the walls of blue air. The village, heaped up
high in its walls, achieved another of those miracles of
balance; it was the same as many other villages that they
had explored, but as it was for the afternoon Tessa's they
exclaimed at its charm and oddity. Inside it was half
dark, noisome and complicated, with whistles of cold air
spouting at them through archway, down staircases dark
enough to be blind and from cellar doors. They entered
the pâtisserie with misgivings, but were let out unexpectedly from the end of a passage on to a terrace that
overhung the void and let them see the full extent of
the farther valley. They crossed on to the railing, spread
out their hands there and sighed at the view. Milton
turned aside to yawn irrepressibly two or three times;
this was the effect that distances always produced on him.
They stood in a row, close together; Mrs. Kerr and Sydney
were side by side.

'Large world . . .' said Mrs. Kerr, vaguely waving.
'Very.'

'Sydney will remember this when she goes back to England,' said Tessa, who though she had travelled a great deal always felt there was only one view. In her memory one gave place to another kaleidoscopically: there was only one at a time.

'Oh, but don't talk about Sydney going away,' said Mrs. Kerr. 'It will be terrible. But surely, Sydney, you don't think of going just yet?'

'Oh, next week, we expect,' said Sydney; 'we think it will be better to get back before the rush begins.'

'*I* shall be the rush,' said Mrs. Kerr. 'I am so stupid: I never realize one's come to the end of the season anywhere until I find everybody going away at once.'

'And then,' suggested Milton, 'you don't get a place on the train.'

'I always seem to get a place in the train: it's very curious. But isn't this a little too unselfish of you, Mrs. Bellamy, letting him take Sydney away from you so soon?'

'It was my idea,' said Tessa at once. She had come to believe this.

'I wouldn't for worlds——' began Milton.

'No, I'm sure you wouldn't really,' smiled Mrs. Kerr. 'But one doesn't have the chance of bringing a Sydney back with one every day.' There was a pause in which she looked thoughtfully down at Sydney's hand on the railing beside her, then laid her own over it. 'They are all going away,' she said to Tessa, 'all the young ones. Ronald's going quite soon, too – down to Sicily.'

'Oh dear – oh dear,' sighed Tessa in placid deprecation of the laws of change. A lump rose in her throat as she too saw Mrs. Kerr's hand lying on Sydney's. Partings were terrible. Ought she to move away gently with Milton to the other end of the terrace?

'But perhaps,' said Mrs. Kerr, 'you two'll come back here together some day. I shall imagine you here.'

'Thanks,' said Milton, and laughed uncertainly. 'Do!'

Sydney took no notice of what was being said; she did not seem as though she had heard. She stood between Tessa and Mrs. Kerr as inanimate and objective as a young girl in a story told by a man, incapable of a thought or a feeling that was not attributed to her, with no personality of her own outside their three projections upon her: Milton's fiancée, Tessa's young cousin, Mrs. Kerr's protégée, lately her friend.

'Sydney,' Milton asked her loudly, '*shall* we come back here?'

'Oh yes,' she said mechanically, 'do let's. Do let's come back here – I'm so fond of this place.'

When they had finished tea they went back to the piazza outside the village to look for the Fiat, and having found the Fiat had to search farther afield for their driver, a brigandish individual in a check cap who returned to them with reluctance.

'Such a nice afternoon,' Mrs. Kerr smiled retrospectively as they slid away from the village; and as the keen air rushed forward to meet them, she drew down her chin luxuriously into the collar of her fur coat. The car swerved violently at the first of the corners, and Sydney who had taken Tessa's place in the middle was flung sideways with her cheek against the fur. 'I wish there were not such a long way to go,' remarked Tessa, who after one look down had drawn quickly back and shut her eyes. 'It's not like motoring at all, it's more like *dropping*.'

'Perhaps——' said Sydney and broke off because it was not fair to Tessa. She sat back quietly and began to concentrate her whole will and imagination. 'If it could be the next corner,' she thought, 'we should go over clean – there is that clear drop. Let it be the next corner . . .' But the next corner was past. The rush of air and the movement had made her come alive again and she seemed to herself to be reasoning very clearly and accurately. There would be nobody really to suffer except poor old Anthony, out in Malay. She did not suppose James's brother and sister would care very much; she did not feel him to have been loved more than conventionally, to have ever so faintly quickened a passion or coloured a life. 'As for Ronald,' she thought, very keen and exultant as though there were a sword in her hand, 'it would be better for Ronald.' She fixed her eyes on the back of the driver's head and began to be perfectly sure of what was coming, perfectly confident.

'We mustn't go over too quickly,' she thought, 'there must be time to say something.' Under the rug her hand found out Mrs. Kerr's sleeve and rested there ever so lightly. She racked her brain for all there would be to say, then relinquished the effort. At all events there would be a moment to look at each other, just to look at each other: that would be best. 'I don't want to look at James – there is always that question of the future. I should be very much embarrassed.' Her mind became quite quiet again and she went on saying, 'The next corner . . .the *next* corner.'

Round the next, barely round it, the brakes jarred, the car swayed on locked wheels and stopped dead. The driver swore, peered ahead left and right, stood up in his place to give point to what he was saying and swore more vehemently. Milton also rose in his place to see better and their view from behind was obscured. They had seen in a flash a long wagon of timber jammed crossways, shouting men, backing, terrified horses. Milton, after a moment, turned smiling to reassure them. 'The idiots,' he said, 'have been making a mess of this turn. They're

all right, but we may have some time to wait till they're
clear. The end of the timber's got jammed against the
rock – they must have been as nearly as possible over.'

'So, I suppose, were we?' Mrs. Kerr said, amused.

Milton nodded, after a half-glance at Sydney. 'Our
fellow *can* drive,' he said gratefully. 'We're here for a
bit – would you care to get out and have a look?'

Sydney shook her head. With both hands clasped on
her lap she sat quite still, defeated. She could not look
at Milton, who helped out Mrs. Kerr and Tessa and
walked with them up to the wagon. In a minute or two
he was back. 'I say, aren't you coming?'

She shook her head again stonily.

'Sydney . . . has this given you rather a shock?'

She was plainly what people describe as 'upset'.

'They've no right to bring those things up here,' he
angrily cried.

'Well, they must build their houses, my dear.' It was
the tolerance of lassitude. She looked over the side of
the car down into the valley: a kind of farewell. It was
a long way below – the depth of it would never be
forgotten.

'Funny we shouldn't have seen it ahead of us,' said
Milton, thinking about the wagon, 'or underneath us.
It's the way the rocks stick out – pretty dangerous, I
must say.'

She agreed. 'Pretty dangerous. Look here, I will
come; but go on with the others. I'll just stay here a
moment or two.'

They were having – up here – a later view of the sun
than their friends down below; by now the tennis-courts
would be silent, the sea fading, the earliest lights coming
out pale and exotic in hotels whose walls still had an
afterglow. Here the sun was still full on the village, level
on peak behind peak; the gold only gave way reluctantly

to a mild rose that chilled and abated and was transfused
by shadows mounting up like smoke out of the valley.
This isolation above the regular approach of night con-
nected itself in her mind with her present shocked sense
of having been flung back on to living. The depths of
shadow from which they were barred away would have
been to her infinitely grateful. Above, in this unnatural,
endless prolongation of the daylight she for the first time
felt life sharply, life as keen as death to bite upon the
consciousness, pressed inexorably upon her, held to her
throat like a knife. Dazed by a realization of their import
she stared at her hands, at her body, at the hills round
her.

Later she had scrambled from the car and was running
down the hill on her stiff legs unsteadily, calling to James.

Round the wagon a tumult was raging of admonition,
sympathy and abuse. Several young men had sprung up
out of nowhere and were straining, shouting and heaving,
alternately propping stones under the wheels of the
wagon, then trying to push the wagon forward over the
stones. Other young men and some women came scrambling down in a state of happy excitement by a precipitous
path from the village that struck down direct across the
zigzags of the road. Friends of the wagoner kicked the
horses in the chest to make them back farther, tugged
them forward by the bridles and almost incessantly beat
them over the head. Sydney saw Milton, scarlet and also
shouting, trying to stop this and being swept aside
amicably as one who knew nothing of the country, of
timber or of the management of horses. Tessa, only too
glad to be out of the Fiat, was trotting up and down like
a little bear in her fur coat. No one, evidently, could have
been sorrier for the poor horses than Mrs. Kerr, but she
was trying to restrain Milton from further interference
because he ran a momentary danger of being elbowed

over the edge of the road. As Sydney approached, the situation was further complicated by a short log working loose from the pile, slipping down sideways and getting locked between the far-apart spokes of the wheel.

'It's all so damned silly!' cried Milton exasperatedly. The crisis brought out in him at the expense of his rationality all that was latently English. Mrs. Kerr shrugged her shoulders and smiled.

'One of those horses is bleeding,' he added in helpless disgust.

'Then come away,' said Mrs. Kerr. 'After all, we're not asked to more than imagine what animals suffer. We aren't asked to be certain – it mayn't be so bad. I think I'll go back to the car.'

Milton only half understood what she said and did not hear Sydney calling him. His attention was all for the horses. 'They ought at least,' he exclaimed later on, 'to have warned us up there in the village that this was ahead.' He turned to find Sydney there, pale, at his elbow and Mrs. Kerr gone.

'Will they be long?' she said anxiously. He nodded, and she put a hand on his arm and guided him up the road again, past the Fiat, where Tessa and Mrs. Kerr were sitting again wrapped up in rugs. Sydney looked at them vacantly, turned to Milton to say something with the same air of vacancy, saw with alarm that the car was still close behind them and hurried him on to get farther out of earshot. 'I'm afraid,' she said, 'that it's quite impossible.'

He understood by some odd intuition; but kept her watching him for a moment or two while he listened intently to the clamour below, the isolated exclamation, the voices. 'What's quite impossible, Sydney? What do you mean?'

'Our marriage.'

'Oh!' he said quietly. 'Oh!'

'I don't know how we could ever have thought of it.'

'I'm afraid,' he said slowly, 'I can't see yet why it's not right.'

She looked hopeless. 'I suppose I can't make you see. But I do know.'

'Since when?' She seemed protected by some kind of exaltation, so he let out his pain in sarcasm. 'Recently, Sydney?'

'Just now. I suppose it was the shock of being alive – oh, how can I explain to you? I had had no idea we were as real as this. I'd never realized it mattered so much . . . Oh, my dear, no, don't touch me. Come farther – come round the bend of the road.'

'I wasn't going to touch you,' he said, ashamed for both of them, half aware that an instinctive movement towards her must have been exaggerated by the effect of distance she gave him. By some defect of focus he had seen her as a long way away. They went up the hill painfully, as though it were steeper, and turned the next corner, which gave her back a kind of echo, a ghost of that early idea of deliverance. Farther up she sat down on a bank by the side of the road; because she looked tired enough to fall sideways he sat down close to her, put an arm round her and propped her up against a brotherly shoulder. 'Now tell me,' he said, 'if you feel you can tell me.'

'*Now* I understand – but it seems as if I ought to tell you what I didn't understand. I think we have been asleep here; you know in a dream how quickly and lightly shapes move, they have no weight, nothing offers them any resistance. They are governed by some funny law of convenience that seems to us perfectly rational, they clash together without any noise and come apart without injury.'

'Do you think *we've* been ruled by this "funny law of convenience"?'

'Yes,' she said without hesitation, but putting a hand out as though to propitiate him. 'We have taken nothing into account. You and me – how could we ever have thought of it? It was just a dream. It seemed simple.'

'It never seemed simple to me. I was going to fight every inch of it.'

'But you're not——' she began, broke off, and in a manner at once intimate and very impersonal leaned closer against his shoulder.

'Not what?' he said, urging this out of her.

'Not a fighter.'

'Not a born fighter, perhaps . . . I thought we could help each other.'

'Never. You could never have thought that.'

'If I am to let you go I shall have to learn to say "Never".'

'Say it now – or shall I have to tell you everything?'

'I would rather you did. But no; the laws of convenience. I think I could guess what is coming . . . Sydney?'

She did not answer. He saw her hand stealing up to her face and discovered that tears were coming out from under her eyelids, and that she was trying to brush them away with the tip of a finger. 'I haven't got a handkerchief,' she said as she felt him detect this. 'I left it behind in the car.' He managed with an arm round her, shifting his position gently so as not to disturb her, to extract a clean handkerchief that he had pushed up his cuff.

'Thank you,' she said, crumpling up the handkerchief and staring at it. 'You are – you are comfortable.'

'So they tell me,' said he, and his mouth twisted in momentary bitter repudiation of comfortableness.

'I'd rather do this alone, if you don't mind,' she said, as the tears began to come faster.

'Very well – shall I walk up and down or will you?'

As she did not answer and did not stir he got up and left her. Patrolling their bit of road at absent speed, with his hands in his pockets, he could still feel her head heavy on his shoulder, and the feeling of intimacy and nearness remained with him. He remembered, looking back with pity for them both, that questioning long look in which they had been baffled by one another under the olive trees. At this moment of swinging apart he was one with her, and was able to say, 'she is right'. Passing by her again and again where she sat he looked or did not look: either seemed to be natural. He could feel rather than perceive her there sitting upright, her hands on her knees, his handkerchief a dead-white blot in the dark. The tide of shadow had risen at last and engulfed them, drawing the hills together and making the valley seem to float up to them, spreading a film of silence in which the clamour from below was diffused. The last of the pink light faded slowly from the hills; the moon rose opaque and lustreless in the still lucent sky.

'Don't come till you're ready,' he called as he saw her getting up slowly.

'I'm ready now,' she said, coming towards him.

His admission was ready for her. 'I do see what you mean,' he said. 'I do understand.'

'Is there anything queer about my eyes – would one notice?' she asked, and turned her face up to his anxiously. He had to peer close in the half-light before he assured her. 'No; nobody'd guess.'

They turned and walked silently back to the car. Tessa was sitting round looking out eagerly for them over the back.

'They've had an idea,' she cried: 'they're going to saw off that long bit of timber. Our driver says it was his idea. One of the men is fetching a saw.'

'And then we can go on again,' said Mrs. Kerr, making room for Sydney. 'Why is it so much more tiring to sit still in something that doesn't move?' Sydney climbed silently in and sat between them. By the time they had been able to pass the wagon, drawn back farther down into a bay of the road, she felt that the evening was already over, that they had been home for a long time, that all this had happened a year ago and only by some delay of the memory still seemed to concern them. As they walked rather slowly up the Hotel steps, weighed down with armfuls of wraps, and the disconcertingly keen lights streamed out on to them, Mrs. Kerr with an air of coming awake again remarked that Sydney was tired. 'If you're not too tired,' she said, 'come in on your way up and say good night to me. We shan't have you many nights more.'

'Thank you,' Sydney said, 'but don't wait up for me. I'll come early if I come at all.' After dinner she went straight to her own room, sleep came up over her like a wave as soon as she shut her eyes, a tall dark wave that gathered itself and waited above her a moment, so that she was conscious of it before she was conscious of nothing. Then all night long she was climbing up the endless road again, corner by corner, to an empty town at the top.

CHAPTER XXIV

KINDNESS

'YET I do think it would be nice of you to go with him as far as Genoa,' Mrs. Kerr said to Ronald, three evenings afterwards. At an end of her gentle insistence, she could do no more; she left the appeal in the air to dissolve or solidify, sighed, turned away from her son and took up her letters. The appeal stretched out and closed upon Ronald's unwillingness, tentacle after shadowy tentacle; he got up and walked round Mrs. Kerr's room, uneasily moving his shoulders, writhing mentally like the Laocöon and feeling himself constricted at every point.

'Well, I am blowed,' he said petulantly. 'I really am blowed!' But Mrs. Kerr was reading a letter.

Ronald could not understand why two people who had come to the place unaware of each other, in perfect integrity and without the intention of seeking a mate, should not be allowed to remain there untroubled now that a transitory notion of marrying one another had been abandoned. Or if they were due to depart, why had they to depart processionally in a long train of Spirits Pitiful; regrets, remorses, condolences, noisy emotions given the licence of carnival? Mrs. Bellamy was 'taking away' Sydney (who now had to be bundled about like a lay figure and spoken of like the unillustrious dead) to a place on the French Riviera, and later to England. Milton was to move on to Florence, even to Assisi; there seemed a vagueness as to whether he might not be trusted in proper abandon to walk over the very edge of Italy into the sea. He had timed his departure, un-wittingly, for the same date, the same train, as Ronald's.

Ronald, appalled by the thought of a journey in company
with one for whom the web of a fatal attachment would
be with every moment attenuating and snapping off
strand by strand, had announced to his mother that
travel with Milton he would not: it could not be done.
He proposed to remain with her several days more.

'We'd see each other on the platform,' Ronald said;
'we should be bound to see each other on the platform,
and we should feel such asses looking all round each other
and then getting into different carriages.'

'Well, don't get into different carriages; talk to each
other.'

'I really don't know how to. You see, he would be
bound to think I was embarrassed. I think he is the sort
of man who would rather expect one to be.'

Many people were embarrassed by Milton, avoided
meeting him in the corridors, moved away when he
came into the lounge, and when they caught his eye did
not know where to look and hurried away to complain
of him. He had expected and hoped that nothing would
'come out' until he and Sydney had managed to slip
away quietly, but in this he had counted without her
directness – he had written a note on the matter to send
to her room, but on reading it through had destroyed it
(it seemed to reek with the meanest solicitudes) and had
sat with his head in his hands, unable to write her
another. Sydney had 'told' Tessa; Tessa, through con-
fidantes fatally chosen and an air for the world of
reserved desolation, let everyone know. He was offered
during the *tête-à-têtes* which circumstances or the con-
scientiousness of a few friends forced on him all kinds
of silences, and found them poor enough meat in his
hunger, his sudden ache for companionship; silences
applied tenderly, like a swab to a wound; silences held
up, like a shield, square and blank; silences poked

across at him gingerly; the silences of Miss Pym, of Colonel Duperrier, of Eileen Lawrence. Sensitive to so abashing his world, he began to feel like a leper. His perturbation as to whether he ought to be here, the increasingly sharp little stings with which consciousness, less of suffering than of being a too evidently suffering man, was brought home again and again to him kept up such a din in his mind that thought was impossible. He could not think of Sydney or of what they had lost or gained. Now and then he would brace himself and with cold exultation look ahead to an ordeal in Florence.

Veronica spoke to him; she gave him all her distracted sympathy, then took it all back again in a breath. 'There are worse things,' she said, 'than not being engaged to be married. I would rather do anything on earth than meet Victor just now – will you walk down with me and look for a court?' That had been early one morning; they had stolen down to the courts together and played singles till other people began to assemble. He gave her minus-fifteen and she won their three sets. 'You know, you mustn't let yourself go to pieces,' she said, shaking her head at him as they walked back together. 'You used to be good.'

'But I'm *melting away* in all this!' exclaimed Milton explosively.

Later, as they turned in at the Hotel gate, she had an idea. 'I say, you do marry people, don't you – I mean, professionally? It would be rather a joke if you were to marry us. Rather a *grim* joke, I dare say,' she added with bent brows, tightening her racquet-press. But that evening, as with a feverish sense of exclusion from everywhere he walked up and down on the gravel, she melted ahead of him into the darkness, trailing the wraith of a shawl from her shoulders, going down to the sea with her Victor to look at the moonlight. She came into the lounge again, shining-eyed, mysterious from having been kissed, and Milton felt that at least she was not unhappy.

He was haunted by Ronald. Ronald, whenever they met, paused momentarily, opened and shut his mouth, seemed always just on the verge of an utterance which was to clarify everything and banish confusion. An oblique glance, penetrating, but addressed to one another's features rather than eye to eye, would pass between them. Then smiling regretfully, as though he had been urgently called away, Ronald would shake back the piece of hair from his forehead and dart off. Milton had the feeling each time of having been weighed and found wanting. There must have been something about him that brought Ronald up dead. He told himself this did not matter, he would not see Ronald again; then the thought of not seeing Ronald again would itself inexpressibly sadden him. The thought of Ronald and Sydney going away in different directions, and of the unlikelihood of their ever meeting came to be even more painful; the injury was personal, as though one or the other, or both of them, had been part of himself. Every time he met Ronald there was the embarrassment, not just of that one moment of failure sharp as the slam of a door, but of a dozen remembered others mounting up behind it.

'I *will* speak,' Milton said to himself at last, and Ronald must have come to the same decision, for the next time they met they both began to talk at once, irrelevantly and loudly. It was this, chiefly, which had made Ronald so unwilling that they should travel together to Genoa. Walking about the room, he was trying with great difficulty to explain this to his mother.

Mrs. Kerr, still with an eye on her letters but with attention dutifully withdrawn from her own affairs, raised herself among the cushions and turned a little round on the sofa to consider her son's difficulty.

'I don't want to sacrifice you, my darling,' she said, 'but if you would do this you would really oblige me. You see, Ronald, the poor man does like you. I thought if you would try and be nice to him – make it all easier – just for an hour or two in the train.'

'It's an Italian train,' said Ronald gloomily.

'I know, I know,' said Mrs. Kerr, and nodded in helpless contrition. 'I'm afraid,' she went on irrelevantly, 'he feels sore about this—— He feels——'

'*Sore?*' echoed Ronald. 'Ridiculous! Sore?'

'I think so, a little . . . with me,' said Mrs. Kerr, and adjusted the shade of the reading-lamp. Her face by that movement emerged from red dusk and was shown to her son like a picture, lit up: a face lying rather wearily back among cushions, full of lucidity and gentleness; less beautiful at the moment than burning in on his consciousness its essential quality, mental or spiritual, that he could not define. Ronald wondered again if this was what he would learn to call love, or whether he would ever experience any other: this feeling of being burnt in upon that left no room for desire. 'I half think,' Mrs. Kerr went on reluctantly, as though she were reading out from the confused blotted chart of poor Milton's mind, 'that *he* half thinks I've meddled. Of course, I have a kind of influence over Sydney, but I should never have used it to interfere in her love-affairs. I have always wanted her to marry, and seen that she wanted to marry, and though I was surprised just at first that she should be able to think about him in that way, they both seemed so pleased with each other that I should have done a great deal to help them on.'

It was a strange and sudden relief to Ronald – he could not have said why – to hear his mother say all this in her matter-of-fact voice.

'Poor old Milton,' he said at once, and could not help

laughing. Mrs. Kerr also smiled, less and less ruefully as his laughter began to infect her. 'Poor old chap,' said Ronald again, noisily. He waited for what was to come next, but his mother seemed to have done speaking. 'Of course,' he went on, at the same pitch of jocularity, 'if it's a case of the family honour . . . anything *I* can do. . . .'

It did sound ridiculous, the way he put it, and Mrs. Kerr smiled again. 'I should feel happier,' she confessed, 'if the poor dear went off more or less happily. You see, he does like you.'

'Oh yes, I dare say he does. I dare say he thinks I have a beautiful expression and wishes I would come and sing in his choir.'

'Something like that, I dare say. But people are not put in choirs for their beautiful expressions. Seriously, Ronald, I'm doing this because I want to do anything I can for him. It seems a lot to send you away from me sooner than you have to go. You see, I'll be lonely,' said Mrs. Kerr, and glanced away from the statement distastefully when it was made as though she saw it as ugly and trivial.

'Oh, mother . . .'

He caught at her hand, but she drew it away again. 'I don't want you to stay and be kind to me. I hope I shall be dead a long time before people are kind to me.' She shivered – not, he thought, at death.

'You're lonely?'

Her eyes took him in, very tiny, and round him the room and the world with its tiny people drawn by their hundreds of tides. She nodded and her thought passed ahead. 'You see,' she said, 'I, who am what is called "an attractive person", am going to be lonelier than other people, the beautiful or the devoted. I shan't be able to crowd myself round for consolation and company with hundreds of little photographs of loving or having been loved.'

'A large number of people seem to have loved you,' said Ronald. Though shaken, he spoke definitely, very dispassionately. It seemed important, so important that his mouth went dry, that his mother should not be allowed to go on looking through him and thinking beyond him with that peculiar expression. 'A large number . . .' he repeated.

'No, no one, I think,' said Mrs. Kerr, after a pause in which she tried to remember. While she spoke she began glancing through her letters abstractedly and with an air of indifference. Then she smiled. 'At any rate,' she went on, having extracted an envelope that had already been opened, 'I don't begin to be lonely just yet – here's such a charming letter, an invitation, from those Emmerys in Paris.'

'Oh, Margot Emmery . . .?'

'Yes, Margot. I am so fond of her. So you, my dear, can run away to Sicily.' She tugged gently at a fold of her tea-gown on which he happened to be sitting and swept him away from her with a gesture, as though he were a little boy again and she were sending him off to bed.

'Well, at any rate,' said Ronald, nodding, sitting tight on the tea-gown and leaning forward to show her he had scored a point, 'Sydney is fond of you.'

'I suppose she is,' Mrs. Kerr said reflectively.

'Then *why* . . .' began Ronald. 'Why on earth . . .?' He stopped again and blinked his eyes, as though he had suddenly seen everything as so complicated that he could only believe in some defect in his vision. Mrs. Kerr gently stirred on the sofa, the loud ticking of the travel-ling-clock at her elbow became suddenly audible. Ronald looking round the room caught sight of his own photograph – 'Ronald' – and thought how odd it was that Mrs. Kerr sitting on the sofa beside him should have a son and how much odder it was that Ronald should have a mother. He found himself arguing very loudly, wisely and dogmatically and was reminded of the only two occasions when he had been drunk. 'You're not fair to yourself,' he kept repeating. 'You're not, mother, you're not really, you *ought* to be fair. . . .'

She looked up at him once or twice from over Margot Emmery's letter, and said presently, 'Well, my dear Ronald, I leave that to you. – Hush! . . . Listen! Come in! . . . Ronald, I'm sure I heard somebody. Do go and see who it is.'

'It's Miss Warren,' said Ronald, having opened the door grudgingly, and Sydney came in.

She came in doubtfully, carrying a pile of books, with a long pair of white leather gloves dangling over her arm. She and Ronald stared at each other vaguely and steadily over the reading-lamp, the only light in the room. In the red dusk over the shade their faces were blank to each other; their features were scarcely visible and their expressions, if they had expressions, not visible at all. As it was a spring night the window stood open out on to the balcony, and now and then the curtains were sucked in and swelled out by a breath of mild air.

'I'll be getting along,' said Ronald to Sydney.

'Oh no, *don't* go.' But the room seemed too small for three people.

Ronald, seeking for and failing to catch his mother's eye, looked round him rather confusedly and finally stepped out between the curtains on to the balcony, where he lighted a cigarette and, doubling his elbows under him, leaned forward to stare at the sea. The exit was not a happy one, in the room behind he remained present yet not present. Sydney put her pile of books carefully down on the table and counted them over, then held out the pair of gloves to Mrs. Kerr.

'I think these are all of your books that I had,' said she. 'And I think these are your gloves: I must have brought them upstairs with me after a walk. I found them among my things.'

'So they are!' said Mrs. Kerr, and looked at the gloves in pleased surprise. 'How nice to have them back – but I never missed them. But I do wish, my dear, you hadn't brought all those books back. Wouldn't you keep them? I shall never have room for them all in my trunk.'

'I shouldn't have room in my trunk either.'

'Not if I wrote your name in them all?'

'I'm afraid I still shouldn't have room in my trunk,' Sydney said, and smiled conventionally.

'Then I shall have to give them away to someone else,' said Mrs. Kerr with a sigh. 'Don't just hover, Sydney – must you go yet? Stay and sit down.'

'I'm afraid I can't. I'm going through my things tonight and beginning to pack – I'd no idea I'd so many. We go, you see, the day after tomorrow, and tomorrow night I shall be going out with the Lawrences.'

'Oh, the Lawrences? . . . Well, I expect it will be very nice for you all to spend your last evening together. Are you really going the day after tomorrow?'

'Yes. So's Ronald, isn't he?'

'He is indeed,' sighed Ronald's mother. 'How time does seem to have slipped away from us all . . . Mr. Miiton and Ronald, you know, are hoping to travel together . . . *Poor* Mr. Milton . . .!'

'Yes,' said Sydney, 'I suppose he is a good deal laughed at.'

Mrs. Kerr glanced at her with raised eyebrows a moment and bit her lip as though she had winced for a moment inwardly. There seemed to be depths of crudeness here that she dared not fathom. 'Not as far as I know, my dear,' she said gently, 'unless, of course, you feel able to laugh at him?'

'I'm not much amused really. Do I seem to be much amused?'

Mrs. Kerr looked at her gently and critically. 'No, I don't think you do. You do look older, my dear, yes, you certainly have developed. I suppose there is nothing like buying experience that somebody else pays for.'

'You're very sensitive to all this,' said Sydney, raising her eyes for the first time. 'What's most beautiful about you is your sensitiveness. If there's one thing one might hope to learn from you it would be to be sickened and turned cold by cruelty and unfairness. I hope that's what other people have learnt from you. I hope that's what someone where you're going next will be able to learn, too.' Finding that her voice was still steady and clear and that she was able to go on she concluded: 'I am very grateful to you; you have done a great deal for me.'

After a moment's pause Mrs. Kerr said, with a glance through the curtains, 'You do remember, don't you, that Ronald's on the balcony?'

'No, I haven't forgotten Ronald . . . Good night, Mrs. Kerr. Good night, Ronald!'

She turned and went back to the door, not quite directly, steering her way through the furniture as though she were carefully following back a chalk line drawn for her on the floor. While her hand was still on the door Mrs. Kerr exclaimed, 'Sydney!' incredulously, then later, 'Well, *Sydney* – what have I done?' Sydney did pause on the threshold and look back uncertainly, Mrs. Kerr held out a hand; then she turned again and went out, shutting the door behind her so quietly that Mrs. Kerr and Ronald only heard the latch click. Mrs. Kerr, catching her breath at the sound of the latch, began repeating her name again in such a tone of desolation and loneliness that Ronald, driven out against something intolerable, rushed through the curtains.

'Why, *mother*!'

'Make her come back. Go after her, Ronald, and make her come back – I have something to say to her.'

'I don't see that I very well can.'

She stared up, arrested. 'Why not?'

'Well, I don't think she wants to.'

'Ronald. . . .'

'I'm awfully sorry.' But his mother had turned away from him in contempt; her eyes were fixed on the door as though under their long, strange, relentless compulsion it must open again to deliver up Sydney. When he came forward she warded him off with a hand. He did not like to look at her, and did not know where else to look, so he stumbled back on to the balcony where he found, still alight, a cigarette that he had taken out of his mouth an age ago and balanced aslant on the rail. He rolled it round between his fingers, considering it, took two or three puffs and threw it into the darkness, then remained standing still there, waiting to be called back. After waiting for some time his tension began to relax again, but looking round at the sky, the sea, the tops of the trees he still saw everywhere his mother's head in the circle of light from the reading-lamp printed everywhere on the darkness.

CHAPTER XXV

GOING AWAY

A ONE-HORSE vehicle with a canvas hood called by the English visitors a shandrydan came round about three o'clock to drive Mr. Milton and Ronald down to the Genoa train. It appeared about half an hour before it had been ordered, and the limp horse in a bonnet, looking as if it had been propped up on its legs precariously, waited on the gravel, indifferent to the flies, long enough to advertise to the whole Hotel that somebody was going away. Departures at this time of the afternoon were unusual, and people coming downstairs after the siesta and people on their way out to the tennis-courts stood about in the doorway (the double doors had been fixed back as for the passage of a grand piano) or gathered round the foot of the steps to smile at the inefficient way in which the concierge, the boots and one of the younger waiters were stacking up the light luggage on the box of the shandrydan. Antonio the boots was very popular; every time he let Milton's leather hat-box or one of Ronald's many dispatch-cases glissade past him and bounce on to the gravel there was laughter and a cry of 'Oh, *oh*, Antonio!' And Antonio, knowing this to be part of a very amusing English song, would smile woodenly.

Nobody was quite sure how much of a 'send-off', under the circumstances, Milton would appreciate, but it was impossible to let pass such an excellent opportunity of embarrassing Ronald. Ronald was better liked than anybody else in the Hotel had been for a long time; it was always easy to be amusing about him; he roused genuine interest and curiosity, and, in the breasts of those who disliked his mother, an active instinct to protect and comfort. In twos and threes for mutual encouragement people were never tired of seeking him out and baiting him, giving him articles in the *Morning Post* to read, tripping him up over statistics or twitting him on an attachment to one or other of the Lawrences. He was the dearest boy, good humour itself, and one could not doubt that he genuinely enjoyed all this. The present prospect of seeing him shake hands all round, reply to a dozen mock-tender addresses and blushingly double his long legs under the low seat of the shandrydan kept tennis-players from courts booked a week ago, wives from buying their husband's tea and walkers down from the hills.

After the luggage had been arranged there was an interval, then Milton took form in the gloom of the lounge and appeared in the doorway, drew half back, glanced at his watch and hesitated, smiling uncertainly. In spite of a very secular grey squash hat he looked for the first time true to type, and several people realized sharply that a Church of England clergyman had for weeks been among them. The professional aspect stamped out the lover: he was once more approachable, showed up even as dedicated to approachability. There was a movement towards him. Friends gained all in a moment smiled for him up at the unflecked sky and congratulated him on his weather, intimates taking him up from before the dawn of that interlude regretted his going away loudly, and turned in anguish to one another with appeals to regret more. He nodded round with successive, finished-off little smiles and once or twice visibly swallowed. Miss Pym, standing down at the foot of the steps said to herself, 'Morituri te salutant'.

People on the verge of departure always seemed to her

to be saying this; there was something about them fated and sacrificial that made her feel self-conscious on their behalf yet somehow rather exalted. Presently Milton thought of something, murmured, and turned back into the lounge. The curtain having dropped for a minute with the usual good effect of tightening them up to further expectancy they all turned to one another again and said in low voices what a real pity it was that he should be going away. All sorts of things that he might have been to them appeared suddenly; with things they might have brought to his hearing for sympathy, taxed him with or asked him about.

Ronald came running down the steps in too much of a hurry to look at anybody. He flung his overcoats and another dispatch-case into the shandrydan, then went round to the box and gravely tested the roping on of the luggage. The pile wobbled so menacingly that he was discouraged, left it alone and ran in again. During another interval he must have kissed and said goodbye to his mother, perhaps in her room, perhaps on the stairs. When they appeared in the doorway all that was visibly over between them. She still had a hand on his sleeve, but it was a light and casual contact of which neither of them seemed aware: she had already delivered him up to futurity. Those who had felt constrained to draw back from the scene of a parting began to return again. Ronald became their prey. Appalled by a publicity as of the scaffold he turned with some desperately trumped-up remark to his mother, but she was not behind him. Apart, at the top of the steps, bareheaded in the afternoon light she was standing, a little fatigued by all this, looking across at the hill that rose over the road and the group of young palms at the gate that seemed to be also serenely awaiting the exit.

'I say, if Milton doesn't come soon we shall run it fine,'

called Ronald in an unnatural, loud voice. Another woman would have jumped at this excuse to hurry back into the Hotel agitatedly calling, anything rather than stand there, just stand there. But Mrs. Kerr stood there, and women's hearts hardened. 'Oh no, Ronald,' she said, 'you have plenty of time.'

Ronald braced up, with his back to the shandrydan, frowned up the steps to search out the interior gloom. A moment, his face lightened: Milton must be coming. Milton was coming, he was half-way down the steps with his hat off, bowing and smiling to left and right, and Ronald was half-way into the shandrydan. Then a voice – Mrs. Bellamy's – called 'Mr. Milton!' and Milton turned back. It was strange, almost eerie, to hear Mrs. Bellamy's voice, because she and Sydney had managed somehow to create an impression of having already departed. Since lunch-time when they had said their goodbyes they must have been up in their rooms. It was recalled with a shock that they were not to set out on their shorter journey up the coast till just before tea-time. Yet Tessa had been already translated, she was an amiable ghost, and her cousin a hard-sounding name with a cold-sounding echo. It was as though Milton running back up the steps with his same formal smile were going back into the shades.

The shades came to meet him not far inside the door. Tessa was breathless. '– We're so worried,' she said, '*couldn't* find you this morning.' She shook his hand between both of hers with more little broken-off sentences. Do so hope . . . did so wish . . . shall remember. . . .'

Sydney, looking unnatural and urban in a dark-coloured travelling-dress, stepped out from behind her. 'Well, goodbye,' she said, and she and Milton shook hands awkwardly.

'Well, goodbye,' said he, and after a moment's

hesitation as though he did not like to seem too abrupt
ran down the steps and got into the shandrydan. She
came a little way after him and stood with a hand on the
concierge's desk, from which she picked up an envelope
and confusedly read the address, then looked after him
again. Her manner was strained and unwomanly: the
impulse that had brought her down here (it could not
have been Tessa's) had been highly unnatural. She did
not wait to watch the departure but turned and went
upstairs again slowly, followed by Tessa.

Milton and Ronald looked up at the windows of the
Hotel vacantly; everybody looked at each other, everybody waited. At last the driver climbed on to the box,
at last he gathered up the reins. Milton and Ronald
sitting stiffly side by side – their legs, willy-nilly en-
twined in the limited scope of the shandrydan, entangled
in rugs and overcoats – relaxed, were bumped violently
forward as the carriage moved on, let broad smiles break
over their faces. Their friends who had been drawing
deep breaths for this moment released an enormous
'*Good*-by-ye!' A hundred jocularities that there had not
yet been mood or occasion for were launched off bravely
after the never-returning couple. One could tell them
anything now, before it was too late, their memories
were from henceforward a limbo. The voices went up
to the sky, together or isolated. Ronald's mother stood
smiling and waving her hand; all round her the handkerchiefs fluttered ... '*Dear* old Ronald ... Steady,
Ronald ... *Sure* you know where you're going,
Ronald? ...' and at the height of all this, 'Cheer up,
Milton!'

Someone flung a bunch of flowers at Ronald and it
struck Milton on the side of the head and dropped just
under the wheel; the stalks were crushed and a slimy
smear appeared on the wheel and came round faster and

faster and faster as the driver took the gravel sweep
magnificently and turned off out of the gate. Cordelia
Barry rushed out, picked up the flowers and flung them
again, but this time they fell quite short, and everybody
laughed.

Milton and Ronald, avoiding one another's eye, leant
over the back of the carriage waving their hats and
shouting jocular nothings. The driver cracked his whip,
the rattling wheels fled faster and soon the travellers,
still waving and with big mouths open inaudibly, had
disappeared. The little company on the steps sighed in
immense desolation.

Before the sigh had come to an end Miss Fitzgerald
and Miss Pym had detached themselves, and complete
with their red parasols and swinging baskets hurried
away. If they were still to make anything of the afternoon not a moment more must be wasted. They were
well down the road under the chestnut trees coming out
into leaf before Miss Pym observed rather breathlessly:
'Strange how they still go on touching one——'

'Strange – so profoundly.'

'These goings away.' She sighed over a diminishing
vista of hundreds. 'Even when they're simply spec-
tacular, not at all *partings* . . . Emily, did you "say" anything?' she added quickly, to hint that the answer should
be in the negative. 'I didn't feel that one *could* . . . I
didn't feel that one could. . . .'

'I must confess that I did. My wretched impulsiveness,' said Miss Fitzgerald, and put on that rather
annoying expression of self-deprecation.

'Impulsiveness . . . oh!' said Miss Pym and smiled a
discreet shade of pity.

'I suppose one must face one's heredity. All the
Fitzgeralds——'

'I know,' said Miss Pym rather sharply. They had

begun to climb the hill; the sun was full on them and Miss Pym, pricking all over with her own particularly uncomfortable kind of heat that went in instead of going out was anxious not to hear about the Fitzgeralds. She was anxious that Emily should not begin to rehearse those unfortunate (but striking) examples of Fitzgerald impulsiveness back through the ages. An inclination to do this was Emily's weakness, and it was always when disappointment, anxiety or lassitude should have drawn them together that they had to be most aware of one another's weaknesses. They had faced this out and discussed it with one another simply and frankly. It was wonderful to have somebody, always there, with whom one could discuss the most difficult phases of one's relationship (afterwards) simply and frankly. Whoever might come or might go, there would always be that. Friendship is such a wonderful basis in Life – or has such a wonderful basis in Life; either, she thought was true. Miss Pym thought of her friend Emily with tenderness, but wished that she would not pant in this exaggerated way to show that she was being hurried too fast up the hill. If she were being hurried too fast up the hill, why couldn't she say so? 'If we're going too fast I expect you to tell me,' she said at last in a controlled voice.

'I thought we must be doing this for a bet,' said Miss Fitzgerald, and panted wrathfully.

'Who did you think I had betted?'

'Isn't it "had bet"?'

They were both silent, and went up more slowly, wondering what they would find to discuss when (quite soon now) they came to the top. The terrace for which they were making had been the scene of profound discussions; there must be something about it, about the tilt of the ground or the way the trees grew. It had not for some time been revisited – in fact, they only seemed